The Machine Doctor (Thirsty Books, 2001)

Odium

Peter Burnett

THIRSTY BOOKS : EDINBURGH

© Peter Burnett 2004

First published in 2004 by Thirsty Books
an imprint of
Argyll Publishing
Glendaruel
Argyll PA22 3AE
Scotland
www.argyllpublishing.com

The author has asserted his moral rights.

British Library Cataloguing-in-Publication Data.
A catalogue record for this book is available from
the British Library.

ISBN 1 902831 73 X

Cover photo: www.illustrationworks.com

Origination: Cordfall Ltd, Glasgow

Printing: Mackays of Chatham Ltd

I thought you should have
something to read before it
all becomes too much.

•

Didn't you like the show?

Rubio's wife stopped in the foyer of the odeum and lit a cigarette. Before they left for the Place de l'Opéra, Rubio obliged her by halting in the crowd. Enamelled cupids stretched towards the corners of the room where larger gods brooded on the departing audience. The symbolism was not lost on Rubio, the characters frozen in their actions by the noise of the Parisians present.

You're acting like an old man, said his wife. You hate music and you hate the public.

Virginie had arrived from work with several wines under her belt and would not harbour criticism of the Opéra. Beyond doubt, she believed that a secret connection existed between the Paris Opéra and a happier society. The same connection was made in department stores and other places where a woman might fall in love with objects and articles, hers was a world that wore probity down to its knuckles, a city of changing rooms, display counters and lunch appointments.

A throbbing calm took over and Rubio looked to see if anyone was paying attention to their scene.

Virginie waited for him to answer, and Rubio fingered the brittle stalk of his cigarette.

I have nothing to add, he said, and he looked into the crowd of white-faced sheep in the foyer. As Rubio watched, the sheep came creeping behind his wife, the meanness on their faces agreeing with her verdict that Rubio had no feelings for society and music. Rubio and Virginie both pulled on their cigarettes before she started up again.

It's called going out and enjoying ourselves, she said.
I know, said Rubio, and he looked along the puckered red line of her lipstick.

He tried to nudge her towards the exit because like the rest of the herd, they were making no appreciable progress to the door.
It's still nice to get out for a change, she said and something of the bitterness dissolved. We don't do it nearly enough.
I'm barely surprised! said Rubio, and he took hold of her arm as a prelude to escape. Don't be like that, she said, and she dropped his hand abruptly.

As they edged for the door Virginie talked about the suite of chamber pieces and identified errors made by the conductor, talking about the similarity of the music to another piece that she knew.

I agree with that said Rubio, it was a very bleak piece indeed.
The music bleared away, said Virginie. It completely bleared away into another piece altogether.

The traffic barged into the Place de l' Opéra and the click of footsteps provided a descant to the cheap grating of the buses in the square. Virginie may have wanted to go to a café and Rubio may have wanted to go home but that didn't matter, they could be anywhere and the same tyrannous conversation would be held concerning his failure or her frivolity.

Let's get home, said Rubio.

Would you not like a walk? asked Virginie.

Where could we walk? asked Rubio.

We can go to a bar, she said.

A bar, thought Rubio, and he looked across the square to the cluster of glass salons at the corner.

He followed Virginie until she pointed to the heavenly wings of an electric beer sign. The great wits were already at work and the conference of the crowd rang like tinnitus in Rubio's ear.

At the bar Virginie searched the crowd, Rubio was blinded by their drinks glasses, cigarettes and sharp clothes. She carried on about the musicians at the Opéra, and she looked towards the door where it appeared that people were having a much better time than she was.

I always wanted to be a concert performer, said Virginie, but my fingers were against me. Too short and stumpy, she said, and she held her rejected fingers before Rubio's face.

The fingers no longer moved, he had not touched them for many days, they presented some angular piano chords on the smeared surface of the bar and he smiled. Too smart a catch for you those fingers, thought Rubio, but he had delayed so long in trying to do anything about it.

Let's just try and have a good time, she said, and Rubio gravely heard her out concerning her ambitions as a concert performer.

When Virginie stopped talking Rubio bid her say more with a gesture of acceptance, too scared to acknowledge the obvious fact of his doubt. Once again, he agreed with her time-honoured theory that she could have been a performer too.

I used to be able to play the Chopin all the way though, she said as her fingers carried out their tabletop arpeggio. I didn't like the way they did it tonight, it's a piece that makes so little sense out of its proper context.

Rubio stared into the Place de l' Opéra, the cars tentatively laid in great lanes before the lights. As the world turned, the traffic drove in the opposite direction, stuck to the gravity bed of the earth, speeding up the process, and Rubio's wife tapped his arm.

Were you listening? she asked. The composer's wishes should always be respected.

I heard you, said Rubio, but he wished that they could leave, or at least change the subject. He listened to Virginie, concerned for the latent violence of their marriage promise, never bothered to disagree, still hoping to leave and go home.

At the end Virginie stood up first and Rubio followed her to the café door, drifting bodiless in his coat and looking for the train fare.

So you liked the show, she said, and Rubio nodded that he had, almost convinced by his fraud.

•

The hour hand extended to meet the minute hand, both upright on the silver ring and reading noon. Where the number three should have been was a smaller dial showing the date, the forty-fifth birthday of Rubio. His shirt was torn at the sleeve so that the watch seemed like stolen property, a sheet metal disk that read KINETIC on its face.

Rubio addressed the watch, the lethargy of the second hand was like a great motion. He held the watch with his thumb and index finger and remembered the shop on the Rue de Rivoli. The shop was fronted with a glass case featuring pretentious lines of cameras packed against copies of the Eiffel Tower. This effect must have registered with Rubio because he remembered it in the desert.

He checked that the watch was steady and stumbled underfoot. QUARTZ it said on the watch, QUARTZ and KINETIC.

The images inside the shop on the Rue de Rivoli were vague, a stand-still glass counter and a half seen sales person. The shop was small with barely room for four customers and Rubio was surprised to see chewing gum for sale. Ahead were cameras, tripods, knives and sunglasses. Even as Rubio became used to the darkness the pale objects and articles seemed feeble, not real like in the window.

Yes, I need a watch.
Absolutely Monsieur. Do you like this one?
No.
This one?
That's a digital watch.
What about this one?
It's kinetic is it?
Yes it is Monsieur.
Let me see it please.

Rubio wrote a cheque and belted the watch to his wrist where the small hand continued like a silver roll of film.

A waste of money, said Rubio, and he looked down the road to where the view disappeared.

•

Up ahead was a point where vision splintered, only the sun determined the amount of interference. Rubio was impressed at how much variation could be found in the sand dunes and pediments of rock that ran into the distance. One is always looking for things, thought Rubio. One imagines there is a house there or even one of the colleagues, although one would be most disappointed to see them there, waving a newspaper and saying, My God Rubio have you seen this?

Staring into the desert Rubio expected one of those café dwelling colleagues to rise at any moment. I wouldn't be surprised, he thought, if there were a terraced café behind that sand dune. My colleagues will always be taking apart the paper and examining the crease on their trouser, thought Rubio, and I will always be walking past, out of range of their shouts.

Rubio exhaled. There was a sheath of dust between the exterior of the lung and the cavity of the chest. The straight plain of the road was like a runway and to cut the sun out, he brushed a hand across his head. The watch pressed on, stepping lively, the short-lived expression of time, and Rubio found the correct step as the gold across the desert settled. There was no café in the sand, this dalliance had gone up like dust, the colleagues were back in France, probably doing something very important with their time.

Where's old Rubi?
Goodness only knows.
It's as well he's not here. He'd go livid if he could see this article.

Laughs and laughs, and then they die away.

Rubio doesn't care for any of that!

(Who was that standing up for him? A woman he hoped!)

No such luck. They had forgotten him the day he had left for Egypt. Away in France, the colleagues were stationed on their iron chairs like soubrettes awaiting the call upstairs, they were all each other's slaves, speaking in sarcasm, insult and adieu. The poise of these roadsiders was inimitable, and when the colleagues talked it was of nothing, as if no sound wave could move in Paris. The traffic passed like paper on the wind, aeroplanes coasted overhead and the metro ran as smooth and silent as a waiter's arm. It was always a film or an overseas crisis, it was always the price of a bottle of Scotch, the very precious Frenchness of it all is what made the discourse of the cod philosophers so unbearable, their time spent in the pedantic purification of ideas, the meetings which made an artefact in and of themselves, the necessity to load their language with disdain.

I should never have started practising thought Rubio.

He pulled a postcard and a pencil from his pocket. On the face was the image of a sphinx half eroded by the elements, its features long forborne in the boredom of time, resting on stone legs. The sun amplified the noise in Rubio's ear, its deathless light made the act of walking harder than it should have been, and he turned the card to look at the sphinx again. With half her face removed, her head was the design of a human ear. The oval window and the cochlea, the area in which Rubio hurt the most, the drumhead, the furthest corner that could never be reached. In the desert the sharpest noises beat the drumhead, the simple noise made by blood passing from his neck to his head. The sound woke him in the morning like a rolling ball of earth and it distorted the stillness of the evening by singing out of tune.

Rubio looked on the horizon and saw the first white buildings of Mersa Matrouh.

Mersa was supposed to be quite a resort, its beaches were the sort of beaches Europeans liked, real Mediterranean beaches, sand curving gently into a sea, a merchant with a fixed expression selling ice cream, everything close to the hotel.

A noise took Rubio's attention, something was coming but he couldn't imagine what. He faced up the hill until a shape appeared like a barrel swelling from the head of the sun. The vehicle emerged as if from an eclipse, a road vehicle from the burning silence of the grave, and Rubio stood mute as the sound of the engine rose. He began on the postcard, and the pencil worked quickly. In a count-down, he estimated ten moments would pass before he would stick his thumb out to the left in order to catch a lift. He wrote the card in the quiet of his watch face, the quantum work of quartz. Moments after, the inaudible count was complete and the postcard was written, the lorry was visible, the driver also, both the sound of the engine and its echo. The vehicle let off a horn piping like a boat. The horn was surprisingly tuneful and it came directly for Rubio, out of the invisible world, a note through the smoke and the cloud of sand.

The lorry hollered past, the ringing continued in its wake and Rubio raised his head as the high-pitched purling begun in his ear again. He slapped his head but it didn't work, the ringing continued its allegro. There was sand in his hair, and a postcard without a stamp in his hand. It read:

> Egypt is the richest country in the world. It is as
> barbarous as it can be. There is no money. It is a
> melancholy business when all the affections of one's
> heart are wrapped up in a single project but I am
> determined. The words of Napoleon: I hope to return
> one day, but first I must discover why it was I left.
> Rubio

With the card in his pocket, Rubio approached Mersa, past a ridge of radar dishes and into a grid of houses where water knocked out of the ground. The road led into a dusty navel of concrete, and Rubio sat and smoked a promised cigarette. Along the yellow road were the basics of a market, several tables and awnings, and near them clean gentlemen Libyans talking trade. In the direction of the sea, sand-coloured buildings gave way to the two towers of a small mosque, the buildings of Mersa were wrapped in white light, roofs decked by the hot sun. He stared at the sea where the sky formed in patterns illustrative of another world, right into the spot where the light doled out the life of the day.

Yes Sir, said a voice beside him and a policeman stepped up. The man's features protruded from a chubby moustache and as always with cops, Rubio refused the urge to look at the man's pistol. Rubio felt for his passport but was distracted by the sea and he squinted as a tough-looking Libyan emerged running from the waves.

I'm just here to have a look at the sea after a long walk through the desert, said Rubio. Excuse the appearance of my clothes.

The policeman was not expected to understand French and he did not.

It's a lovely beach, said Rubio and he made a generous motion with his hand.

The policeman stared as if spoiling for a fight until his attention was taken by the Libyan who ran up the beach in the direction of his home country. The sun shone into the runner's brown back, for a heavy man he was fast upon the sand.

Yes Sir, said the policeman. It sounded as if an inquiry were being made.

Rubio saluted the Egyptian police and walked two steps away. The policeman watched him leave and made no attempt to follow, merely spoke again, a definite question for which there was no answer.

Rubio took a chance and walked towards the incomplete chunk of a hotel building and once on the high ground of the pavement again he turned and waved at the cop.

Impassive in moustache the policeman stood his ground with his hands by his side and Rubio carried on to where the sea washed up against the concrete shell of the hotel. Rubio felt his money roll sheathed at the bottom of his pocket, and sliding it free he began to count, switching the notes from the left hand to the right. His mind fell to his favourite game of calculating how long the holiday could be, based on the amount of money owned, a game that had as its centre value, the assured sum of five thousand. He palmed at the notes and muttered, passing them from one hand to the other.

Here was one thousand, a week away from home, and here was two, another week including the treat of a good meal. Here was three thousand, which was the expectation on the waiter's face as he served in the dream world of an Egyptian restaurant, and here was four, a clear month in sun.

Finally Rubio counted five thousand, a draft agreement between himself and Egypt stating that in time he would have forgotten Virginie and the wily enemies of his surgery. The money was a guarantor, a freeze on the depressions of Paris and its banlieue and the promise of at least a five-week campaign of exploration.

●

The radio declared its intention to create wall-to-wall Phone-in-Land, where they, the unstable, might work off the humours promoted by football, war, obesity, terrorism, dead celebrity and everything that grated on their milksop attitude. Some patients talked non-stop from the moment they entered surgery.

It was a pain in my throat doctor and now it's reached my ears. I think the sawdust has made it worse and I coughed up a lump. I was giddy after that so they sent me home. When I was walking home I felt fine, but then last night, boum, much worse.

It was the doctor's duty to undertake examination and listen to the symptoms. Patients would consider it important to tell Rubio how old they were, any statistic and its unwanted consequences, they took private advice and came to surgery with their side-show well prepared and Rubio was thereafter expected to remember all their names and diseases. The doctor would be in the family for years, like a hound or a chest of drawers.

Virginie had a notion that Rubio would graduate from the medical surgery in Sarcelles to work in the parlours of Paris. By Virginie's logic, experienced doctors treated the well-off while inexperienced doctors practised on the poor in the banlieue, and so she tolerated the humourless stone walls of Sarcelles as a stopping point in her ambitions to live on the boulevards. Cruel of Rubio therefore to be the only man who in her words aspired to live like a pauper, the only doctor who wished to remain in the outskirts of Paris away from the velvet greys of the Capital.

You've got something against people, she said. You don't like to see them having a good time.
It might be that, said Rubio. But I wouldn't put it in those terms.

How would you put it? she asked.

Rubio had not been looking for trouble but a situation had arisen, marriage had opened a private closet in which there was room enough for two, and nothing else.

You can't stand to see people have a good time, said Virginie, but Rubio said no, and didn't budge.

Out of the window were a disused canal and a half-empty tenement block. Sarcelles must have looked to Virginie like a scene from Hades.

That's what they do in Paris, she said, they have a good time. They eat good food and they see good films. What's wrong with that?

Nothing, said Rubio.

He sensed the pros and cons collapse and looked at his feet. Virginie's argument was a chain of reason, his answer was unproven analogy. Virginie remembered everything, and Rubio despaired, counting the buttons on her amazingly decent garments.

What have you got against the cinema anyway? Virginie asked.

Films are terrible, he said.

Rubio's shoulders sagged, he was ducking the issue but he couldn't recall a single film that had in his opinion any merit above its obvious crowd-pleasing sound and colour.

They make these films for idiots, he said, so people become idiots in order to enjoy them.

You snob, said Virginie.

It's true, said Rubio

How can you say that? she asked. Do you mean French films or American films? Is everything on film, every last frame, bad?

Virginie was taking the cinema issue personally but Rubio continued, he had brought them both to this ridiculous impasse.

Cinema is a tragically fruitless and expensive waste of time, he said. Its actors are glorified children. Why else would they cry when they receive awards? Why would we pay to see their exhibitionism when we could just invite some of your friends round?

Virginie's eyes broadened because Rubio had gone too far, he couldn't even remember what he'd wanted to say although he had relished allowing the thought a pair of wings.

There are thousands of films said Virginie, and you haven't even seen ten. You've not even seen ten films and you know all this without having been to a cinema.

Rubio shrugged and tried to back away from her.

I know what it is, she said, you're anti-social, that's what it is. Do you have a cure for that? Do you have patients suffering from spite, because I hope to God it's curable.

Rubio said nothing in honest silence.

Anti-social, she said, and you won't go to the cinema with me because you're too embarrassed.

Rubio left the final remark carelessly astray in the air, and said, I tell you, the cinema is rubbish.

Behind Virginie, the scene from their window. Entirely natural, the delicate collapse of the housing stock of the banlieue, life in the still water, even in the broken stone of the buildings they were pulling down. It was something you could trust, not like the streets of Paris, all made up for fools and holidays, Paris was like a TV show with everyone constantly interviewing each other.

You don't want people to have a good time said Virginie, and you're scared of enjoying yourself as well.

I enjoy myself, said Rubio.

Virginie sneered.

You enjoy yourself reading an old book about Napoleon or eating a bowl of noodles. This is you enjoying yourself, said Virginie, and she made a bowl with her hand.

A bowl of noodles! she said. Noodles and carrots, the staple diet of the Vichy regime! That and a book about Napoleon and the Jews!

Rubio knew the argument. What was planned as a night out became a meditation on the cinema and a discourse on noodles. What next? Once that train gets going and the carriages start to rattle, then it'll ride down anything.

Do you see what I mean when I say I'd like to enjoy myself? asked Virginie. That's why I want to go to Paris this evening. I want to go to the cinema.

I don't want to go this evening, said Rubio.

He fancied that he was calm but he scarcely dared look at her.

You just want to sit with those colleagues of yours, am I right?

You're right, said Rubio.

Don't be funny said Virginie, and she folded her arms.

The folded arms were a good sign so Rubio left it there. He

was like a ship and she was like the sea. He could wait for her to settle so that he could continue, but like the sea, she mechanically beat him back. When they argued the sound was like white noise to Rubio, and so he conceded early with a smile which Virginie did not accept as genuine, and ultimately he went to Paris with her.

They took the train to the city as a couple and patronised the cinema, a light comedy of manners. There was nothing to look at in the dark of the auditorium but this filth, strict attention was demanded by the screen and rows of swollen heads stared in judgement at the light. The patrons of the cinema stared open mouthed while Rubio imagined the sharp clashing as the actors were impaled on London railings, half hoping for a horse to hoof an actress in the heart.

Was there an expected benefit from this experience?

Rubio closed his eyes until the actors had bowed off the screen and gone back to England. He waited until Virginie had seen her fill of the film's final credits – for she insisted on this – before he ushered her through the lobby at high speed to save catching one word of the ghouls' post-show conversation.

They are always surprised after their films, thought Rubio, so surprised that they seldom mention the fact that they have just seen the same film from the month before, and again from the month before that.

Ushering Virginie through the lobby, Rubio lit a cigarette and sighed out the smoke. Around them milled determined people, riding the contours of consumer optimism.

It's all that the hopeful deserve to be entertained like that, thought Rubio, and he led his wife with a worsening weariness into a bar where she delighted in analysing the drama, while Rubio stared at her trunkless head and proceeded to get drunk.

●

Tourists emerged as the sun cooled at six o'clock. It seemed at that time as if Mersa Matrouh were a European colony.

Europeans can colonise anything, thought Rubio, they're doing it all the time. Americans buy and sell their catches, but the subtle European embraces a culture and primes it for the featherbedding of tourism.

Colonise is too mighty a word for the European when infest is available, thought Rubio. Ants build colonies from scratch as well as taking over dead ones. Infestations however are pests, bodies invading against the local grain.

The sun turned to a faded cheek of light and the tourists came like white grubs from old wood. Rubio noticed the first ones on a hotel balcony, a young couple like two stalagmites on the fourth floor, and on the street more of them appeared, pod-faced Europeans in couples that gave Mersa the uncanny feel of Left Bank Paris. Rubio bowed his head as two English girls came near, he touched his face, perhaps to hide it, and the girls walked by with their holiday sacks bouncing. At the side of the road stood men in white head wraps and Rubio let the two girls pass and wandered onward to the sea. The beach was chaste, the corniche a mangle of lanes and windows, broken wood and jetsam. Rubio felt his money roll boxed in his trouser pocket, he slipped his hand around it and squeezed. He worked his foot within a hollow of sand and looked up to see the two girls half way to the water. Rubio felt a familiar crack in his skin as he smiled, as if his parchment-white face had dried like an old sheet of fruit. Ultimately the two girls launched forward and ran into the sea, both were overweight and their attempts to swim remained an image of indulgence.

The patron of a café in Cairo, mistaking Rubio for a personage of distinction, talked to him concerning France.

I am to marry a Frenchwoman, said the patron. I am to go to Paris too.

The proprietor wore a grey suit, he was a large man and his spoken French was impressive.

Egypt is beautiful said Rubio, and France is full of snobs. All of Europe is!

Snobs? asked the proprietor.

Yes, said Rubio. They think they are superior. Do you see? They are people who think they are better than other people.

The proprietor clicked his fingers.

Yes, very much. We have snobs in Egypt too!

Someone shouted and Rubio watched two boys with a basket approach the beach, they were selling water there at the cooling end of the day, water and nuts if anybody dared. Rubio moved up the sand towards the town, now hungry as if patience were giving in to an interest in his own well-being. A current of darkness drew over the sea and on the air was an ounce of cold while from the mosque came the alluring call to prayer, veiled and iron in the shade of the tannoy. Towards the desert, the sound of donkeys assumed the role of an echo and Rubio signified his regret with another cigarette. At home, the colleagues may be settling to a glass of kir beneath the arch of a plastic canopy, discussing the recent war or insulting absent friends. Rubio listened to the muffled roll of the water at the foot of the sand, the soldiers faced away to the mauve electric lights of the corniche, and the loudspeakers called the town of Mersa to forgive. He watched the dark edge of the night as it approached with the ghost of a sound from the sea, the darkness absorbed the waters and rippled on the beach. The call to prayer stopped and Rubio fingered the KINETIC watch, looking for a sign that he may be linked to the earth by this pendulum around his wrist, that it somehow validated him. He walked toward the corniche where the end-ways of the buildings showed no light.

Here is where the conquerors came, he thought, celebrated by the triumphal arches of Europe, in the Place de l'Etoile and in Rome. Generally speaking, no opportunity should be missed to humiliate the conquered people, and the Emperor in question may be given places of honour on these monuments. The invading army ate dogs and camels and drank brackish water, the olive groves and broken ground were like the scenery of Languedoc but the heat was that of hell. Glorious pages were added to the military annals and the Great Nation sang a *te deum* to celebrate its new territory.

A thin selection of tables and chairs ran along the wall of a coffee-house and Rubio looked again to see if anyone was there. Garlands of plaster crumbled on the pavement while parked cars lolled into the road, their eyes shaded by their hoods. From the corner, an oil light glowed from a doorway and voices rose from within. Rubio walked towards the noise, the light fell sidelong from the foil of a broken door and he approached, confronting the suspicion that something exciting may be happening.

Likely gambling, thought Rubio, picturing a coven of Arab card players face to face in smoke and coin.

The wind brushed against him and he heard indistinct words, a louder voice was clear from the doorway and Rubio looked as if there were somebody behind him. The cars in the semi-dark all looked away embarrassed and Rubio turned to where the oil light glowed.

Five men played cards around a table and they all turned to Rubio, who waited with a hint of guilt. Rubio held a hand up as if he were announcing his intention to trespass but the faces in the oil light glowed in horror. All five men spoke while the wind pushed their cards obliquely upward. Rubio stuttered an apology but the cards collided with banknotes and the game fell apart. Chairs dropped as the men rose and one man, his lips slippered with curses, held Rubio by the collar and pushed him into the street. Rubio fell against a car and groaned, and the other men followed, the stuffing of their mouths spilling out around him. Rubio was on his back and his apology was lost in the crash of the broken door. He yelped as the men began to tug him down the road.

Please! said Rubio but he was not heard.

The men picked up speed and Rubio felt the rasp of the stones, he jerked his arm free and gazed in sudden fear up the stitch of their robes as if ready for a beating. He said nothing, the ringing in his ears forbade him, and the men stared at him with clenched hands and simple disbelief.

Rubio watched the gamblers slope back to the doorway, right to the point where they turned to look at him. He brushed his sleeves and felt for his money roll which was not there. He thumped his pockets and took one step forward, he dropped on his knees and slapped the earth. The card players were watching and so were the vehicles.

I've lost it said Rubio gently as his fingers scraped the ground. I had money in my pocket but now it's gone.

The card players did not move and Rubio crawled forward to see if the cash-roll stood out against the dust. Two of the men were looking now. Their heads inclined, they walked beneath the dimmest streetlight, brushing aside stones and litter with their feet. Above Rubio, the stars staggered in the sky while his hands felt in distress for the money roll. It was somewhere in the street, crisp beneath the starlight, nudged homeward by the scorpions. All the men were searching now, talking to each other and treading carefully on the knife-edge of the evening like actors at the rear of a stage.

The campaign is not a defeat, thought Rubio, and he felt his pocket again. Tipping himself to his feet, it seemed unreal that such a loss should be possible. Stay upright and regroup, he thought, find a hotel and billet, the holiday can't be over so soon. What would Napoleon have done to challenge the obstacles posed by circumstance? He would have countered with genius and triumphed.

Rubio looked up the road where the card players appeared to have found something of interest. He heard their voices through the ringing in his ears, the meter beat that had bothered him since he had arrived in the country. Rubio had not really lost the money. In the morning he would wake, the light on the coast would breeze in with an air of openness and he would turn out his pockets and the cash-roll would be there. Just now however, his stomach pressed towards his mouth in hunger, so he left the scene of his defeat in order to find some plain camping on the beach for several hours until a decision could be made.

•

If love is reachable, thought Rubio, then it's not through the perfection of the city. Dream built motor cars approached in lines on great roads, emerging from double tunnels which resembled the barrels of shotguns. In these hard-headed centuries, there is an obligation to be materially secure, thought Rubio, and nobody knows what a doctor has to put up with. With every person bent on their own salvation nobody wants to hear that what they've got is incurable. Salvation is unheard of, but why shouldn't there be a millennium for each one of us?

Meanwhile, crowds roamed Paris on the search, every one of them a masterchef and critic, their targets were the combined gourmandising of the small screen, a step by step creation of a culture where nothing lasted out the day. Dreamy-eyed Parisians stood at shop windows, their only realism being the delectable work of their clothes, and Rubio had studied them and learned this fact by heart.

Where was Virginie?

She had joined them and had found another husband, one that shared her opinion of department stores and not Rubio's slow crabwise movement for the street door. Virginie couldn't bear to be parted with the freedom of the department stores, they were the most positive and gracious churches in the city. For years Rubio had avoided his wife's shopping trips, so when it came to the end of the week he always had a house-call to make in St Cretin, or there was paperwork to be ready for Monday.

Just go yourself Virginie, he said. Enjoy it and I'll see you later.

Rubio made a hundred excuses but for some people it's not enough that you don't participate. He passed her money and felt absolved, as if giving to the church. Virginie needed to go to Printemps and find a new set of crockery or some dried flowers for the fireplace, she had done everything that it was possible to do with dried flowers and Rubio had stared into these laurels with the dismal plight of a caged animal. Together, Rubio and Virginie were so tenacious. Like insects locked together in flight they fell and rose as one, they ached at the abdomen and hips, until they were crushed by the wind and split in two. A dilapidated love gone to seed holds on, thought Rubio, but both must bail out or it's curtains for everyone on impact.

He had memories of department stores that were worse. In a department store, the child Rubio had become absorbed in stroking a fur coat. The child Rubio gripped the coat and asked his mother if he could stroke it and she said yes and let him run his hands through it. After he had stroked the coat several times his mother had seen enough and told him to stop, she was tired and the price of everything was grating on his father. It was one of those painfully dull times, a whole decade of it passed during which periodically something woke him, such as the coat. The child Rubio therefore gripped the fur and scratched, refusing to break with the experience, it was tall and grey, a sheared racoon or a chocolate brown fisher, long guard hairs and a compact woolly underfur.

Later his parents were gone and Rubio was still playing among the coats, travelling parallel to the racks in search of fresh fur.

We had to get them to put out an announcement, said his father, but he couldn't hear that, not him.
So we waited, said his mother, half an hour until we'd had enough.

Eventually Rubio was found with his hand within the nap of a fox skin cap, his other hand reaching for a full skin Whiskey Mink with collars and cuffs.

Hiding in the coats, said his mother, so we dragged him out and got him home.

Hiding in the coats, said his father and slapped him across the face.

Rubio returned to the department store with Virginie, and while she twisted clothes across her arm he would whine and joke, his humour a mild protest against the lengthy process of home-building.

What's that sofa going to look like when the dog's slept on it? he asked of a young couple with crisp clothes and smiles.

Why buy a baby a painted cot that it can't appreciate?

The ermine is a weasel, he used to say, and the best racoon comes from Russia not America.

The abiding image of the department store left Rubio with memories that would never be redeemed, no matter how scrupulously detached he tried to be. In this way his memories became an open wound, a flick book of thoughts that never granted him leave to look elsewhere. The memory of Virginie was a page that stuck in the flick book, an image with the suddenness of a shell-burst, she was a special woman who could cause a traffic jam by a mere appearance, this was her trick and she performed it keenly. Whether she read a magazine or peppered chops with rosemary, Virginie was always busy in Rubio's memory, and wherever in the world Rubio was, her image alighted and he had to stop what he was doing.

The 200th celebrations of the Terror brought out the cynicism in everyone and Rubio and Virginie took the train from Garges Sarcelles to witness the commission of several civic acts involving fireworks. Their love was a modernistic evasion, their marriage a set of lies agreed upon at an old fashioned altar. She was always up to the minute and looking for the latest recreation, while he the fossil man was just about extinct.

It was in the department stores that Rubio's tinnitus began. Those obsessed by Christmas collided with those who'd had too many golf clubs to the head, everything was reducible to the pursuit of pleasure and people filled their homes to every corner with the short established bistrot atmosphere they loved. In the multi-level paradise of Paris, chubby Saturday types ranged among the duvet covers, clocks, and pans, while the word nice was repeated as if it were the true responsory of this earthly religion.

Virginie was one who also said that it was *nice*, the word rang in her speech with the greatest commitment. The word on the fascist flag was *nice*, as if there were objects and articles that were *not-nice*, things un-French, and un-societal. *Nice* was the elemental horror from which the city in fact emerged, it was the reverie of their future because Paris was alive and immediate, not petrified like Rubio was – but nice.

•

Day was dying and the street deserted. The Hotel Bel Air, sweetly picturesque, remained the only monument to Imperial France in Mersa. Rubio read the sign, the name Bel Air evoked delight while the glowering shutters of the building had lost all firmness and agility. Bel from whence beautiful, he thought, and Air suggesting easy-breathing. Bel Air – perhaps a satellite in California, or a thin cigarette for people with open top cars – Bel Air – the biting surface of the sea as the wind rides across a bank of sun-loungers on to which the guests are tucked tightly into place.

The reality was a garrison of expressionless windows and a dusty stone step. The pavement outside the Bel Air was an imitation of the European, flat cement and an invitation to drink coffee among the crashing boredom of your friends. A torn umbrella beneath a canopy was whiskered with dirt and an advertising board pointed up the street to where there was food.

Fuul Ahmed Mohammed.

The picture on the advert bordered on the comic, a white plate of mashed beans and salad, the neck of a bottle of cola. Rubio leaned into the door of the Bel Air and thought of the colleagues and the moment he had told them he was making an adventure in the land of Egypt. What would that crew of cultural critics make of his circumstances now? He could hear their sarcasm and see their eyebrows raising an additional fraction at the thought of his situation. They broke off from their flights of mockery to make a personal attack and Rubio felt relieved to be unseen by them. Bullied by hunger, he lit a cigarette and pushed into the hotel. The door seemed unreasonably heavy, but Rubio worked against it and rehearsed his way through some words in his mind.

I am lost. I can give you this good watch if only you can let me go upstairs, what say you?

The tiles of the Bel Air seemed freshly washed, creating with the light-coloured roof, the effect of a drained swimming pool. Nearby two boys played chess, clicking the pieces over the board so quickly that Rubio wondered if they knew the rules. The only other person was a European woman slouched on a far away chair, she wore a red robe and sat in the pose of a vulture, black hair and a bottle of beer, smoking too. Rubio watched to see if she would show her face but she was drunk, glaring at the bottle that it might leave her in peace.

Rubio was five steps from the counter when a thin man appeared and spoke to him like a lizard in a styptic local tongue.

Yes, said Rubio and he slid his wormy French passport across the counter.

The man took the passport and leafed over the front page, he didn't look at the paper but into Rubio's eyes. Rubio stared across the marble to where the man stood with the passport held open above his shoulder. The man indicated the picture and Rubio said yes, unsure of what was being asked.

Frenchman, said Rubio in the hope that another formal start may be made, and he looked at the passport image of himself. In the photograph nothing had changed, the same caricature perched in an acid white rectangle in the corner.

I speak English, said Rubio in Arabic, it was the most reasonable statement there was on any continent but the Arab was not moved.

Rubio clipped the watch from his wrist and placed it on the counter. He wished to slam his Frenchness down and demand that the man accept it but the man stared black-toothed upon him and said nothing, forcing Rubio to glance at the slumped European woman staring at her beer.

You have to understand said Rubio. You have to give me a room for just one night. Do you see?

The drunk woman tilted her head back and as Rubio offered his watch again she fell from her chair and the beer bottle cracked on the floor. The bottle clattered to a halt but the sound was cut short by a movement like a click in his head, a soft pedal was depressed in the woman's voice and he heard her say in French, leave me alone, my husband is upstairs.

Rubio turned and the hotelier grabbed his collar which cracked with dust.

This is Egypt, said Rubio, and you should accept my passport, but he was led towards the door, and the door was pushed open for him.

Rubio hoped that the door would open to the desert, he wished to be hurled into a sea of sand, to spin down the celestial mechanics of a dune, to lie against a rock and wait for night. The Arab said something sharp, it dimly represented a request to leave, although it sounded like the innards of the language rather than the meat. The drunk French woman was on her feet and in the heat of a rash decision Rubio threw his hand into his trouser and pulled his passport free again.

My nationality said Rubio, pressing his passport to the hotelier.

Look at it, said Rubio, but the passport dropped and was kicked away.

The patron pushed Rubio through the door and Rubio pressed his hand to his ear where the drum in the inner tube was vibrating like a propeller.

I'm leaving, he said.

The drinking woman glanced at Rubio with thunder in her eyes, the look was specific, a hallucination of immovably stuck threats as if she despised him. Her condemnation left Rubio weak, ready to return to the streets of Mersa and its malevolent inhabitants.

I'm French, said Rubio, and the hunger pricked his stomach.

He fell outside the hotel and hit the pavement next to the wet lump of something dead. Face disfigured in the sunlight, Rubio felt on his wrist a patch where the watch had been and realised he was lying on a dead cat. Children gaped with mouths like wells, while men looked up from appliances of wood. Rubio lay in the litter of the street and looked into the hotel where the woman was now drawing on a cigarette, her lighter guided by the patron Arab. The flame made contact and she begun to puff, and the man picked up her beer bottle while she pursued the smoke, drunkly.

Next to Rubio, the dead cat's teeth squeezed thorough its gums in a final fighting grimace, an oozy notch of blood running from its eye. Rubio walked two steps into a foul sack of something musty and saw it to be a woman. Her eyes were yellow and what she said to him he could not hear, she stared at him and tapped her lips for a cigarette. He threw a smoke into his own mouth as he leaned into the hotel's window and the woman tapped her lips again. Rubio concentrated on the cat.

All is not lost my friends. I suppose that, when I reassemble my forces, I shall be able to keep the enemy occupied and give France time to do its duty. There is still time to retrieve the situation – and great victories have been preceded by great defeats.

The words of Napoleon, something from a textbook about the tough Egyptian campaign. Rubio swayed on towards the back of the hotel where he believed he may try again. He repeated the conqueror's words and smoked, astonished rather than angry that he had now lost his one and only watch.

•

Sunday: no breakfast because Rubio didn't believe in such. No newspapers because Rubio never took a newspaper. No work because the surgery was closed, no cinema because no wife. No shopping because no wife and no lounging in the garden, because that presupposed the meagre notion of free-time.

In the morning Rubio read the final chapter on the French army's disastrous Egyptian campaign and left a cup of coffee to grow cold. At midday and tired to extinction, he found a suitable place for the book on his shelf and filed it.

He dressed at the mirror and watched the sparkle passing from his eye as he crossed his necktie. An hour later he stared along the rails at the station while the local kids readied their pens to vandalise the train.

Rubio sat in shame on the RER and he thought about books and wondered if he should treat himself to ordering some more.

The train reached speed and drove from the darkness of Sarcelles, the happiest point of his week. There was de Tocqueville's Democracy in America bound with a black spine, his favourite edition and sure to look good within the dimensions of his collection. He played with his fingers and considered the investment that such a book might involve. There was the merest sensation of leaves outwith the train, the trees shone tender and green in the light, the carriage passed through a further area of banlieue that was earmarked for destruction and Rubio fantasised about the book. After that, he was in the din of Paris and facing the cannonade of motor vehicles.

Rubio crossed the River Seine into the crowded circle of the Latin Quarter, St Michel. Here flower shops spilled clammy bouquets on the pavements and pyramids of books were for sale, everywhere was the same constipated accumulation of goods, a demonstration that nobody could digest everything that was consumed. Turning a rack of paperbacks, Rubio looked for his favourite black-spined editions aware that he had come to Paris out of some gnawing obligation to participate in this weekly festival of indulgence. He walked beside families and tourists with couples in dark glasses, and who knows, he thought, any one of these people could be in the surgery tomorrow morning with a skewer rammed into their shoulder.

On the Left Bank there were greater and more trivial arcades to ponder, but they were all identical, same obsolescent spoons, same tabac, same table and umbrella. The arcades were barely populated the rest of the week as if humanity were out of season, and then on Sunday morning they ground to life when the people arrived in the vellum-jacketed hell of their motor cars. In the evening the same masses of people left behind them cups and litter, the monuments of their conversations and the smell of their excited children.

Dr Burneto, a man Rubio's precise age, and Louis, his young son.

The two doctors shook hands and Burneto took off his hat and fanned himself. Rubio had the impression that Burneto had been practising this fanning action for years, motions adopted from the cinema. Louis was a shy boy and his finger went to his face when Rubio appeared.

We're having a walk, said Burneto, he sounded so proud of the fact. He was proud of his hat, he was proud of the Left Bank and delighted with Paris, the world in which Burneto moved was like a boast.

Then we're going to look at the barges, said Burneto, and holding his son's hand to his stomach he said in a quiet voice, aren't we?

The boy smiled but Rubio stared like a macaw.

How are you doing? asked Rubio, all he could remember were adult niceties.
Very fine too, said Burneto.

Burneto's free hand was all go, making a fuss of himself, wiping his forehead and tilting his hat. Once the hat was tilted the hand went in and out of his coat and produced a small pocket knife.

I'm just going to the river, said Rubio. Would you care to come with me?
Yes, said Burneto, and Rubio turned and got in line.

Walking in the epicurean wonderland, Rubio felt warmer towards his two friends, although the price was dear. Misery was thrust upon him in the form of the merry conversation of Burneto who talked about his breakfast and how there had been a calamity with their usual supply of rolls. The baker, it turned out, had gone to the football on Saturday and not come back, and Burneto despaired loudly.

Football, he said, is the greatest inanity, an art whose best creation is a tongue-tied teenage moron with an expensive haircut.

Burneto continued his tale. The substitute rolls had been no cop at all and the neighbourhood had been out in force desperate for the yield abundant of their habitual boulanger. Rubio nodded. The anecdote had been an elaborate way for Burneto to show his family's swamp of comfort, but Burneto was so busy painting the scene that Rubio had forgotten the point.

That boulanger has to have the football! I said to him, what is your fascination man? Explain it to me – but all that baker could say that football was like religion. The religion of the baker is football! He insists that it is a passion. See?

The three of them headed down a cobbled alley that made two turns to the Seine. Tidy back doors and flaky walls separated the buildings and the foot traffic melted away as they reached the main road. With the rolls story established, Burneto continued with the rest of his Sunday morning, because it had been the papers next.

Did Rubio see them?
No he didn't.

Well there's something, said Burneto. I won't tell you but you have to see it for yourself. I won't spoil it for you but you must see it. Look, I must buy you a copy because I know you'll love it.

Rubio held his hands up and promised to get his own newspaper but Burneto's voice rose in excitement before he became absorbed in a passing motorbike.

Did you see that bike? he asked and Rubio agreed that he had.

All three watched the motorbike drive into the sour grey of the Quai St Michel and Burneto tried to remember what he had been talking about.

How is Virginie? he asked as the three reached the familiar lead of the River Seine. Above the river were the white-faced windows of the Mairie.

Fine, said Rubio, she's fine.

Burneto was pleased with this and he tried again to remember what it was that had been so interesting. He stood at the roadside watching the oncoming traffic with a queer and irregular eye.

How's Sylvie? asked Rubio.

Oh very good, said Burneto. We had a row today but I blame that baker. He's a strange duck. His football is a way of punishing us. He can't really like football can he? A man like that?

Amazing said Rubio, and he chanced another look at Louis.

The boy stared at Rubio from his father's side, weighing him up. Burneto sighed with a deal of effort and Rubio tried to think what to say.

Actually Virginie and I aren't together said Rubio. She left last month.

Rubio pondered the Mairie and heard Burneto rise to the exciting news.

Oh so, said his friend, what bad news that is.

Not especially, said Rubio. It just means that I've been working hard.

Yes, the surgery, said Burneto.

He looked on Rubio's face as if it were a shelf of deadly boring books. Rubio's surgery was the one thing could possibly quieten Burneto, it was a poor little surgery in the purgatorial area of Sarcelles. With all of Paris to chose from, those expensive sore throats to heal and the ear infections of the Olympians, to work for so many years in Sarcelles was to cudgel oneself. Burneto, like Virginie, could not work it out.

So are you moving? he asked.

A typical question, a slobbish Frenchman of a question.

No I'm not, said Rubio. I like it in Sarcelles, it's just right for me.

You're a queer duck said Burneto, and Rubio took a good look at the perspiring face of his old friend. The sun shone across him and on to the gothic towers on the opposite bank.

You know best though, said Burneto. You'll always get your own way.

Rubio groped for a meaning in his friend's statement, but Burneto had started speaking again.

I really must get on, he said, and he looked down the street from which they had emerged. It was very nice seeing you. You must call because I'm sure Sylvie will be concerned. You'll need to come for dinner.

Yes, said Rubio.

An evening with the uncultivated galoot of Burneto showing off his various acquisitions. This book, this painting, these plates, it would be torture as Burneto zigzagged Rubio through a series of photographs and grim white teacups he'd bought for a song. As a couple these barbarous evenings were hardly bearable but without Virginie it would be worse, the hell of the married mill.

I'll see, said Rubio, I'll maybe give it time.

This was the correct statement, the most accurate selection from the script.

I understand said Burneto. Still you should count yourself lucky. Take some time you know.

Blundering advice, but Rubio thanked him anyway.

Last of all, before Rubio walked away, he watched Burneto and son cross the road, big man, small boy. He stared at Louis and was unsure. Father and son carried off their parody until they were out of earshot, their divers inarticulate sounds hovering between bashfulness and certainty, the collective comfort of their bond.

•

Rubio arrived at the rear of the Bel Air where he squeezed through a broken door to a courtyard. Empty balconies were joisted in bleak colours, beautiful accompaniments to the clear sky, and he walked beneath these and slipped under the vaulted arch of the back door and was on the premises.

This time the reception was empty, there was no sign of the patron or the drunk woman, no sound from the dimpled plaster of the stairs which wound beneath a punched iron balustrade. His stomach felt like rock, a pain rose in his limbs and he gazed into the well of the hotel stair. The walls were bleached blond by the sun and insects ascended between the broad ledges of the windows.

A floorboard thumped and Rubio was surprised by the presence of a European man. The man's face formed a staring prism of features, while the remaining portions lined up and an English voice said Hello.

I've been robbed, said Rubio balancing on the stair.

He noticed that a digital camera strapped to the man's wrist filmed his horrid confession in its small glass eye, while the tourist looked from above it with an expression of polite disgust. Rubio put forward his hand for help and thought about what to say, but the young man maintained an arm's length distance. Rubio understood that he had interrupted terribly, the man was another traveller, they flocked through Egypt like the bones and flesh of a death to come.

I've been robbed, said Rubio, and I'm sorry but I'm stuck here.

The young man held his bag to his chest as he walked away. The air in the hall flowed with the short-lived joy of desert dust and a minute later the hotel returned to the way Rubio had found it.

At the corridor on the first floor an open window invited Rubio to a sea view, so he rested on the ledge and looked at his depleted carton of smokes. For those occasions when you can't face a full meal, thought Rubio, there are always cigarettes. Each tube contains the dried spoil of a once exotic plant, a fount of sorrows to drown your own, and each moment one of them is burning, thoughts take on a wild and clear tone. Rubio lit up and drew enough smoke to suppress his discontent. Below was the shining sea, the orbit of cool water was otherworldly but it was all that materially separated Europe from Egypt. He stared from the stone slab of the hotel while the sun pricked his face, the same figures from the day before lay on the sand, as though stranded on a reef in a dying ocean. Below the Bel Air were concrete houses and television ariels, dynamically ugly against the flat sky, Mersa was a grid of streets and blockhouses circling a hill, there was one road and one people, a fallen aqueduct and two rows of columns which led nowhere.

Rubio's feet were cold and he rebuked them in his mind. The possibility of his feet not working didn't bear thought, their course of revenge upon him would be complete enough when they walked away and left him.

Hey mister?

There stood a child, a pale-faced French-speaking boy.

Hey my son, said Rubio.
The words felt lucky, as if Rubio had found a gentle voice for once.
What are you doing? said the boy.

Rubio leaned into the window, a concrete square broken much beyond what he considered safe.

I'm trying to get upstairs, he said.

The boy was dressed in a T-shirt and neat knee pants, he took Rubio's hand and pulled.

It's okay said Rubio, you can leave me here.
Yeah, said the boy, you're going to stay and get drunk – and he struck at Rubio, punching him on the shoulder.
I'm not drunk, said Rubio and he reasserted his grip on the window frame.
Yes you are mister, said the kid, you're drunk and falling over.
I don't have enough money to get drunk, said Rubio almost with a shudder.

We've got money in our room, said the boy.

Sure thing, said Rubio, but the kid frowned as if in discovery of a problem.

We've got piles of money on the bed, said the kid.

Your Mum and Dad? asked Rubio, but the kid said nothing, a premonitory sign of trouble.

Rubio looked up the corridor in case the parents had seen him. If caught with the child he would be accused of something debased and have to play the stainless gentleman, culpably French. The parents could spell his salvation, in a room upstairs they were perhaps preparing cigarettes, laying them out like medical tools to save his life. They were folding newspapers and probably even had gin, and that would be Rubio right back into the Teutonic Fold.

He lit up the last cigarette with a cheap matchstick and looked for the kid who was already down the corridor and waving him on. Rubio held the cigarette straight and collected himself for society. He desired sleep and coffee, cigarettes and breakfast, enough to get back on the road, maybe even the loan of a few dollars. He moved off gracefully and wondered if his story would wash with Mum and Dad or if it would have to be the full fait accompli, the exchange of addresses, the tiny inflections required in presenting oneself both as safe and interesting. He prayed again for gin and cigarettes, the carefully graded toxins of France laid out and available to him so long as he remembered etiquette.

He dragged on the smoke.

Stupid, he thought, it's too late for any of that.

Rubio walked after the child, the corridor was of a bygone age but the atmosphere had been destroyed by the alchemy of dust and cleaning fluid. He saw the hotel room door was open and half expected a man in a suit to step out and offer him a handshake, perhaps someone he already knew – and with this in mind he walked to the door and looked inside.

A two room suite and in the first room, a mess of blankets, clothes and bottles, stained floorboards and a repose of empty bags. The sun on every surface and to the left was an open door and more clothes in a rocky pile.

Rubio stepped in and said hello, the kid was not around.

Bottles spilled over the fabric of many blankets while the fan on the roof turned at medium speed. Objects appeared to Rubio as he walked towards the bed, a suitcase and two rucksacks, a woman's shoes and a child's toys. A patterned blanket covered the bed and this too was scattered with bottles of Egyptian wine, notoriously expensive and ill-tasting. Spirits from Europe combined with plainer varieties of drink, and on top of this a crumple of old dollars and torn receipts.

Come on, said the kid, and Rubio pushed the door and saw a second bed of blankets with the woman from the foyer on her side. He swore quietly and lowered his cigarette.

This room was worse, the closed shutters killed everything and the fan was broken. The woman was drunk or dead, she lolled off the bed with her face unseen, almost pressed into the floor which she had been using as an ashtray. Rubio kicked away a bottle and took the woman's pulse, her wrist beat out a life and he moved some hair to look at the face. He squeezed open the eye, it was green within the milk and stared at him like the purest marble. When he moved the woman's arms a bottle fell into a sticky puddle which held a damp, unsmoked cigarette, the liquor bubbled free and soaked into a blanket.

The kid watched.

Drunk, he said.

You sit down, said Rubio. I've got to see if she's okay.

The kid pressed himself to the wall while Rubio turned to his patient. A woman about forty, she was free in sleep, perhaps only in sleep, and he moved her to her side and cleared her hair from her mouth.

Clean up those bottles, said Rubio to the kid.

His voice sounded too loud, a contradiction to the stillness of the scene.

Make them stand against the wall, he said.

That's not allowed, came the voice.

Just do it, said Rubio, get all the bottles together and put them in a line.

He lit a cigarette from an open packet on the floor, it was stronger and more satisfactory than the imports he'd been carrying. The woman snorted and Rubio pulled away some blankets and shifted some articles from the bed.

What's she done? asked Rubio. Is that your mother?

The kid pouted from his upright position at the wall.

What's she up to? asked Rubio, his voice contributed to the general dejection of the room.

I've got to get ice, said the boy. We both like sweets so I have to get them too.

That's good, said Rubio, that's really good.

He walked to the window.

Where are you from? he asked.

The boy pointed out of the window towards the desert.

We're from Siwa, he said.

Oh, said Rubio. Siwa.

The Oasis of Siwa, the labyrinthine stone paradise in the sand, there was definitely nothing to drink there, not alcohol.

Are you on holiday? asked Rubio, but the boy said no, speaking into his shirt as if he hadn't understood the question, perhaps indicating that it hadn't been the correct question.

The boy fell on his side, mimicking the posture of his mother. He lay in a sulk while insects ducked around the bed. In the sink was a clump of wet bottles and on the sideboard cosmetics and jewellery were scattered in a heap. Rubio moved his fingers through the jewellery, the longest piece was an old style silver chain embroidered with a sprinkle of stars.

Line up those bottles, please, said Rubio, and he indicated the epic sweep of empties on the floor. He picked his own bottle of beer from the sink, the scent of the alcohol previewed a rush to his stomach and he looked through the bottle at the miniature floorshow of bubbles.

Is your dad about? said Rubio but the kid said nothing.

Come on, said Rubio, but the kid looked away.

We'll see what happens when your dad comes in, he said to the kid, and he sat in the corner to wait.

Rubio smoked, he drank a beer and tried another one. He searched the room and found more money, Egyptian pounds and US dollars, some crumpled in an attempt to hide them. Under the blankets were tins of preserved foods, make-up, paperbacks and bottles. He read the rear pieces of the paperbacks and ate burnt almonds, allaying hunger until he broke into a tin of meat. Once he'd eaten, Rubio smoked again and decided to write another card. He had several left, the same image of the sphinx, perhaps an angel, perhaps a devil, certainly not a man or woman, her image had been reduced to the last extremity of recognisable form by the course of time.

He wrote:

> Colleagues! Why should not our whole nation
> become Muslims? The two objections are as
> follows: the necessity of giving one tenth of one's
> income to charity, and the ban on wine, a beverage
> indispensable to French life. Why then should
> Egypt not be Christian? The single objection should
> be the drunken Catholic's lack of benevolence.
> Rubio

With the postcard propped on a chair next to his earlier unsent version, Rubio watched the light cross the floor. Below the window human figures coalesced and dissolved at the street market and Rubio broke the seal on a bottle of Scotch.

After four hours she awoke. It was evening and she didn't see him, she was looking for a drink or a smoke and Rubio addressed her by raising himself and standing to attention by the window. Bladders of skin beneath the woman's eyes were marked with the gum of where she'd slept and she yawned, turning to see who was there.

What are you doing?
Her accent was not expected, Swiss perhaps.
Your son let me in, said Rubio.

She picked at the bed for cigarettes, looking for the right carton, her eyes less awake than the limbs, slowly scrambling through the blankets. Rubio wished that he had done something about himself, tidied for the inevitable, and he reached over and offered the women one of her own smokes. She pulled her hair back and looked at him again.

Is he out? she asked.

Yes said Rubio, he's out.

He lit the woman's cigarette and the smoke flowed up as she drew.

Can I have one? asked Rubio, and she waved him yes, and returned to digging through the clothes, leaning forward as she dug deeper. The woman worked her arms through the rumple of blankets like a cat at morning exercise while cinders of ash dropped from her cigarette. The blankets were fed behind her to a hump on the floor and Rubio was about to say something when the woman found what she was looking for, a strip of tablets. She lowered herself to the mattress and spilt a section from the pills before she fell over where the blankets had gathered up.

Hell, she said, and she clutched the strip of tablets in her hand.

Her red dress, so straight a moment ago, looked like it had been put on the wrong way. She drank from the neck of a bottle and swallowed the pills.

This is it, she said when she'd finished drinking. What time is it?

My watch is at reception said Rubio.

Reception? she asked.

She pushed the burning cigarette into the floor and stood up, looking at Rubio as a problem to be solved. She would have competed well among the ensembles of local drunks at Sarcelles, she would have been a terror on the station steps. Rubio felt in his pockets where a torn hole allowed his finger to touch his thigh, and she walked past him to the bedroom where he heard her saying the word *ice* under her breath. When she returned she brushed her hair from her face and watched him smoking.

You can't eat the fruit, she said. The bread's good and they deliver it to you in the morning.

Ah said Rubio, it sounded like the dreadful re-enactment of a stage play.

Shit, this is the morning, she said. I could do with a lemon too.

She picked up the gin and stared to the vaulted neck of the glass. She looked into the side of the bottle as if there were messages before her in the spirals of the alcohol.

Christ, a lemon, she said.

She poured two glasses of gin while Rubio watched.

I can't drink it like that, he said, and she shot him a glance from underneath her hair. He watched the measure vanish as she drank and so he tilted back his head and did the same. The gin burned his nerves while outside the voices of donkeys rose, the tortured sinners of the town.

She held up the bottle.

We trade in gold, she said. What's in this bottle could feed a family for two months.

One more drink and a pause. She filled up Rubio's glass and then her own.

I got it in Bur Said, she said. To have this much drink is probably illegal.

She laughed but it was a snort, a frail release of air.

I'm a doctor, said Rubio, a sentence which proved significant enough to damn him in her eyes.

She drank again and chewed on a lemon rind until it was time for a cigarette which she drew on like a true disciple.

What about another lemon? she asked.

She faced Rubio as if to let him know that the conversation was over, her stare petitioned him for action. Rubio rummaged in the rags of his pockets while she opened the bottle and poured more in her glass, calculating a powerful measure.

You can just shut up she said and she walked to the adjoining door where she paused in a blaze of oppression.

Who let you in anyway? she asked, and she was gone.

When Rubio heard the body drop on the bed he helped himself to a whisky and raised the glass as if offering a forgotten toast. He heard a bottle's crash from next door, a smash on the wall and an idle moment during which she coughed and swore again.

Come doctor. I expect we had better go and have a look, see what the old girl has done to herself now.

In the next room the woman's eyes had closed and she lay high on the bed buckled in pain. Where a pillow should have been was the dim mouth of an open bag and in the bag were more cigarettes and another offering of pills. Rubio picked at the tablets and read the label:

> Patnamil – 150 mg
> Patients should be advised to be alert for warning signs
> and symptoms of liver dysfunction (jaundice, anorexia,
> gastrointestinal complaints, malaise etc.) and report
> them to their doctor immediately if they occur.

Anti-depressants, thought, Rubio, and he drank the woman's whisky while she mumbled into her pillow. Across the room a bottle of vermouth was a charming sight, upright on her suitcase, the bottle free and tender, its screw-top a parapet of leaded plastic. What sophistication came in the model Italian bottle, sculpted to her hip at the window when she took a drink? The charming bottle suited her countenance but her expression was the opposite of any advertisement.

Rubio claimed another mouthful of whisky. The woman lay level on the bed, her lips passing air like the mouth of a dying fish. Rubio took the whisky to the window, a glowing cover of lint-white dust had settled on the town and smoke rose above the hoot of a traffic horn. The stillness travelled forever, over the dunes to the hungry eye of the sun, Rubio heard the door of the hotel room so he put down the bottle and welcomed back the kid.

Hey boy, said Rubio. What's going on?

The kid twisted his face and walked to where his mother's breath shivered in the darkness, Rubio watched him pick something from her dress.

There's money here, said the boy.

The kid held a torn Egyptian note and Rubio crouched.

What's your name? asked Rubio, he cracked on his haunch bone as he moved.

Daniel, said the kid.

The kid gazed as if he'd been stuck in this jam forever, his little fists gripping his shorts.

Daniel, said Rubio, that's great. I'll be back with some food Daniel, and I'll get you something sweet. You stay here and I won't be long.

The kid burped his answer, Okay.

Rubio picked a small bottle of whisky and clicked the door closed. He walked down the stairs of the Bel Air, his hand trailing on the wall, the light dipping through the coloured glasses in the roof. Hearing a buzz of conversation from nearby Rubio missed a step and to rectify his gait he gripped the wood until it led him to the ground. The street was quiet and the windows slouched in their frames while the plaster lagged into the cracks. Rubio hustled the small bottle of whisky from his trouser and drank until he felt the sting in his lungs and coughed. He twisted the cap around the neck and carried on towards the clipped donkey shouts and the call to prayer, playing with the woman's cigarettes in his left hand.

Staring at him from across the road were the two girls from the beach. Rubio shoved the bottle behind his back and in a spirit of lunacy raised his arm as if to grant hello. The girls looked on in curiosity and so he smiled, their mouths open in surprise. Rubio waved and retreated over a hole filled with rubble towards some of Mersa's block apartments, emerging near the oil-yellow window of a café. His eyebrow twitched and he scratched at an exposed clast on his wrist where the watch had been. Like a longstanding public drinker, Rubio downed more whisky and began to appreciate Daniel's mother's desire for ice.

•

I was back at the airport, thought Rubio, I was on holiday by myself for the first time and inevitably I had my doubts. The airport officials seemed less than sure themselves, sitting at their benches and asking intolerably cryptic questions.

The purpose of your trip?
I am following in the footsteps of the great. Egypt is a place of great beauty but its immediate attraction is its history.
Business or pleasure?
It's, as I've said, both.

The official relented and agreed, he stamped Rubio's passport with permission to leave France and returned to his repose. The voice of the airport tannoy broke above the concourse, and the listeners strained their ears while the air quaked with information. Rubio owned the least amount of luggage that had ever been seen at Charles de Gaulle, the least of bags and the least of families in procession. He had also come to the airport an uncanny six hours before his flight.

A hot day in France. Rows of aeroplanes, rifle-slung police, and Rubio pretended he knew where he was going while the announcement boards scowled messages. The yellow figures on the board spelled Welcome to France while at the same time avoided the idea that France was glad to see you. Although Paris was gentlemanly in welcoming you, its coffee machines were rattling like a salvo of artillery and it talked about you with aversion once you'd left. When an aeroplane took off it hung a moment in the sky while mist blew out behind.

There the planes and then the planets, thought Rubio, each passenger comfortable as the cast serves up alcohol along the cabin. The fliers drink gin and wine while jet fire mutilates the air, cracks and slashes the clouds.

He watched a party of Americans negotiate with a taxi driver who stammered a joke that caused the French words pun with an English insult. The Americans ignored him and pointed out sights familiar from home, one American raised his hand to an advertisement with a chunky camel face, promoting the tender herbage of US smokes. The American party was not bullish about their stay in the airport, but rather made a success of their visit with icon following icon. A disheartening café chain called Bargain Basement Brownies and a cosy swathe of Red n'White cigarettes. An orange vitrolite bar selling Muffins, a joint where 3.3 billion hamburgers had vanished worldwide, and the second largest espresso bar chain on the continent, Black and Blue Iced Brews. Rubio watched the American party leave, their necks tilted back so that they tended to look upwards as they made their journey. The Romans he thought, and indeed they all wore sandals.

A Japanese asked Rubio directions, he was looking for the Oofer. Rubio with his small handbag at his side squinted and said Hotel? but the man's eyes glowed brown like cork, and he asked again for the Oofer. It sounded simple but Rubio shrugged.

You'll have to go away said Rubio. You'll have to find someone who knows what you are talking about.

The Japanese laughed at this scant sufficiency of information. Looking at the foreigner's sable eyes, Rubio felt an anger that he wished to express by pushing the man away. The man didn't leave him however and generously asked the question again, this time with a newspaper.

You'll have to go away said Rubio. Please ask someone else.

When the Japanese left, Rubio returned to watching the aeroplanes. Behind the row of smaller jets, a jumbo hauled past and mounted the sky, lifted generously away and took on the viewless form of a flying metal bar. The plane was hoisted upwards and shone, the ample silver pole made its ascent and an announcement began, the voice sounded across the complacent faces of the crowd as if it was squeezing out the brains of a chicken.

Woo bass ter gone own ter fine ter wont fainter.

People curled up peacefully beside their luggage while the glow whacked down from the glass sky. Guards passed on the prowl and the speakers continued to utter their instruction. Rubio looked wrong. He had never worn casual clothes in his life and his colour drained as he thought about the implications of his trip.

It may be nuts he thought, it may be all a game. They'll skin you alive in Egypt, and what is there to see? I should have gone to Corsica and caught sunstroke. There's even more Napoleon in Belgium than there is in the Middle East.

Rubio stood in the gallery of the concourse while air stewards walked by with tiny valises. Gripped in Rubio's hand was his only bag, on his shoulder the span of his old suit jacket was reduced to settling on his bones. He approached the bookshop, pulling himself away at the last minute and heading instead for the tabac. A clock was running, and soon he'd be spread-eagled on a bed in Egypt, God knows where, but there just the same. Planes reared into the sky and people poured from doors and down escalators, a row of telephones hung like shells upon the wall, each one of them occupied with a traveller, and Rubio wondered how he had managed to come so far in his plan. He stooped on a bench beneath the glass that divided the airport concourse from the domain of the planes and the aeroplanes tarried before they slouched up to speed and went into the sky.

Later, it was time to fly and Rubio followed the call towards the appropriate gate. Almost everything he could see, from the planes to the cars on the circular road looked like an aspect of a toy universe. He followed this universe's unreal inhabitants and began to merge with other people who were travelling to Egypt, he waited in line behind another man, looking at the back of this old fellow's neck, and only then did he begin to remember Virginie. Bodies moved forward to the gate and Rubio with them. He stood in the queue as he had always stood in queues, witnessing the plod of life at its dullest tick and tock.

We wait like a pack of wretches, he thought, running down a slope while the doctor rides behind, ever so gently applying the brakes.

The gentleman in front turned his head because Rubio had spoken aloud. The stranger seemed to smile and agree, his lip twisted as if he were trying to stop himself from laughing.

Rubio's last holiday with Virginie had involved three days aboard a train serviced by waiters who were buttoned up to their chins. A European break, it was called, luxurious travel on a train as swift as dust blown by the breeze. While the train hammered away at Europe, Rubio and Virginie fooled around with cocktails and made jokes about the scenery. They looked out on still lakes and forests until the train slowed and they were obliged to shop in cities where Rubio hung his head at his wife's talent for spending. In the evenings, Rubio drank whisky from a silver flask and muttered at the bony parts of Virginie's elbow. He criticised everything that he could see from the train window and over the duration she learned to hate his nasty bickering.

Is there anywhere in Europe you actually like? she asked as he spied on the bitches of Berne from the passing train.

Give me a break, he said. I've gone over it a hundred times, I'm just amusing myself that's all.

You haven't a friendly word in you, said Virginie as Rubio did for the slobs of Florence.

Don't overdo it, he said, we're supposed to be on holiday. I'm enjoying myself watching these idiots.

When the train returned to the Gare du Nord, Rubio returned to Sarcelles while Virginie delayed that journey, continuing for the nearby boutiques. When she returned in the evening she had become a china and glass enthusiast after visiting the cristsallerie. Rubio commented that the peacock-tail ceramic she had bought was the greatest waste of space he had ever seen, and she replied that she did not care and that she loved it.

A moment later and Rubio was on the aeroplane to Egypt, the door was slammed and the man next to him was playing thoughtfully with his seatbelt, children's laughter was heard and the engines vibrated nearby. The smile of the steward did little to improve the interior of the cabin, and it struck Rubio as he looked out over the vague heap of the airport buildings, that his holiday had begun and there was no going back.

•

Rubio took pulses and inquired after people's relatives, he abandoned the narrative format of the consultation and queried his patients' diets. The patients couldn't tell the difference, they were swallowers of pills, passive spectators in their treatment. He looked into babies' newly formed mouths and nostrils. The mothers were always angry with their children which were a perpetual source of failed endeavour. A young woman with a troubled infant arrived, the child was held at bay in a small cradle that reminded Rubio of the seat of an aeroplane ejected, the pilot held bodily in a plastic cloche.

Baby Gerard is it? said Rubio. I hope he's doing well?
In some respects, said the mother, but the way she muttered didn't offer any support for her claim.
Let's have a look at him then, said Rubio.

The mother grabbed the body of her hair and placed it to one side before it flopped back in front of her eye. Rubio pushed his chair away and raised the cradle into space, the baby's eyes watched him all the way.

On the couch then, how about that?

The infant's capsule landed smoothly and Rubio gazed at the young innocent. With its watery expression and bored roundness all he could think of was what the baby would look like as an elder man in a restaurant. He looked into Baby Gerard's ears and felt the generous development of his perfect belly. The child's mind was on a plate of meats and he was ordering a second glass of wine, he had dismissed the consultation and gone for lunch in a shady square where he sat inspecting mussels, duck, lamb and more. Internment in Sarcelles had inspired Baby Gerard to fantasise constantly about being seated in a restaurant, served by waiters in ankle-length aprons, the shock and jolt of the consultation had interrupted this escape.

What have been the symptoms? asked Rubio, and he touched the baby on the chest.

I don't know, said the mother, but I can't put it off. I don't know what to do.

Rubio opened the baby's collar and felt about the throat. Air drew through the fibres of Baby Gerard's nostrils and choked him slowly, the air turned stale in the badness of his lungs and he lay immobile, doomed to a long wait.

He looks very well, said Rubio. When did I last see him?

I don't think you did, she said. The other doctor saw him. You saw me when I was having him, and then for my pills.

That's right, said Rubio.

He spoke to the mother but she wouldn't return his look. Facts clouded facts and he tried to remember if she was married, he glanced at the open file on his desk but was unable to make out his own notes. The child looked up with an arch intelligence that Rubio interpreted as hunger, its yeasty white face seemed more alive than that of the mother.

I'll take him out of the cot, said Rubio, and he lifted Baby Gerard free. The child didn't complain but stared as the meat of his face grew harder. Rubio's face obviously disgusted him, all bumps and puffs, the wear of age.

He seems to be fine, said Rubio, holding the baby up.

The mother turned, her face had almost disappeared behind her hair.

60

What is it? asked Rubio.

He scanned Gerard to see if he had missed anything. His finger was inside the baby's tiny shirt and he pulled it to one side to see if there was something promising beneath.

He's unhappy, said the mother.

Her words carried their own painful meaning and Rubio felt in the pillow of skin that passed for the baby's neck and was glad that he found only smooth flesh.

He's nine months, said Rubio but the mother said nothing, her expression unchanged.

Rubio felt the child's legs and the dreaming mother nodded at his medical rites.

Can babies get depression? she asked.

The mother asked this question like a fencing move, she stabbed the idea into Rubio with little chance for him to prepare, and he wondered at the fundamental features of the illness, the evaluation of a malady that in so many cases, failed to prove to him that it could exist under one single name. Rubio busied himself with unnecessary examination of the baby, the taught ritual of eyes, nose and throat while he wondered which of these he could cure.

Can they get depression? whispered the mother, and Rubio replaced the baby in the cot, determined that it was well.
No they can't, he said, but the medical textbooks shook their heads while the facts of the matter slid into confusion.

Once the baby is in existence, he thought, it bears an unpredictable character. Its most pertinent traits are those it knows by instinct, an utterance of the experiences related to dietary needs and various speculations on death. The baby's face is the swelling surface of a gumboil, its voice the combination of sounds made by a cat and a peacock. The doctor, fortunately, is only there to help, at the end it's the parents that know them best.

Rubio coughed and Baby Gerard winced on the foam of his blanket.

I expect it's partially possible for them, said Rubio, and he felt beneath the child's body, not knowing what for. Depression is a difficult thing however.

The mother muttered and turned her back on Baby Gerard, but Rubio knew he could grant no medical credibility to infant depression. It was something that she had made up, obliged herself to believe, taken comfort in at an inappropriate time.

Can you prescribe something for him? she asked.

The mother's reasoning had not changed since her own consultation, she drifted with the same gist towards medication over practical advice. Meanwhile Baby Gerard put on his hat and asked for the bill, the waiter retreated and the child conducted an autopsy over the leftovers of his meal. He finds pork distasteful today, thought Rubio, and wishes he had partaken of the beef, which the family at the next table are enjoying.

There are no drugs suitable for a baby, said Rubio. I could suggest something more in keeping with his own constitution if you feel he has a depression, although I've not heard of this before.

I need to do something, said the mother. He's suffering terribly and it isn't fair at his age.

The child's eye shone at Rubio. Baby Gerard had stayed up the previous night to watch the horror thriller and he stared like he remembered it all, prematurely geared to the carnage of adulthood.

I cannot give him drugs, said Rubio. This child is only nine months old.

He has depression said the mother firmly, and she glanced at the child as if it may have overheard.

What has your husband said? asked Rubio, still under the solemn vision of the child.

He works in the car plant, said the woman. He'll get more overtime in the new building.

Rubio closed Baby Gerard's shirt. Something in the mother's grief reminded Rubio of her last visit, it explained the baby's early resistance in one respect, Baby Gerard's fear, the vital spot of his own fate in the new building of the factory where his ancestors worked, his cool attitude to life with his mother.

It is impossible that a child of this age can have such depression that you describe, said Rubio, and he tied two of the straps in the baby's capsule. Please bring him back in a month and in the meantime plenty warmth and don't forget to sterilise everything.

The mother left with a grunt of offence at Rubio's lack of medical sympathy, he knew she would take a second opinion and that he would see her again. He watched them go and sighed that the next twenty years would bring them both back to the surgery in order to prove that he'd been wrong that fateful once when he'd denied the infant its right to the embrocation of a drug therapy.

•

The whisky was finished and Rubio was wondering if he should open another bottle. In his hand were two mummified lemons with skins like cracked parchment and he supported himself on the wall and surveyed the previous binge. He stroked a cigarette from an open packet on the bed and lit it as the kid woke up.

I've brought some lemons said Rubio as the child's nose twitched at the smoke, the kid sat against the wall, his brown face budding with doubt.

She'll like these, said Rubio, and he raised the lemons and pretended they were his eyes, although the kid stared, unwilling to laugh.

She's not my mum said the kid – and Rubio lowered the lemons like lodestones.
Jesus then, said Rubio, whose mum is she?

The kid waited with his hands on his lap and kicked a bottle which knocked over another one.

Where is your mum? asked Rubio, and he thumbed in the direction of the other room.
Is she looking after you? he asked.

The kid's face didn't budge but he spoke with a trace of intolerance.

My dad's at the oasis, he said. He's at the Siwa oasis and that's where we're going.

Rubio glanced across the muddy patches of light on the wall to the other room. Her chamber was dark, the colour of remorse, a dungeon of dead furniture.

You wait here, he ordered the kid and he placed the whisky bottle on the floor.

She had not moved far in his absence, maybe to the table and back. In her wake were a trail of clothes and a black pool of whisky on the floor, alcohol licking into the wood. Her head lolled off the foot of the bed and her feet were aimed at the pillows and Rubio smelled something that he shouldn't have, cold urine. He brushed away a strand of hair and looked into the eye – it was a clear chrism of syrup that stared inward and not out – and that was enough for diagnosis. There was no stir of air from her throat, no gulp when he straightened her neck, and he held her head and seemed to forget that he was a doctor. There are forty-seven ways to tell if somebody is alive or dead but one expression tells all, he thought. Her shape opposed the bed, abruptly motionless in the red dress after death.

He went to the window and stepped on something that crunched, there was a necklace on the floor, now trodden in two parts. He bent to pick it up but stopped short. Led by such tokens investigators would find him, it was now a sin to handle anything.

Here's the plan, said Rubio to the child, we'll leave Mersa on the next bus, we'll walk out of here and let your father call the police. We'll take some money and we'll be in Siwa by this evening. We'll have some food and leave her for a few hours and have your father phone from the oasis.

The kid approached from the corner of the room, he looked towards Rubio and swung his arms as if a soldier. Both of them looked at the mother, the milk of her eyes neutralised by the poison, her hand held a burned-out cigarette that had turned to stone, the bed covers had frozen into the same arid dunes that crossed the desert and Daniel marched by and saluted her.

Let's go kid, said Rubio, and he clicked his fingers and waited by the door.

The police would come looking for Rubio and slap the Hippocratic Oath in his hand. He had stolen this woman's cigarettes and her money, he had taken her child while she lay in the debris of bottles, and Rubio would suffer for it if he didn't return the child to its father. Through the hotel window, the horizon was a thread of hazy light, visible between many ragged buildings, and Rubio covered the woman's sunken head. He took Daniel's hand and said, *come on*, and guided him to the corridor which stretched with a slight upward tilt towards the stairs.

●

Virginie left Rubio, glancing at him like a twist of lightning. She critically cocked her head in repeated disappointment and said good-bye. The argument concerning the purpose of their relationship had brought them directly to the subject of its conclusion. Rubio had endorsed the marriage with great patience but had refused to set up surgery in Paris, to minister to the rude beings that made their home there.

Will you shut up! she cried out, one full shout that hurt the innermost of his ear.

There's no need for that, he replied, but his calm made her wilder than ever.

They'll kill you here! she said.

Do you know, he asked, the average consultation fee in Paris is now higher in Euros than I can recall it ever being in Francs?

So what? she asked. Do doctors work for nothing?

For the last time, Virginie listened to Rubio blame the médecins qualifiés of Paris for ruining honest treatment. He looked at the map beside the telephone, the arrondissement system made it clear where Paris ended and Europe began, a ring road distinguished what was irreproachably French from what was slag. No other city had such definable barriers. A doctor working in Sarcelles, Montmercy, St Denis was not a doctor who worked in Paris, such a doctor therefore lived in Sin and could claim none of the medicable properties of the Capital City.

When Virginie escaped from Rubio she left Sarcelles and the banlieue, she lived in Paris and became a better person. Sarcelles was forgotten, an area of catalepsy where megatons of fresh meat were delivered in refrigerated vans and eaten by the unstirring zoo animals of Rubio's surgery. Across the canal from the apartment lay a complex of tower blocks, focal points of planned new growth poles. Empty trellised walkways crossed lean-to sheds and other concrete formalities. On paper these strongholds of tough luck were known as the1985 strategy plan but in the absence of this vision, they formed a segregated netherworld, a jumble of housing and small industry. The diseases of Sarcelles were unique to the banlieue, while in Paris, art, ambition and the tempting semblance of the best food in the world contrasted with this hoary main of scarcity. In the days of their wedding knot, Virginie spent as much time in Paris as she could, away from the antiquated illnesses and the derelict concrete plateaux of Sarcelles, but Rubio clung to his toil and the ungrateful public for whom he worked.

Why do we even stay here? she asked during arguments – but Rubio had only a sketchy idea of how to answer.

They need me, he said. This is a depressed area and somebody must look after it.

They need to clean up this hole, she said while Rubio screwed a cigarette into his mouth and agreed.

A sore throat came to the surgery one spring, hung up its coat and opened wide. The sore throat coughed, seemed to cumulate something in its mouth and then swallow it again, all the while staring at Rubio as if gathering the courage to ask something delicate. Finally, the throat folded its legs in a display of dignity and said:

Have you a pension doctor? Do you mind if I ask?

Rubio placed his pen where he had been doodling on the prescription pad.

Yes he said, I have a pension, all doctors do.

And insurance too? asked the throat, quite gently. Perhaps you have some insurance cover for a terminal illness? It's not often that doctors think of that, which is an irony I expect. Do you know Doctor Rouilly?

No I don't, said Rubio, and he took the throat's card.

Rouilly works in the Medical Centre at the Hospital, said the throat. I only mention him as an example because his pension wasn't established entirely in his favour. If you have a few minutes I can tell you about it.

Go ahead, said Rubio to the throat.

Rubio sat back and heard about how government pensions were imperfectly built for doctors and how with the throat's help he could remedy that potential shortfall.

It works like this, said the throat. There are two main types of pension. What in your view are the two main types?

Rubio noted a marked improvement in the health of the throat as it spoke, its voice no longer confined to the suffocation of its

68

illness, its coughing now expired. The throat was shaved pink and its mouth and eyes worked on the same axis, it employed them in parallel to pivot its useless ideas.

I'm a doctor, said Rubio. I don't know about the types of pensions.

You'd be surprised what you know already, said the throat. You'd be surprised if I told you that you already know the answer to my question.

So what? asked Rubio.

Monsieur you can ask your wife, said the throat. I'll wager that your Lady Wife has worked it out and could tell me the answer in words that we all understand. The two main types of pension – you see – are the Big Pension and the Small Pension.

Rubio nodded, party to the stage show, uncoiled in his seat with his head back for the next punch-line – and the throat rolled on.

Next, it said, what is the biggest problem with retirement planning?

I'm sorry, said Rubio, just continue.

Rubio could see all the way down the throat, through the bars of flesh and into the settled gut from where these questions were raised. The throat was not thrown by the lack of repartee and watched Rubio shake his head.

Okay, said the throat. But I'll wager you that your wife knows.

She may said Rubio, but she's not here.

He saw Virginie with her paper files. The increasing cunning of the insurance companies would never catch her out, she was an adult at this business and would have definitely known the answer.

Virginie had been to insurance offices to make security arrangements, all their chattels and their insurance were certified in lien, she had been the surety and Rubio had been the hostage. Now that she was gone, Virginie operated the same devices for her new husband who was probably equally as ungrateful.

The biggest single problem with retirement planning, said the throat, is underfunding. Yes?

Rubio's pen lay on his pad. He wished to pick it up and doodle but refrained as if such an action would intensify the interrogation. He wondered if he would cease to be a doctor when he retired and took up the throat's suggestions. The pension would commence and Rubio would relocate to a cavity in the North like Meudon, but would he still be a doctor? No practice, no patients, Rubio could barely see it working, he could barely imagine a day when he was not a doctor. And the throat? The throat wasn't anything. The throat was trafficking in the invisible, it was selling old age, issuing promises for when its clients were tossed overboard into the seclusion of a waste-bin.

Choices you make before retirement, said the throat, will determine the choices you have after you have retired. Yes?

Rubio nodded. It was all the throat needed to continue.

The throat drew a bundle of pension literature from its case and placed it on the desk, it moved its hands as if to indicate that it was safe for Rubio to touch. The brochure was bright like a summery dress, it was futuristic and on the cover was a retired professional man who looked like he had clocked off life with a smile and had gone to seed.

Question then, said the throat.

Rubio said nothing. He wondered how to identify with the brochure. Retirement wasn't long – only twenty years to go – and in that time, Rubio was to prepare for his transformation into the straw hat wearing, vineyard wandering old buffer who was smiling from his gums on the leaflet.

Question, said the throat. How can you guarantee a good performance for your pension?

Rubio shrugged but the throat wanted more, the throat wanted an assurance that Rubio would commit himself to a strike. Rubio looked ahead for an answer, the desired response to the brochure on his desk.

The money you pay into your pension will be invested in the stock market, said the throat, so what I'm asking you is how can you guarantee a good return?

Rubio wondered what to say, the jaws of the trap were close and the throat was drawing him near, so he shrugged, unable to progress.

You can't guarantee it! said the throat suddenly. That is what this brochure is about Doctor, so I'll leave it for you and your Lady Wife to have a look.

The throat went on. He had a great turn for oxymoron and talked of death benefits, tax efficiency and retirement options. Surely all of this was taken care of however? What is bureaucracy, thought Rubio, if it cannot manage my benefits without sending in characters like this to regulate my surety against death?

After a minute Rubio took his pen and sketched a semi-circle while he abandoned the idea that there could be life after five o'clock. He listened to the throat's rasp and imagined his money being siphoned away in the direction of the Bourse.

It's not so much the world we're living in, said the throat, but it's the world we're going to live in.

Rubio began a count from ten to one. On reaching one he would rocket out of his chair and shatter into the roof.

In the next decades, said the throat, it's going to be as difficult for doctors as it is for anyone else, so a good step in the right direction is to provide for yourself.

Rubio drew a dagger on his notes and decorated it with dripping blood. He would prescribe the throat white arsenic. He would say: put this in your coffee and you will feel much better. How the throat could explain the future in such detail one spring morning, Rubio did not know, but from this day to the grave protection ruled. Retirement may be the bitter flip side of work but the throat would smooth everything out, that was the promise.

If the state provides for you, said the throat, then you'll have this pension on top of that!
Which pension? said Rubio.

He wondered if he had agreed to something but the throat didn't answer. Instead it opened the brochure and pointed to a heading, The Perfect Pension Provider. Same line and same locale, the same professional to serve the same needs of the people of Sarcelles, and Rubio asked him again: which pension? The throat explained it, smiling as if this were a comedy while Rubio looked on his scribbled prescription pad.

All I'm saying is that the time may come when you need it, said the throat. I can leave something for you to look at and you can get back to me. These pensions are for doctors who wish to enjoy retirement and not worry about it in the meantime.

I'm not a doctor said Rubio.

The throat's face was white, it had been about to smile but had stopped, unable to find a phrase to counter Rubio's end stop.

I'm sorry? said the throat in a croak.

Rubio said it again.

I'm not a doctor.

Goodness said the throat. What shall I do with this prescription then?

Give it to your chemist said Rubio, and your chemist will give you something to ease it up. I'd do it soon because I've a feeling it might be worse tomorrow. I think you know the rest. Good food, sleep, plenty of rest. Cinema. Yoga and prayer. Non-violence, intensive journal keeping, escapist fantasies. A vocation of poverty, maybe a wilderness sojourn. Jogging. Otherwise it'll get worse and it could be very painful.

When the throat said thanks it looked nervously at Rubio. It retreated to the door leaving the leaflet open on the desk, showing the small print of the Perfect Pension. When the throat had closed the door, Rubio put its pension literature in the waste paper basket and turned the diary page to see the next two days. He thought about what the throat had said and looked at the medical trappings of the consulting room. This was a complete surgery, perfect in many ways, and he pictured himself in the doctor's chair and reflected how strange that only a moment ago, listening to the throat, he had not felt like a doctor at all, under any description of the word.

•

In the medicine bag Rubio counted a tangled thicket of instruments and devices, forgetting what they were for. On the bed his mother maintained a remote but ever-sliding breath, capturing air in her lungs and whirling it slowly out.

You're cooking? she asked, and Rubio nodded that he was.

Chicken like yours, he said, hoping that she would not be strong enough to ask him for some.

Bring me some chocolate, she asked, and Rubio lifted himself from her side and left the medical tools in the mountain mass of his bag to make a final shopping list.

He carried home a plucked chicken and a block of chocolate, he pulled the chicken's body apart but the bird was black along the line of the wing and smelled of a lung fever he had once treated. Rubio broke the chocolate into fatal looking shards and carried them to his mother on a plate, he left her making snappish sallies at the broken lumps and returned to the cooker. The bird's knees were drawn up to its chest and it lay in the oven like a conch.

During the second week of his mother's illness her breathing became more difficult, she ate less and only wanted a glass of orange. Every day a glass of orange and some yoghurt for her sour temper, several pills of her doctor's prescription and a few words about the Lord or the postman.

Life paused as if a breeze had been caught and his mother's face became whiter. She needs more light thought Rubio, and he opened the curtains. Instead of a frown, her head appeared to shine with the gauze of a smile when she saw the daylight. The last few motions were carried out and then she closed her eyes for good.

Rubio called Virginie but the line was engaged on more important business. He weighed the phone in his hand a moment before he called Burneto and asked him to come over, saying yes, his mother had rejoined the Catholic faith.

Do I need to bring the priest? said Burneto.
She's died is what I mean, said Rubio.
Okay, said Burneto. Twenty minutes.

On returning to the bedroom where his mother lay, Rubio thought about the priest, a fang of a man with a thousand pardons in his Bible. Rubio glowered at the prospect of the priest walking up the stairs, the worst of all possible men, a suburban and plastic parson, coming to claim Rubio's mother for his vapid after-world. He picked a flyspeck from his mother's blanket and touched her neck like a medical man. She was warm but her temperature was fading as the skin relaxed upon the bones. The newspaper lay unopened at the bedside and Rubio knocked it on the floor where it split untidily. He wondered if he should cover his mother's face and touching the sheet he decided to wait until Burneto had taken a look.

When he needed a cigarette Rubio left his mother's side and stopped at the window. The apple tree in the neighbour's garden approached a blossom but the flowers were dirty, the remaining trees leaned against the wall, bedded in the distillation of muck that the neighbours called The Orchard. Everything had worked out, the priest would arrive on the doorstep and confirm this. The reversal was complete. The living house of God had become God's last earthly facility and the death would be ordered in the files, the body dressed and each part of the event dissembled and then sold on.

Burneto arrived at the back door and tramped through the kitchen to the stairs. The next stage on the journey had begun and the low whisperings of Burneto's shoes were leading the way to the next station. This was the progression, it was happening all the time. Whenever some person's mother died, manners kicked in and Burneto arrived, a sweet and simple doctor moving as delicately as possible.

Rubio? He heard his friend's voice from below.
Up here, he said.

Burneto's hat appeared and then the body, coat and bag.

How are you doing? asked his friend and Rubio said fine.

Burneto motioned shyly to the door of the bedroom and Rubio said yes, allowing his colleague access. His friend's genuflection was a thoroughly dishonest action but he carried it out as formulaically as his examination. He felt her neck and checked her breath and heart, he touched her wrist and clipped his stethoscope to his ears, all the while knowing that she was dead. A modest medical rigour was applicable and Burneto was there to tick the boxes, his duties were official. He padded around diplomatically attempting to fulfil every medical procedure in order to render to science the art of manners, and Rubio watched him, irritated at the palaver. Burneto was a great professional. Like all the best doctors he systemised his examinations into ritual shows that played for the patient's pleasure. People were used to seeing their doctors in a confessional humour and liked the action to be predictable.

Are you done? asked Rubio when he'd seen enough.
I expect so.
The perky voice of Burneto.

Rubio went for the bathroom where he lit up. Here was another room that required attention, more cupboards to be emptied, a toilet he wished to drain, a hot water tank he'd gazed at all his life. He used the sink as an ashtray and leaned against the door. Burneto appeared from the bedroom and offered a hopelessly sympathetic look.

Would you like me to call an undertaker? asked his colleague.

Yes, said Rubio, that would be helpful

If it's a consolation, said Burneto, you should know that my own parents were the same.

Both of them? asked Rubio and he pulled hard for a nutritious blitz of smoke.

Yes, said Burneto, they were both sweet folks, like your mum.

Rubio ignored the platitude and tapped at the cigarette. Burneto was behaving like an utter dog, standing there with his hung expression and saying, how about a coffee?

No thanks, said Rubio and he blew a beam of smoke.

Dog photographs formed a flying V above the toilet. The dogs in the pictures were chewing bones or crouched like prize winners in wicker baskets. Rubio picked a picture from its perch and carried it to the hall where Burneto was walking down the stairs, running his hand on the banister in mortal contemplation of the wood.

I'm making one for myself, said Burneto. It's just as fast to make a couple.

Rubio followed his colleague to the stove, and pained by the sight, he watched Burneto assemble a coffee maker that he couldn't remember having seen before.

Listen, said Rubio, there's probably no coffee.

Come on, said Burneto, sit down. It's not pleasant but the initial shock you know.

Rubio dropped the picture of the dog into the kitchen bin and Burneto stopped what he was doing.

I say, that was probably worth something, don't you think?
Rubio said nothing and tapped ash over the photograph.
I'm sorry, said Burneto, and he stopped with the machinery of the coffee maker and touched Rubio on the arm. I know what it's like he said. Wait until she's gone. There's plenty time.

Rubio obeyed his friend and walked to the back room, another trove of unnecessary activity. Papers in the closet, a bureau and a rack of books and magazines, a half-finished crossword at the fireside, dated the week before. The Papal tapestry above the sideboard and the set of holy books were an extravagance, they were older than his mother had been but ensured the room was complete. There was a clatter of dishes just as if his mother had been there, but it was Burneto, playing the crank in the kitchen, opening jars and looking for things. Rubio heard Burneto examine the cupboards for food, cleaning plates and rattling cutlery. He expected Burneto to appear in an apron, but when his colleague poked his head in he was still bound within the refrigeration of his coat.

I told you old man, don't worry.

Everything to perfection, Burneto offered his cow look into the room.

Look, said Rubio. An unfinished crossword.

Burneto glanced to the fireside where the newspaper lay open on Rubio's mother's trolley, a glow crossed his face and he said, take courage old man.

By the time Burneto had served the coffees, still in his coat,

Rubio had crumpled the newspaper and crushed it into the fireplace. Burneto didn't notice and put the coffee on the trolley where it had been.

Now the undertaker, said Burneto. Do you have any idea of what she might have liked?

No, said Rubio.

He looked into the cup of coffee – a shimmer on the surface made it oily sick.

Is your mother still alive? he suddenly asked and he looked at Burneto who was wrapped in the warm scoop of his coat.

No, said Burneto. You were at the funeral you remember? That was ten years ago. She was as an old dear when she went. They just begin to fade sometimes.

Yes, said Rubio, it's true.

He remembered the funeral after all, the colleagues in the purity of their black suits when they had barely met the woman. The same physicians bound in black would be at his mother's funeral too, a thought not worth the time of day.

I wonder if you could go now you've done the examination, asked Rubio and Burneto's eyebrow raised as Rubio bid him stand.

Burneto unsnagged his coat from the ornamental iron fender and Rubio led him through to the front door. In the hall was a row of coats upon the pegs and Rubio realised that one of them had belonged to his father.

A few moments alone with her, said Rubio. Then I'll do the business with the priest. Maybe we could eat together later?

Ideal, said Burneto.

The poor man's face was heavy. Burneto had come to do his

duty but he was being thrown out without even being allowed to drink his cup of coffee. As soon as Burneto was in the porch, Rubio closed the door and looked at him through the glass, as if his colleague were an exhibit.

I have to say goodbye to her, said Rubio.

Burneto opened the street door and was sucked out into the world. When the door had closed Rubio stood until the noises of the empty house had returned. He felt his father's unfamiliar coat and looked into the kitchen. The task was to strip the premises of all its confidences before it was sold to the next young comers. He picked up the telephone and dialled Virginie again. When he heard her voice it sounded as if she had adopted a new accent. She was deeper and more precise, less Parisian and more English.

It's me, said Rubio with all the emotion of the grave.
Oh yes, she said, not impressed.
I needed to talk, he said. I'm phoning from my mother's house.
Could you hang on? asked Virginie.

Rubio heard her walk from the phone and then return. A broad fog emerged to cover his memory of their marriage as if it had not been a real event.

What is it then? she asked when she was ready. How is your work going?
I'm still working but I've thought about packing it in, said Rubio.
Really, she said. For what?

Rubio hadn't thought of packing it in but now it seemed to be the thing to do. He was going to pack everything in, pack up his mother's house and have a rag trader take it away on a cart. Slaves would lay fagots on the pyre and the cart would empty its contents on the blaze, then Rubio would do the same with his own place. Why was he still living in the same slab-sided apartment that he used to share with Virginie?

I don't know yet, he said, but it's just the way things are going. Reaching that time? she asked.

Unsure what was expected of him Rubio said yes. There was now no way to introduce the topic of his mother's dying.

Do you remember Burneto? he asked. I've just seen him.
God, said Virginie, your old partner.
Hardly, said Rubio.
I thought you hated him, said Virginie. Is he still a doctor?
We're all still doctors, said Rubio.
He's so reserved, said Virginie, he would sit there with his hands clasped. Do you remember?
Yes.
He would be sitting there while everyone else at the table was talking and Burneto would have his hands clasped!

Rubio grunted and went for another cigarette.

What was that about his hands? he asked. He was here just now, the usual fool, blameless in life, he drives me crazy sometimes.

Why are you telling me all this? asked Virginie.

Rubio looked at the telephone and wondered whom else he could call. There was no ashtray here but he lit up anyway.

My mother died, said Rubio, and he shuddered at having to hear the sentence.
Oh no, said Virginie, I'm sorry.

It's okay, said Rubio, and he sank into the soft lap of the hall chair.

There was a pause while Rubio worked on what he had to say next. The house was cold, as if his mother had taken every calorie to the grave. He waited until Virginie spoke, unsure of whether it was his turn to say something or not.

What happened? she said after a moment.

Rubio wondered what to say. In Virginie's world death was an affair during which people reverted to a script. She was abundantly piquant in life but knew nothing about its end.

I saw her, said Rubio. Strange, but I felt lucky to see her go like that. I called Burneto but I wish I hadn't now. I should have called her own doctor.

That's terrible, said Virginie. Is there anything I can do?

Rubio knew that Virginie was going to say that and he wondered what she would say next.

I just wanted to call you and let you know, he said, absolving her from action.

Was it sudden? asked Virginie.

Her script was out of order, the poor woman. What she knew about life could be written on a scrap of toilet paper. Rubio wanted to smash the telephone down but managed a laugh instead.

I'll call you for the funeral, he said, and he flicked another harmless chunk of ash on to the floor.

It'll be a couple of days, he said.

Okay. Let me know if there's anything we can do.

Sure, said Rubio, cold blooded.

Virginie's *we* had included her husband, although you could hardly count on him for support at a time like this. On cue, tomorrow morning Rubio could expect a bunch of flowers, signed from the husband as well. He nearly said to Virginie, don't bother, but why should he spoil her fun? Why remove her script at this difficult time?

I'll see you then, said Rubio, and I'm sorry for butting in.
You look after yourself, she said, and don't be too sad.

Rubio replaced the phone and looked up the frost line of the banister to the room upstairs. There would be one more trip to see the mother and then he would go around the corner and drink wine. Later he would search through the boxes and papers, looking for those elusive clues, the keys to the past, anything in the tomb that could set his memories adrift.

As he reached for his father's coat to try it on for size, it occurred to Rubio that there was nothing more to do, that family life with all its charms and stresses was over for good. There was nothing more to get upset about. His father's coat was a dirty specimen that had not been touched for years, and when he wore it, Rubio swayed forward, almost giddy with the knowledge that he knew nothing and cared for nobody.

·

A brief morning sandstorm left the bus momentarily lost, tie-down lines on tents snapped until the wind died and the vehicle was able to move away towards Siwa. The bus driver clapped his hands as if to clean them of something distasteful, sand grimed everything and Rubio stared down the road to where the sun indicated its end.

If there had been one to ask why I felt such manifest irritability, thought Rubio, I doubt whether I could give them an adequate response. Indeed, if my outward demeanour is one of petulance, my inner consciousness is rather of a nameless dread and of the need for my senses to remain taught and on the alert for danger.

He pulled a postcard from his pocket and repeated the sentence, fidgeted with the pen while he searched the broken face of the sphinx.

Daniel tugged his arm, but Rubio stared at the Egyptian on the near seat, the man's large black hands awkwardly playing with a cigarette. The bus window was sparked with dots of clay and Rubio reached to pick at one, unsure if it were outside or inside the vehicle.

You were asleep, said Daniel, and Rubio stared into the empty court of the desert, the mouth-like cavities of the passing rock.

No I wasn't, said Rubio, I was just thinking about writing a postcard.

You were asleep, said the kid and Rubio ignored him.

Later, when the vehicle crawled to the side of the road again, chatter rose and Rubio saw that they had arrived beside a brick cabin in a flat saddle of sand. The bus came to rest and people moved to the door.

Come on, said Rubio to the kid, and he shunted Daniel to his feet and out into the sand.

Across the road was the squat shadow of an army base, the iron curb of a disused hut, a broken jeep and a flag. Beyond that there was no difference between the land and sky.

Look, he said to Daniel. Look at it all.

The sun licked the cheek of the earth and the horizon ran so perfectly around them that it was like being at the centre of a plate. Where the sky formed a line above the landscape, here sat the sun, deep in its yellow casement, and Rubio took a cigarette from his pocket and rested his hand on Daniel's shoulder.

Do you need the toilet? Rubio asked Daniel.
He lit his cigarette and filled himself with smoke.
Well? said Rubio, how about it?

Behind the rest stop were several short stone walls that concealed toilets. A donkey tied to a post stared straight ahead, a bridle skewered to its jaw and its head covered in flies. Rubio walked Daniel past the donkey towards the open plain which ran to the same obstinate stop in a distance. The sand was like the sea in its consistency, as if it were nursing the vain illusion of movement.

All our negotiations need to aim at these points, thought Rubio. Return Daniel to his father and obtain more money in the form of a loan. Explore the oasis of Siwa and establish what if any links with Alexander the Great or Napoleon. Finally return to the coast.

There was a light scuffing from behind and when Rubio turned he saw the boy running in the direction of the sand. Daniel tore away from the rest stop into the wilderness which ended at the sun.

Daniel? said Rubio, not loud enough for the boy to hear.

Rubio walked to where the desert began and stood in far-gone contemplation watching the kid run directly into the emptiness.

Daniel!

The kid had made distance now, fifty metres towards the horizon where the sun hung like a threat. Rubio glanced behind and caught the sarcastic eye of the donkey, a calculated sneer from its gums and teeth. Who can run faster, it asked, the five-year-old boy or the forty-five-year-old man? Forty-five-year-old man is already mortally influenced by his own failure to communicate, and as for five-year-old boy? He doesn't even need to try.

The sun swivelled low and Daniel leaped over a flat rock towards the hood of the sky. Rubio spat and began to trot, almost immediately feeling the loneliness of the desert. His voice clove to his throat as he began to fear where Daniel was going, a tiny figure running over the flat plate of the world to nowhere.

Come on Daniel! shouted Rubio, but his voice died in the dipping hillocks of rock. He pulled his cigarettes out of the torn shirt and gripped them in the pale of his fist. The jog continued in a driving silence and Rubio's footsteps bore forward on the sand, patting one after the other on the trail of the boy. He wondered how often the drunk woman had to chase Daniel through the sand like this. He heard her crying his name and tripping over her dress, he pictured the avalanche of her approach as she beat the earth and cried. It's strange how you meet someone who despises you and the next day they've reconstituted themselves in your imagination as a priceless entity, he thought, because I actually liked her. It's strange, but that scarecrow of old cloth made an impression, it's as if we had been married. That's the problem with marriage, he thought. You should never meet your wife, your husband, you should maybe see them once a year for a short holiday. The confrontation between man and wife develops not under the sign of love but as an avowed compromise that guarantees the union until one takes the courage to die.

A sudden downtrend in the sand and Rubio fell and rolled on his side. He bashed to a halt and as the breath was hauled out of him a mouthful of sand was kicked inside.

Daniel ran like a missile into the sun, Rubio wanted to shout but the weight on his chest told him it wasn't worth the effort. The pressure in his ears was unbearable, his stomach jumped into his throat and he sat down in a spin. He tried to see the kid but darkness pushed upon his eye and he wondered if he was even facing in the right direction. As the deafness reared, Rubio thought he heard a noise, the sound of Daniel's running feet, and he bent over to take a breath. The taste of the whisky returned, a swarm of needles in the stomach, he began the trot again and his knees cracked, he suffered an image of the joint in question and thought of the surgery.

Rubio gulped involuntarily and a watery secretion of whisky ran up his throat. The kid finally changed direction and turned several steps before he tripped. Rubio thought of what they would say in France concerning his kidnapping of the boy, it was roughly worked out in his head, his appearance in the court where the word *freedom* had a more formal meaning than it did in the plain lingo of the day. He stopped to rest his weight and shouted, Daniel!

The boy stumbled and fell, and Rubio stepped on towards the low light in the sky.

The boy lay in a sun-sprinkled star when Rubio approached.

Come on Danny, what is it? You still want to go to Siwa, don't you?

The boy nodded as tears swerved off his face and chin. The rest stop had sunk into the land behind them. Surrounded by its herd of road vehicles it had become a blob of light that could be mistaken for a large rock.

We've go to get back on the bus, said Rubio and he wiped his head, dirty with sweat. The bus'll leave, he whispered, we have to get back for that.

The ground was close, the earth made savage by the reins of heat. Bacteria swam across Rubio's eyes and the sun's pattern on the equator dizzied him as if the magnetism that kept him upright was failing. All the stones, the tiny grains of dirt and inches of black shrub that tried to bust through the earth, they amounted to nothing while at the same time were the entirety of a kingdom. The boy seemed to experience the same doubt and gripped his legs.

Kiddo, asked Rubio, what were you running away from? Is it me?

Rubio had hopes that Daniel might answer yes. The kid was chaperoned by an itinerant doctor, he had no mother and the few surviving fragments of childhood were falling away. Why should he care about doing what he was told?

Come on, said Rubio, I'll get you back and we can see what your Dad's got to say.

Daniel nodded, his blunt nose held a tear. Rubio placed his hand on the boy's head and they started across the diameter of the land to where a glossy plume of dust arose from the roadway. The high drone of the engine thumped in the distance and the two of them faltered towards the road, Rubio pulling the kid's arm.

Come on! shouted Rubio and Daniel's calm expression modified to tears.

In the white of the sky, inches from his face and many thousands of miles above, Rubio wondered if he could make it the final few steps to the road. He made out the burned solar face of the desert bus – the vehicle was turning in preparation for departure. On the bus were faces black and dim. A cloud of dust played and Rubio waved his arm as the high-pitched purling in his ear began.

Hold on! he shouted, an optimistic idea that anyone on the bus could hear him.

By the time the bus had hunched over one pothole and the next, Rubio was banging on its wing, choking on a layer of dust. He kicked the vehicle, hoping to knock a deep socket in its body, and it bounced to a stop and the door hissed open. He pulled the kid to the door and as the driver welcomed them back, Daniel yelped and pulled his arm away.

I'm sorry Daniel, he said, but I didn't think we'd make it.
That hurt, said Daniel and he headed for the rear of the vehicle.

Time caught up with itself and the bus moved on. Rubio stared at the smeared hem of sand that ran beside the road. He dreamed of a long lie down during which he might consider the next twenty years worth of patients, their skinny hands, the clank and iron of their depression. From the bus window he watched the glaring dunes. The sand was rich beyond the colours of the sky, smooth in a haze of yellow with nothing of the world's master revealed. It's little wonder that religion came out of this place, thought Rubio, and less wonder that it's so very futile back at home. . .

He planted his feet on the floor and began to sleep. An envelope of cool gases formed and his mind regressed as his patients appeared in a belt of unhappy faces, each one a brief caricature of their malady. The noises of the bus departed and he tried to work his way into the chair on the assumption that it would cocoon him like a pillow, hold him in the gentle cradle of his shape. The opposite was true however and Rubio's neck felt as if it were locked, the muscles overlapping each other in a search for comfort. The sand dunes froze as if in a cold shade, as if the bus were a tiny molecular weight on a cooling layer of iron. Clouds collapsed to stars lit by the moon, erratic in the brightness, a jewel box with horizontal branches stretching into the land. The sky was sustained by a surging sea of hydrogen dust and atoms, while the universe behind it was silent with the steps of supergiants.

Rubio bumped awake and he looked along the ragged edge the headlights made where they contacted the dark. The play of light wrote a line of Arabic and the bus swerved as if the driver were trying to steer a horse. In the darkness the faint hump of the horizon suggested rocks and hills, the bus bounced through a gouge in the road and the engine gave a raw rasp, something which seemed to impress the driver a great amount. Rubio took a postcard from his pocket and reconsidered his line.

If there had been one to ask why I felt such impatience this day, he thought, I doubt whether I could give them any response. Indeed, if my outward demeanour is one of sensitivity, my inner consciousness is rather of a hopeless dread and an awareness that my senses need remain steady and on the alert for danger. . .

The driver shouted to the passengers from his powder blue seat, the bus broke through the hush of the night and the passengers grinned at the violence of it. The vehicle shook as if its dented aluminium skeleton was choking, the clips and bolts shaking in dismemberment. Rubio slipped the postcard into the pitch-black of his pocket, where the sphinx shrugged and returned to sleep. He remembered Daniel and turned to see the kid speaking to a couple of soldiers at the back of the bus. He tipped his hand to them but they did not see him.

If there had been one to ask why I felt such impatience this day. . .

Rubio's hand found the cigarettes and he saw the plum faces of the colleagues as they read his postcards. They were stirring coffee and thinking of something to say, until one remembered him and laughed.

I had a card from Rubio – he says he's entertaining himself with the affairs of France – as close to hell as can be found on earth. All the heat and thirst stuff you'd expect – and he says that his irritability and boorish impatience – whatever they are – are at an all-time high. He says he's otherwise having a nice time and that the weather is wonderful. . .

With Siwa at hand, the driver shouted. He pointed from the window and gestured with a sense of wonder. Rubio saw a colonnade of rock against the sky, shapes that indicated a change in the landscape, mighty darkness, pleasing in appearance, the shades of two lands in the crack and jump of the suspension forks. The driver spoke but his words meant nothing, mocking signs in a chain of excited phrases. Rubio lit up as he observed the first lights of Siwa, the glow formed a line on the horizon and brighter chinks appeared from a rocky foothill. The driver leaned on the steering wheel and skidded the vehicle in the moonlight. The engine wailed and the first streetlights stressed a row of buildings with no windows, blocks which vanished and were replaced by sheds and shacks. The effect was of touching down among a wasteland like broken swords. The collapsed form of the old town of Siwa rose in a mound of gaunt brown sand lit by an inhuman gleam of spotlights, this mountain of houses was an abstraction, a pile of doors and walkways leaning gently skyward, the work of human insects over many years. The bus drove to a square and before the motor had shut down, Rubio was out of the vehicle and beneath the yield of the old town wall.

As his senses gathered, Rubio watched the kid stroll over to a concrete building called the Hotel Youssef and turning around, Rubio saw the other passengers struggling with bundles of cloth and plastic.

Daniel, he said, and he followed the kid over to the awning of the hotel.

Next to where Daniel curled on a bench beneath the hotel's strip-light, Rubio laid out his cigarettes and postcards for sleep. One road ran into the palms and the other stopped at a small acropolis of sand topped with weak towers and a minaret. The bus hacked away through a corridor of salt-impregnated mud buildings which merged around it as a single block.

Where Rubio lay on the porch of the Hotel Youssef, in between the ravine of doors and windows, Paris was once again a distant fiction, something he might read concerning a time long past.

I'm sleeping here for the night, he said to Daniel, but the kid curled nearby with his back turned.
Goodnight, said Rubio, going for the cigarettes, sinking back to wait for a response.

•

The clatter from the edge of the letterbox elbowed Rubio from where he lay at ease in his arrow pose he had barely disturbed the covers.

Will you have children? his mother used to ask. She repeated the question monthly and he felt dead feelings stir. Rubio's mother knew that her son the doctor would never father any children, his marriage bed a God-forsaken site. When she asked the question he politely answered no, the sight of several births had already been unforgettably horrible, even for a doctor.

Rubio kicked the covers and stepped on to the rug, the trade-mark feel of home. He moved the edge of the curtain to see the tenement houses in the old square, the swastika on the cabin of the bus shelter. At the end of the street two African women pushed baby buggies on the platform of the pavement.

In the next room he checked on his dead mother, hard against her pillow, her shoes huddled together in the shade at the corner of the room like refugees. The bedroom was hospital grey, the small essentials of her life were arrayed in ones and twos upon the mantelpiece, her gaze upon the roof. Once satisfied, Rubio walked downstairs like an undecided guest, first to check the letters that had fallen into the porch and then to take apart the kitchen, to combine coffee with the demolition of the past.

His census began with the cake tins and all of them submitted to his cleansing. He wiped the shelves to the very darkness of the armoire until all was brought to light and sectioned for disposal. The pans she used to use were anchored in the iron age of the War, while on the draining board were the tea-towels of many nations, sunny days in the fishing towns Brittany and the Tower of London. Rubio pushed his mother's kitchenware in a cortège towards the stove and at about ten o'clock when this game was at its height, he heard a step upon the front porch and the dignified chime of the doorbell rang like lead. It was an old trick of the house that obliged the bell to resonate in nerves that normally lay untouched, the sound snaked between the legs of the furniture and returned to the eardrum even after the note had died. The silence was guilty and Rubio caught his reflection in the glass of the cupboard.

Now it's too late to go answering the door, he thought. Excuses will have to be made, embarrassing moments on the doorstep must be avoided as must the dread agenda of funeral formalities – the body needs be taken downstairs and the neighbours must be informed – the sandwiches should be ordered and the old Gauls from the provinces will have to be lettered with the details.

In anticipation of being spotted by the uninvited, Rubio reached through the tripwires of daylight and clicked off the electric switch. To his surprise, he feared the funeral and its guests, Burneto and the colleagues, his wife and every other mourner in the wedlock of remorse. Rubio had Burneto to blame, France had Burneto to blame. Burneto lived in a model universe, it represented the ultimate in reason, the revolution of good sense that kept him and his plans so tidily on course. The mourners were coming and Burneto was running the show, configuring a network of funeral guests and facing death in the modern style. Burneto would have called the florists and the newspapers, Burneto would be carrying the coffin down the aisle just like Burneto would be mourning discretely in every degree, for it was not like him to do anything at an inappropriate time. The mourners were coming but the funeral was only a stopping point between their homes and the cafés to which they'd retire when she was buried. The way they arrived, the way they touched the cable of cord that hung from the coffin, the way they bowed away to their habitual cups when they'd had enough of the scenery. . .

Rubio could still hear a person in the vennel, an insistent visitor determined to remove the body from the tomb. He listened until the footsteps departed towards the street and when he spied his cigarettes by the stove, he reached out and grabbed them.

Crouched while the sun wheeled past the window, Rubio sat with his back to the wall and mourned beneath the cigarette smoke until Burneto appeared at the kitchen door with his stupid question pre-prepared.

Didn't you hear the bell, old man?

Harnessed in his cardigan, Rubio smoked and made up a story that he had been in the cellar. The house had no cellar and Burneto knew it but Rubio persisted with his story until the undertaker walked in and said that he was ready. Burneto skulked in the area of the kitchen, a room laid bare and placed in boxes. He twittered about his son and his surgery and to shut him up Rubio asked him to follow to the front room where there was more work to be done.

Make yourself useful, said Rubio. Have a look in the standing cabinet and see if there's anything of value.

Rubio signalled Burneto towards the front room which held the treasury of the house. He hadn't counted on his colleague's tact however, a trembling decorum which disallowed Burneto from even looking at antique items while the body was still within the bounds.

Go on, said Rubio, and he opened the glass door behind which his mother's whatnots lay bathed in dust.

Inside the cabinet were plates and ornaments, statuettes and crystal glasses, spoons and toneless ceramic dishes of many colours. Rubio knew exactly what Burneto was thinking – he was wondering how on earth Rubio could possibly sell these treasures, but if it hadn't been so vicious a thought, Rubio would have sooner smashed them.

Value? said Rubio, and he turned to Burneto who retreated into the shell of his overcoat.

I'm no expert, said Burneto, meaning that at least in his own opinion he was. He leaned towards the cabinet.

I could give you a rough figure I expect.

Go on then, said Rubio, and he pulled an ashtray from the side table.

Burneto stood like a love-sick bird before the cabinet while Rubio stared from his father's former armchair. As a rule of thumb, thought Rubio, Burneto will flatter my mother's collection, just as she flattered it by putting it in a glass-fronted chiffonier.

Burneto looked across the display and said – may I? – asking if he could pick up a plate.

Of course, said Rubio and he took out the cigarettes.

Burneto held the plate like it was a bomb.

Ah yes, he said looking at the underside.

There was a light thump from the hall and there she was coming down. It had been a pleasant day before Burneto and the undertaker had arrived. Rubio had been downstairs, remembering her as only he could. It had not been unreasonable for him to keep her there the extra day. As far as contacting the undertaker was concerned, he had expected that like any other act of procrastination, it would be done tomorrow.

Burneto smiled because he had discovered something uninteresting in the sack of inapt facts he depressingly called his knowledge of antiques.

English, said Burneto, having identified one of Rubio's mother's plates as coming from that frozen land. Face to face with the plate Burneto's features were mirrored unpleasantly.

Pink and yellow flowers on a cream ground, said Burneto as he gained more confidence. Underneath the name of the manufacturer in gilt. So where would she have got this one? A trip to England?

Rubio could recall nothing of his parents' holidays. She could have picked these things up anywhere. In those years, people had delighted in collecting jolly crockery, everything in the cabinet belonged to a time when these obsessions mattered.

It would have to be the nineteen thirties, said Burneto holding the plate up to the light. All he lacked was a film crew and a camp of similar antique buffs to flatter his intelligence. Possibly one of a set of three, said Burneto. Did it come with any others?

Burneto suited his overcoat, it was the colour of an old sycamore and the perfect get-up for the amateur antiques inspector. Burneto held the plate close to his face as if to sniff it and then he stared once more into the cabinet.

How much is it worth? said Rubio.

Well, said Burneto turning the plate, I'd say it would fetch a fair amount with the right buyer. I'd certainly say that it increases the value of the cabinet as it stands.

Give it here.

Burneto wiped the plate with a handkerchief and gave it over to Rubio. Mother was gone but the plates remained the same. The decadence of her body had infused the collection with her own disease, her smell was there, a vein of flint in his nose. Burneto was right about the plate. Pink and yellow flowers and leaves on a cream ground. It was a revolting item of tableware with the manufacturer's phallic logo printed on one of the tiny leaves. Mother had probably known the plate better than she did members of her own family although Rubio could hardly blame her for that. He had no desire to keep the plate and gave it back to Burneto, disgusted that this dispersal was going to be more difficult than he had imagined.

Very distinctive, said Burneto looking under the plate again. You can see here that it's been scored several times. It gives it the kind of character you'd be looking for.

The plate was returned to the circle of the shelf as the undertakers bumped through the hall. Burneto paused and then selected two red decanters that had splintered the light for as long as Rubio could recall.

Cranberry, said Burneto, and very nice too. These pieces are older than your mother, don't you know?
Rubio shrugged.
How much? he said.
At least as much as the plate, opined Burneto, maybe more. It's difficult to say. I don't know much about these things but still

I'm rather taken with them. They certainly are a delight.

Burneto held the decanter by the stem and rim, exercising his continued penchant for always being right by staring through the glass like there was something that only he could see.

Have it if you like, said Rubio. It's really nothing to any of us.

I couldn't do that, said Burneto and he bashfully returned the piece.

I don't care, said Rubio. Do you think that you could drink out of it?

I don't know, said Burneto. I wouldn't imagine that many people have.

No, said Rubio, they haven't.

He heard the undertakers in difficulty at the front door.

Burneto, may I ask you a question?

Burneto was in among the collectibles and had found a rather tasty ceramic lady of which he very much approved.

Certainly, he said, and he turned to Rubio, holding his figurine, a contrast to his own shape. Rubio stopped. Burneto was consumed by the cabinet and couldn't wait to be left alone with it.

Do you think you could look after the lot for me? asked Rubio. That includes the case itself. Why don't you sort it all out and see what you can't get for it?

If you really want that, said Burneto, and he looked at the figurine of the lady with interest.

I do, said Rubio. I want you to take care of it all.

Burneto's brow crossed, a sign that his mind, teeming with facts and probabilities, had uncovered an objection to the plan.

After a second in contemplation of the ceramic lady and her yellow parasol, Burneto spoke his concern, now adopting the perverse doctoral tone that indicated he felt Rubio to have lost his reason.

It's just that these items might have sentimental value, said Burneto and he looked up from the dancing figure with an expression of care which made Rubio want to throttle him.

Sentimental? said Rubio. What are the sentimental reasons for possession?

Burneto offered him the lady figurine while Rubio looked on it sourly.

This piece you would like, said Burneto. She's so demure, and this delicate umbrella, it must have been something that your mother treasured very much.

Burneto stood with the figure between his fingers, a distinguished doctor defending the rights of innocent china.

I've never seen that before in my life, said Rubio.

He drew on his cigarette and stubbed it into the ashtray.

She really is splendid, said Burneto. I think we should just leave her in the meantime and see what happens with the others, don't you?

Rubio stared at his friend.

I think we should sell her immediately, he said. I think we should dispose of this stuff the way I suggested and I think that if you like that figure then you should take it.

I didn't mean it like that, said Burneto.

Burneto turned to the cabinet and replaced the figure in its sinister arrangement with the other fragments. With his hands behind his back he gazed onward just as the coffin made a final bump into the porch. Rubio opened the door and there was the undertaker's young assistant, a boy in black paying attention to the new coffin. As Rubio felt for his cigarette lighter, the young man stared at the box and did not turn, so it was Rubio who looked away. Burneto was close behind, pressing.

I need to go to town, said Rubio. I've got to be there in an hour.

I'll drive you, said Burneto, and he carefully retreated with the silver spoons he was holding.

No, said Rubio.

An emphatic locution, a small word he wished to make a mountain between himself and his friend. Rubio held his hand out and said, I'll walk.

Burneto's smile returned and he spoke as if to a child.

Come on now Rubi. I can easily drive you there. It won't take me a minute.

I'd rather walk, said Rubio. You stay and do the cabinet.

The undertaker was guiding the last of the coffin out of the door and when Rubio passed the man turned his eyes and allowed a strictly professional smile. Rubio took it to be a good sign and ran up the stairs to see what had happened.

The bedroom was empty. The undertakers had drawn the curtains for their black purposes and had stripped the old bed and folded the sheets. No blankets, no body, so trace by trace she went away. He walked to the window and watched the coffin slide into the vehicle, a charming last moment in his relations with his family.

The unrelenting attention to the colour black and the sobriety which the undertakers brought to the affair was a perfect counterpoint to the whitish sheets his mother had left. Rubio witnessed the undertakers close the hearse, absorbed in duty to the point of walking in straight lines to the car doors.

In the hall the undertakers offered him instructions as to the funeral arrangements and handed him a clipboard to sign. Both undertakers then folded their auras like giant wings and were gone. Rubio closed the front door leaving Burneto alone in the house, exercising his diffuse expertise on the collectibles. Rubio could sense his colleague's delight, the combined vices of antique evaluation and death, the rational achievement of all his life as he tutted and hummed his way through the hallmarks. The bend and bearing of a spoon, the mantling quarter of a pewter dish, his almost mathematical method of boring everyone on different styles of furniture.

Rubio looked towards the blocks of the near estate and wondered which way to go. The wistful almost hand-drawn face of his father appeared and Rubio moved off towards the town. All the way to the station, shops and houses had been spoiled with chintzy cornices and cosy swathes of plastic credit card signs. He passed beneath the silent shadow of a bare tree and was comforted only by the amusing image of Burneto bending biscuit-coloured at the old cupboard, a man in love with whatnots.

•

Sarcelles burned daily with desire, half in love with football players and half in love with singers. Rubio listened to his patients for three and a bit hours in the morning and a further three in the afternoon, although their questions remained for him to settle in the long watches of the night. Two nurses were casually coming and going, filling out airline reservations to Egypt, the Sudan, to anywhere with an ancient wilderness of sand. Rubio was issuing passports to the exhausted citizens who had quit their jobs, he had produced a pamphlet detailing the benefits of an empty landscape to those who were too weak to face France another hour.

Sandals compliments of the house, said Rubio. Go to the desert and take it from there, life will be different after that.

Whatever you say doctor. . .

Rubio wished that he had prescribed wilderness sojourns instead of his drug therapies. The old town of Siwa was the perfect rest stop for the dejected people of the surgery. Walls had collapsed in drifts of sand and twisted plastic twined around the telegraph poles and ran in streaks down the lanes. Light progressed in single frames over the ragged edge of the town and at each moment, Rubio expected a wave of people. The sun flecked the ledge of another naked tower, more air evaporated and further empty windows were revealed. The collapsed houses were the result of a Biblical disaster, and Rubio drew a cigarette forward from the box and rubbed it across his mouth.

In the sludge of morning sunlight, Daniel was stretched on the veranda of the Hotel Youseff. The kid blended in as if he had been moulded to the boardwalk. The blue of his eyes stared at the bracelet of light across the old town as if trying to work out if he'd been brought to the correct place.

Do you know where your Dad is? asked Rubio.

When the kid stepped off the veranda Rubio grabbed his arm. Daniel struggled but Rubio tightened his grip on the bone. A cockerel sounded and when the front door of the hotel opened, Daniel had wrestled free and was gone – in a matter of seconds the kid had vanished into the broken stone of the prehistoric old town.

Looking from the front door of the hotel were the red-rimmed eyes of a man, and Rubio turned his head, looking for the kid, wondering at the hotel's patron.

Ingleezh, said the man, and Rubio threw down his cigarette.
French, he said. I'm French not English.
Ingleezh to you, said the man, and he sighed idly. We make in Ingleezh here.
Okay, said Rubio and he held his hands up.

In the hotel's foyer the stealing figure of the owner crossed to an alcove where there was a desk and a television, and Rubio walked towards him with his hatred for mankind unstirred. As Rubio strayed into the dark, the man took his place beneath a photograph of President Hosni and various proper lines from the Qur'an printed on a tasselled background. The man shook his white robe and slapped the desk with the palm of his hand.

Yes, he said, this is cool in the day!

Rubio waited at the counter to see what was expected of him, while the man splayed a fan of passports like a hand of cards. Rubio stared at the passports and then at the picture of President Hosni, strong and portentous, interrogator and prophet. The corner of the picture was torn and the President's brow pitched forward sharply. Several lines slanted from behind the President's head, lines that if interpreted broadly could be construed as curtains. The figure's expression suggested kindness overlaid with the political iron required of every Egyptian Army officer. The man at the counter flapped the passports but Rubio hadn't thought about this document for hours. After it had vanished, Rubio's passport took on an entirely new character, a scrap of card stapled with the plastified likeness of himself, a piece of art reflecting his claim to come from France, as if Frenchness implied divine origin. The passport represented the polemic directed against all Egyptians, the will to move from country to country, a fact hardly considered abnormal outside of Africa. The formulaic words: Nom et Nombre, a stamp and the Fees Received, President Hosni's permission in short. Rubio's right to travel was the essence by which all images of himself were justified, and that had been the last time he had seen it, somewhere in or around the Bel Air.

Rubio pulled off his shoe and from it unfolded some money. The notes were clean but the man seemed unimpressed and squeaked again for Rubio's passport. He held the passports symmetrically in his black hand while President Hosni expressed his familiar in absentia desire that everything continue above board.

No, said Rubio to the dark man, and he pointed at the passport. He realised that he held all of his money in his hand and wondered if he shouldn't have divided it between his shoes. A second later Rubio watched the money go, it left him peacefully as the man replaced the passports in his drawer and offered Rubio a pen with which to put his mark inside the register.

Your room, said the man, and he offered Rubio a key.

He pointed towards the upper floors and Rubio walked away with the blessing of having the last of one's money taken.

Rubio dragged the shutters closed and once on his back, he looked into the ceiling which was painted in the same unbroken shade of sand which now covered his life.

He was too sleepy to seize on the right words, but there were two hands moving down from the hotel room ceiling, as if looking for something, or hollowing a space. Shadows drew close and Rubio's stomach churned, shapes on the wall danced and the peculiarity of the motion made him sick. He looked down. The hands were not on the ceiling but within himself as if his stomach were a bowl of sand, as if the motion from above was now inside.

What are you looking for? asked Rubio as the hands dug away, searching for the knot inside him, exploring him in sweeps from one side to the next.

When Rubio opened his eyes the day came awake in Siwa. It could be time for a cigarette now, he thought, with the impression that he had aged a little more. It was happening all the time.

Rubio lit the cigarette and the smoke began to please him. He smoked for a moment and imagined that he was back where he belonged, in a doctor's surgery in Sarcelles, issuing tired medical lines and speaking loudly to the old folks. He leaned over his desk with a look of concern, everybody's doctor until the day he died. The calendar photographs were the same each year, as were the inclined faces of the filing cabinets, the elongated medical tools and the cross-section of the human-throat. The flank of the brown chair was always warm from the last consultation and the progress of the great clock on the wall tired him with its repetition. The people of Sarcelles were depressed perhaps, but Rubio was always there for them. The simple statement of the matter sounded funny but dusk had fallen on Sarcelles and the menacing uproar of television had drowned their feeling. In Paris the buildings sat like expired buddhas and Rubio walked under trees pricked by winter. The water of the Seine was a darkness of smoke drifting between the banks, and on the next bridge various objects with cigarettes hanging from their mouths stared at him with unexpected confidence. Rubio was always crossing the same square, looking for the correct road North, leaves blew like sharpened blades and always in the distance were those same characters. He wandered in the footsteps of pilgrims and geographers, tourists, school groups and weekend visitors, Paris was a religious temple, a museum whose ample merit was lost on its neighbours in Sarcelles. The northern banlieue was an unmarked tomb, St Denis the dead bastion of the Red suburbs, now unquotable and old.

Things die slowly encased in concrete, thought Rubio. One day I'll have the explanation of my patients' miseries.

An aeroplane crossed, a jetliner thirty thousand feet above, and in the horns of the mattress, Rubio rolled to his side and pulled the sheet over his legs. Voices laughed in the hall and he thought of Daniel as he lit his cigarette. It was almost like a real breakfast the way the smoke throbbed inside him, frugally effective.

When he was ready Rubio walked to the window and looked to see what there was for him in Siwa.

Near the hotel was a makeshift café and beneath its straw awning was a group of pleasure-seekers, young and European. Coloured adverts crossed the roof and created a holiday atmosphere. The foul intimacy of home was preserved by the back-packers, the voices laughed and they sat in the drab shapes of their loose clothing.

Rubio took a box of cigarettes and made his exit. The padlock rattled, the key turned in the bloodshot eye of the lock, and Rubio wondered how many nights he had purchased for his money. Hotels in Egypt were busy but always gaping for more custom like the mouths of dead gods. Travellers from Europe and Australia appeared in multiples and couples, differentiated from the Egyptians by their affluent social rituals, mediated by their relative wealth.

Rubio pulled on his cigarette and threw it down. He turned the remains into the floor, working the mess of burned tobacco into the sandy substance underfoot. His old shoe turned in a sweep and the cigarette disappeared – what was left had spilled out and become black. It was his isolation, it was his spectacular failure – the pool of his ambition would never become still and Rubio would never see below its surface.

Downstairs, the hotelier was spread out upon the sofa gazing at President Hosni. Hearing steps he glanced at Rubio and outstretched his fingers. Rubio reached the bottom of the stairs and stepped over the man's feet.

Good day, said the hotelier in English.
And to you, said Rubio in return, the official language of the Commonwealth making him sound overly polite.

Rubio felt for the cigarettes. The packet was sturdy, full of the stoic little fellows who were now wholly supporting him. He tipped one upwards and stuck it in his mouth.

Outside, there were more people than Rubio had expected. Men and woman worked nearby stalls and filthy shapes could be spied at greasy windows. The decay from the palm trees spread through a shambles of wood that had been transformed into a vegetable shop, and from the old town sound travelled and died so that Rubio felt he could hear a conversation from a half-mile away.

He looked across the road to the restaurant where the travellers sat in untidy European accord. Their conversation fed into the shambles of the oasis. A girl talked while three boys sat like monkeys in the melancholic performance of cool. Rubio ducked his head to step beneath the awning and realised that these young travellers were speaking French. He took his cigarette out of his mouth and greeted them as a fellow national with his hand up as if in self-defence.

Salut.

The girl looked at him in surprise, as if an animal had talked. She was younger than Rubio had imagined, half his age or less. The girl greeted him and the others stared, the moral force of their expressions seeming more adult than their age.

I've just come to say hello, said Rubio.

He stood assiduously still, the air breathed past him slowly and the clustered lights above them brightened.

I'm a doctor, said Rubio and the four young people conferred in glances until the girl moved a chair out.
I'm Bernadette, she said.

Rubio held the chair and said hello to each traveller in turn. Something lurked in these people's glances but Rubio smiled. It was a seedy effort, a faked greeting from the carrion of his burned face.

How long you been in Egypt? asked Bernadette, returning Rubio to the reverie of their conversation.
Under a month he said, and it sounded right. Two weeks in Cairo and then in Alexandria and Mersa.

Rubio recoiled from his own speech. Each question was posed in grey prison clothes and delivered as if to his enemies for punishment.

I was in Mersa for several days, he said.

He could not protest, only find amusement in his own shocking courtesy. Rubio had nothing more to offer and so he cut immediately to the truth of his situation, flicking the cigarette lighter in irritation.

I don't have any money, he said, a statement that focused the attention at the table marvellously. The three guys present were interested, the idea seemed curious and their shock was evident.

Was you robbed? asked an Australian voice, it seemed unsympathetic, as if Rubio should be proud to answer yes.

I was, he said, twice in Mersa.

Twice! said the girl and Rubio nodded.

I gave the rest to the man in the Hotel Youssef and apart from that I've just got my cigarettes.

God! said the girl, and she sat forward.

Have you reported it? said one of them, an English voice, the classic indignation of his race now evident.

No, said Rubio. I think it was my own fault.

Jesus! said the girl.

The party paused as Rubio peeped into the brown of the sun. His story was wretchedly passing as adventure among the hard-travelled youth. Pop music beat in the background and the monotonous superhumans eyed him, the surveillance of a higher authority.

I'm really hungry, said Rubio. You don't think you could help do you?

Shadows crawled across the back-packers' faces and Rubio sensed their doubt, their contentment turned to a mirthless worry that they may have to intervene.

They'd love to help, he thought, but their help is always indirect.

They understand charity as they understand ethics, a passive operation. I forget that their greatest care is etiquette, here as at home.

Rubio asked his question again to no reply, he felt the same nagging hopelessness his patients used to express.

God! said Bernadette. It's terrible that you were robbed!

The conversation halted while Rubio watched one of the boys plugging numbers into his phone, doubtless a message to another no-hoper in a caramel-coloured burger joint elsewhere in the world. These kids were like his own dear colleagues in their lack of empathy, their fear of anything other than their own pleasure. Theirs were the guns firing over the ocean, theirs was the Kingdom, and they covered the earth with their morals like creeping wisps.

Rubio turned to face the sandy mound of the old town and saw another young man approach, the best-dressed foreigner he had seen in Egypt. In the distance this young man was the height of a hill, he carried a shoulder bag and his parted hair was a desert miracle. As this boy approached, Bernadette and the other three paid close attention as if waiting for the last constituent in a plot they were hatching.

This is Yunni! said Bernadette. He's been out on safari today. Ah, said Rubio, the best word that he could manage.

When he arrived, Yunni's mouth flagged into the half form of a smile while he waited for one of the others to say something.

He's cool, said Bernadette and she cocked her thumb at Rubio. He's a doctor and he got robbed!

Yah, said Yunni in judgement, a German judgement. He wiped

his hands and sat down and Rubio saw that even the young man's short trouser exhibited a crease. Rubio offered a handshake and the formalities were complete, allowing for another rude pause.

So you have come to Siwa? said Yunni. His accent was that of interrogation, the precision spectacles, the pressed shorts and leather bag were as clean as if they had been taken down from a rack that morning. Most foreign kids dressed to look as poor as they could but this one travelled in the abnormal get-up of a businessman.

He's cool! said Bernadette.

Rubio realised he hadn't answered Yunni's question, if that is what it was. Bernadette smiled but that was no good, none of these people seemed any friendlier. The travellers partied from the first world to the third, they always found an old illuminated Coke sign and a pinball machine, the simmering rivalries between their own country and the one they patronised were strained by their lack of action. To top it all, Rubio was tired of being called cool, because every motion made him more French, less cool, more heated, poisoned by the cheerful fire of their conversation.

Okay, said Yunni, let's go to the hotel.

Yunni glanced at the Hotel Youssef and the others gathered their cigarettes, cameras, novels and coins.
Yunni stood up and said to Rubio, are you coming?
I guess, he said, and he stood up too.

The party left the awning of the restaurant and walked towards the Youssef, the belly of the afternoon hung above the centre of the oasis and the locals watched the white-skinned convoy as it approached the old hotel. The head of President Hosni sheltered in its picture frame as Rubio and the travellers trooped towards the stairs, all as limp as a pack of slaves. President Hosni, in the accustomed surroundings of the Hotel, extended his stare like that of a powerful animal.

Do you know of a boy called Daniel here in Siwa? Rubio asked Bernadette.

Bernadette didn't turn her head.

Nope, she said, and they filed up the stairs.

He's a friend of mine, said Rubio, his father is a friend of mine.

I don't know him, she said.

They reached the second floor and Bernadette undid the padlock to a rear-facing room. Yunni entered first and the others followed. There were clothes and bottled water on the beds, and realising that there may be relief in this aimlessness after all, Rubio took out the cigarettes. Yunni stood at the door, tall enough to fill the frame with the granite of his white expression.

I'm selling grass, he said. It's five dollars a finger. If you can't buy you can't come in. Can you buy?

Bernadette's face rested in the shade of the door. Rubio had the feeling she had let him down, a girl more at home among the web monkeys of France than she was in a desert oasis.

We'll see you later, she said. We'll be around so watch out for us. I hope you find your friend.

The door closed leaving Rubio alone on the landing. Nearby was a rotten cardboard box into which he dug his foot. He pictured Bernadette, smoking grass in the maze of her luggage, only distantly associated with the great names of Egypt. Rubio reached for the wall to steady himself. He moved towards the stairs where there was a noise from below, people sweeping up. This poor concrete hospice was the end of the road and Rubio returned to his room. The sound of sweeping was approaching on the stairs, there were voices coming too, dull gibberish from above and below. Rubio slipped the key to the padlock and fell on his bed where he rolled to a heap near the wall. The sweep ran east to west on the bare floor outside and Rubio prodded the flakes of plaster in the wall. Outside, the broom rushed the floor like a whiplash and Rubio pressed his palms into his face so that several stars of green light formed and flowed away. The youngsters were stoned on Yunni's grass and Yunni was counting his money – profiteering on the dark continent. The dope crackled in new-rolled joints, the sound was trapped in the gooey buds of the drug and a rootless fanfare played into the minds of the young travellers, a discord to rival any city street. Their anomie broke and Rubio heard the sound of their laughter through the floor and in his ear with the maiden grace of organ music. He felt for a postcard but realised that the only course of action now was to return to Paris and spend all his money.

There were plenty things to buy with that money, Virginie was right. There was gambling, bird watching, a holiday in the lakes, classical music boxed sets of the great composers.

Everything was available at home.

Plenty emerged in the form of satisfaction without end, it was the cure to depression and the incertitude of living . Rubio beheld the charmed image of his own house where his own boxed sets blushed on a walnut shelf in a sparsely decorated living room. Near the boxed sets, he stood with a glass of spring water. His curtains rippled in the summer as if from the rarely heard sounds of conversation and the tinkling of coffee cups. Rubio was pleasantly somatised by the music, he had retired and now he collected books and musical recordings. He had credit and was like everybody else, not to be undone, and he touched the buttons quite contentedly on his new CD player and sat for the afternoon with his eyes on a medical magazine.

•

The tone of her voice, the open sunshine of the Place de la Nation, Virginie had known from the off why earning-power was important. When Rubio bumped into her, coincidentally on the Cour de Vincennes, the only monument in Paris to a Napoleonic defeat, Virginie was carrying newly purchased boxed sets of the great composers, a laboratory of musical art in a plastic sack. She strolled up with her shopping bags and said *hello* with all the dogma of politeness.

I'm on my way to a fortieth said Rubio, shuffling out of the light.
That's nice, said Virginie. Are you forty yet?
Yes I am, said Rubio.

All these fortieth birthday parties! she said, we were at one last weekend.

Virginie delighted at seeing Rubio, the man who never changed.

Still smoking? asked Virginie when Rubio took out his cigarettes, and he said yes while she smiled at his lighting ritual. She pulled one of the classical composers boxed sets from her bag.
Look, she said, I have this to keep me company tonight!
Fine, said Rubio, I'm sure I couldn't afford that.
I'm sure you could, she said, and they kissed goodbye.

Virginie could have been anybody and not just his wife. He would forgive her boxed sets and her make-up, her summer season clothes and her husband's bank balance, but her happiness was what truly grated. Virginie was so innocent that she looked no further than what could be bought. Her greatest crime was that she sought out comfort over bitterness. Rubio watched but Virginie did not quite vanish into the crowd. Instead she walked to a newsstand and turned like an actress to stand beneath an advert for the autumn look. A bus wheeled round the corner from Vincennes, faces inside the bus were all signs that everything had gone wrong, their expressions seemed to represent the death of Rubio's enthusiasm.

When the bus passed she had gone and the smugness of Paris blew up once again, from the water-heads of the fountains to the café tables.

Virginie had joined the hysteria years ago. Behind her sunglasses her eyes popped with anxiety and she rushed away in a blizzard of tissues to set the world to rights among the hyena-like moaning of her friends. She sat in a shopping mass of fragments at the foot of the stairs, a talus of commercial goods unwrapped, and she examined the receipts as in appreciation of flowers for the first time.

My wife is a critic of everything but herself, he used to say to the assembled colleagues. I have so many patients like that too, their depressions are gleaned from the newspapers and cereal boxes. What they want is doctoral sympathy, justification, and a dose of Peisinol!

Rubio was glad to see her go.
To see her rude red lipstick no more.
That was how it went, shuffle up the marriage aisle and let everything take its course. With a common accord Rubio and Virginie took their vows and reinforced the emotions that provoked their wrath.
You're a cynic, she said. The greatest shit on the face of this earth.

How often do I have to tell you, he said. I'm not a cynic, I'm a sceptic.

What difference does that make? she asked.

All the difference. You're a cynic and I'm a sceptic. It's cynical to spend so much money when you're professing to be so ethical. It's sceptical to be aware of that.

You see? she said. It's rubbish. You don't even know what you're saying.

Virginie's voice was clear despite the deterioration of Rubio's hearing. Bottom out and top out, her voice hauled him over the coals for any number of offences until without a shadow turning on her face she yelled at him, hard enough to rattle the glass in the kitchen window.

Do you see what you're doing to me? she asked.

Virginie was leaving and Rubio could not even ask her to stay. The thought of being alone made him unsteady, as if he would really become a child again. Maybe, he thought, this is just a freakish turn.

Virginie calmed.

I have to go, she said. I have to get my shit together.

Rubio nodded, the enduring nod which always made her angry – it was the way he kept so calm that bothered her. When Virginie was mad, Rubio was sober, and she was always getting her shit together, going mad, and then getting her shit together again. In one hand Virginie had her magazine. It was another palliative in her inveterate lunacy, her ecology and human rights periodical, it espoused good values, internationalism, conservation of the planet in the face of new clothes and automobiles. The magazine sickened

Rubio and it embarrassed him to see Virginie with it. It was as well she was going. His criticisms of her were becoming that small.

Rubio pretended to amuse himself with the button on his cardigan. Once Virginie had been his wife but now Rubio could criticise her all he liked. Virginie and her shopping, Virginie and her magazine, Virginie and her recipe for goose drumsticks, Virginie and her new husband whose name was Michel. She carried on with a second marriage, wilfully ignorant of her first one. As if life wasn't a rathole enough, he had to be reminded of the fact.

●

Rubio walked to Burneto's fortieth birthday party as the day became cooler. He trailed along the Quai de la Gare past a recobbled dock and entered a series of ragged streets hemmed in by office blocks. Rubio's thoughts echoed with the patients of the last week and he dwelled on the interchangeability of their symptoms, the similarity of their complaints.

There were a few of the old gang swinging when Rubio arrived at the jazz bar, the same crowd from university. Burneto could be heard talking from the door, while the others were similarly self-contained in the watery death of their beers. In surgery, doctors present a faithful and caring intimacy with life, but when they get together, they are arbitrary, wrathful and destructive.

Rubio is here! shouted Burneto from among the stately pillars of his colleagues.

The other men looked up, their faces frames of conceit and superiority. Rubio shook hands with the people he knew and then the people he did not, and within a minute he was immersed in greetings and thinking about how soon he could leave.

118

I never thought I'd see you again, said a buffoon in a waistcoat and earrings. It's been six years!

Six years, said Rubio.

Rubio's words were lost as the colleagues returned to their doctoral frivolity, he got to drinking and the band played jazz, thuggish music which defied the idea of talent. He thought about the boxed set of records, the comfort of spending money, and he walked to the toilets where his regret became stronger. A piddling thin selection of friends like that can stay together for ten years, thought Rubio as he urinated into the closed corridor of a designer toilet. They can manage it until they're forty, he thought, but after that it's not tenable and they're going to be swallowed up by a greater purpose – such as caravanning. They gripe about the price of houses and judge the city's health, someone's mother has had an illness and people fake a moment's concern. The depression attacks and they fend it off like puritans, earnest neurotics who burst into the obvious insanity of drunkenness given half the opportunity.

Later, the friends stood in the street outside the jazz bar and a taxi took them to the card game they had planned. The ageing party led the forty year old Burneto to a bachelor kitchen near the Porte de Vanves and about an hour after his piss Rubio was looking across his host's music collection, indulging in an imaginary vision that they were all his. He stared along the row of compact discs and wondered what it would be like to own so many uniform beauties, a wall-space spread with your own intellectual absorption to render the unlearned visitors helpless. There were boxed sets too, records and discs, tapes and video cassettes, and Rubio picked up two tapes of Bach and put them in his pocket.

Drinks! said Burneto. He was absurd and futile in his merry-making.

Others poured whisky and cracked ice cubes while the remainder gathered near the forged pine of the kitchen work surface.

Are you alright doctor? said someone. You'd better get your money ready!

The card game began and the men giggled with the sudden excitement of their gathering. Rubio sat between two head-wagging colleagues, their bizarre mannerisms included clicking their fingers to the music. He felt in his pocket for the tapes which rested in the darkest dye, deep in his coat, and he winced at the way the group retorted to everything that was said, as if disagreement were an obligation. Rubio had drunk too much and he disliked everybody he knew. Virginie was in bed of course, she had played her fabulous boxed sets and read the accompanying booklets, calling over her husband and showing him the pictures. Her husband had joined in and said, look at that conductor, he's bearing over that orchestra like a twisted tree!

Was there a sense of relief when Virginie arrived home and dropped her shopping bags? Did the purchase make her home a better place? Rubio had his tape cassettes of Bach so he would know for himself soon. He turned from the game and pretended to look out of window, but his heart beat stiffly as he stared at the darkness.

Rubio! Are you in?

Those were the colleagues then, men exempt from the trials of family life for one night only, all at the age of forty. Doctor Rubio was among them, sick of himself and drinking wine. The men flipped gambling chips on to the table, some had cigars and others had joints, the formality amid their childish behaviour unnerved

Rubio as if he were stoned and they were straight. None of these men enjoyed women, but all of them enjoyed books. One of them talked about prostitutes, he seemed to think that the prostitutes in Paris were a commodity and noted that a girl he had visited had a questionable quality. Rubio held on to the two Bach tapes in his coat pocket and when appropriate, he laughed. The heroes of modern life shuffled the cards while whisky glasses were placed in a circle, the banter turned to politics and the politics turned to a caustic shouting match.

Doctor?

The man who offered Rubio the joint revolted him, a colleague from the ashen world of the 19th arrondisement, a grinning thumb raised and the moulder of his old bones visible in his teeth. Rubio had passed over the hill and into the medical profession's most groundbreaking decade when doctors were dabbling in illegal drugs. His surgery in Sarcelles was dated by about forty years, he had lost his way and wound up in the Porte de Vanves. Rubio passed the joint to the next poor soul, but Burneto interrupted and laughed, he clapped his hands and began a story that consisted entirely of the phrase *all these blacks*. This could only be Paris, thought Rubio, the racist swine, all the tricks the collabos learned in the War, replayed endlessly in the privacy of unexampled prosperity. The Nazis might have gone but they left their bureaucracy behind. Paris has always been God's gift, a fact set in rock by Napoleon for those who have lived by his same standard ever since. Rubio looked at the others, their faces smudged like steamed glass. One of the men was looking for the correct long player, touching the records as if they were crystal. Cards were dealt and the needle ripped the vinyl before the sound struck up, Rubio stood as if emerging from a play of wires and scrap paper.

My surgery, he said.

Across the table and over the furniture of this once elegant apartment, every bit of the scene was typical as Satan would require before he destroyed it. Paris skyline, public clocks, porticos and rotunda, the sound of jazz rising from the trench of Burneto's birthday. Card players with open mouths, wet cigars and thin hair all round.

Rubio said goodbye and walked from the flat, he closed the door on the card game and started on the stairs which curled like a moving picture below him. Cars buzzed past and Rubio touched the wall of the building. A group of young people crossed the road while a café cast a glow on the pavement, the magic of the alcohol had been replaced with a collection of tasks that Rubio simply could not manage. On the taxi journey to Sarcelles he listened to the pounding of his heart, a compressed beating in his throat, blood moving fast with the fear of a car accident. Rubio's colleagues were playing cards, enjoying the confiscated cheer of their middle age. The taxi ran into a tunnel and Rubio caught his breath, he smoked a cigarette that caused a breeze in the blood as the wicked worked its way into to the brain.

When he awoke, Rubio was in the surgery. His legs were weak and he stared ahead at a mother and young boy. The young boy's trouser was at his ankle and his leg was scarred with a recent cut. The peculiarity was that twelve hours had passed and that Rubio had been drawn with them as if by some strange current. Home, bed, smoke, sleep, breakfast, smoke, shaving, walking to work and then the illnesses of Sarcelles. He looked at the clock and collected himself for the benefit of the patients. They sat ahead of him, the boy with his leg and his mother.

You can put the trouser back on now, said Rubio quietly.
Are you sure? asked the mother. You haven't had a look. . .
I'm sorry but there has been a mix-up with this file, said Rubio.

The kid awaited his mother's instruction. It was not a dream, it was disappointing reality complete with the files of many exhausted city dwellers piled on the couch. Rubio grabbed at his pocket for the tapes of Bach but felt only his house keys.

Doctor? said the woman.

Her stare weakened Rubio with its promise of revenge.

I'm sorry, he said. I'm a little faint. I've been working too hard.

Rubio avoided the ill will of this mother's eye. She stared and said, *it's only Monday*, as if Rubio could have exhausted himself in the three hours of the week he had worked so far. There on the pad was a morning's work. In his own hand, Rubio had prescribed Peisinol twice, and one Thelxepeia. On the pad were three notes torn, three carbons and his own domestic signature beneath. Rubio walked around the desk like a stage actor approaching the curtain. He bent down and said, yes now, as he looked at the scar along the young boy's leg. He could taste the green of sickness in his throat as he examined the scar and he wondered what if anything he had eaten for breakfast.

Depression is nothing to do with these symptoms, he said to the mother. That's why I cannot help, that's why these drugs can't guarantee you anything.

The woman grabbed her son's trouser and the sleepy child came to life in a flash.

You'll be hearing from us, she said, trembling with hatred.

Rubio checked again that it was Monday and tried to see if he could recall this woman's name. He had seen patients daily for fifteen years and now he was going to ask himself to remember a name. The mineral misery of the surgery had got to him at last, eyes open or eyes closed, shapes flitted past, patients in the narrow nave of the waiting room, their heads bowed to face him like bullets in the chamber of a gun.

•

Rubio watched the sunlight burn the shade away. He thought of Daniel and made a silent promise to find him.

Downstairs, Youssef was not at his counter. Battle lines had formed on President Hosni's brow and dust rose in degrees like an aerial army, the sun tiled the road in dirty gold and the heat pressed forward in a wall. Nobody saw him, Siwa was empty, flies twitched and donkeys gazed with closed eyes, there glistened an expression of softness around their faces.

The old buildings of Siwa sat like a puff of dust in the stillness, a village carved into the rock with towers supporting irregular windows. As he entered the old town, Rubio stared up to a bank of dried mud which formalised into a tower. Yunni the German was taking notes. He was a stick man among the collapsed rock, observing the mouth of a pit and writing in a notebook which he clipped in an appropriately sized pocket. Rubio balanced on a jamb of wood and watched. Yunni wore the same shorts and pressed shirt of the day before and held a camera which he directed at the wall ahead. When he was satisfied, Yunni re-entered the town through a gap in the brickwork, continuing his studies elsewhere.

Rubio stepped into a split in the rock that led to several ancient doors. From the murk of a collapsed house there came a knocking and peering over he saw a child working on a mortar like a ghost. Before a red and black door stood a man in a grey frock coat as if he had been waiting there. His head rose clean from his coat, an ogre in dark glasses.

124

Looking for your Daniel? said the man in French, and Rubio nodded that he was.

The ogre approached with an outstretched hand and Rubio took it, the dark glasses stared, outshining the sun in their ferocity. Rubio noticed that the man wore Siwan neck jewellery and that there was the edge of a concealed tattoo beneath it.

Mitard, said the man and he flapped his coat behind his body and slapped Rubio's hand in his.

Nice to meet you, said Rubio and muttered his presumptions about this man being Daniel's father.

I am he, said Mitard, and with a chafe blustering he cleared his throat and announced the word *tea*.

The corridor into the rock house sloped darkly. Rubio was unsure why he smiled, and he looked away over dreadful banks of books to a wall pinned with magazine cuttings. This procession of cut and paste merged with a red slogan in Hebrew which ran the block of a roof beam. On the door was a Buddha image, the golden smiler sitting in auspicious glee. Every other image was witness to recent civil unrest, a launch of tear gas, the Mac Attack in London, protestors dressed as animals and Mitard's own defaced items of advertising.

Mitard slid away his dark glasses and his hands crossed his heart as he shuffled into position on a cushion and pointed that Rubio might do the same.

An impressive collection of books, said Rubio and he indicated where the soft wood of a shelf supported a wall of many volumes.

These are religious and political books, said Mitard. I rarely use them, I de-construct them as the ongoing body of my work. Boundaries become harder to maintain when the multiplication of logic leads to a multiplication of valid claims of knowledge such as one so often encounters in religion and politics. That is what I aim to clarify.

Rubio crossed his legs and felt the familiar crack in his joints as his knees locked into their most despised position. Immediately his legs began to rebel by cutting the blood into splinters which numbed the nerves within their grasp.

Is Daniel here? he asked as Mitard heaved into a similar position. Somewhere, said the man, and Rubio picked at the sole of his foot, blistered and sore.

Rubio thought immediately of a cigarette and looked about him, finding the stolen emblems of Seattle-based java giants shredded into arrows. Rubio stared and muttered the words, *very interesting*, avoiding praise for artistry, ignoring the possibility of admiration.

Magazines are recycling plants, said Mitard, frontierlands where everything is displaced, or perhaps washed up at random so that in them our isolation is thoroughly exposed. They show commodities as they actually are, as opposed to the items which you may actually buy. In fact, magazines offer Platonic ideals in contrast to the increasingly disappointing purchases themselves – don't you think?

The blood froze in the knot where Rubio had attempted to cross his legs and he shifted to allow the fluid connection of his body once again.

How is Daniel then? he asked seeking other objects of discussion, looking along the line of books.

Daniel is well, said Mitard, he is once again in what we call a safe zone. Each departure leads to responses in kind for the child, new relations and interactions are always interesting for him.

We had quite a journey, said Rubio, and he reached for the tea.

The tails of Mitard's frock coat splayed like fins, Rubio drank from his cup and replaced it beside the curl of the cable of a personal computer. He tapped the floor beside the machine.

Don't get too many of these in the desert! he said, allowing Mitard to respond in the same dull and winding voice.

I'm writing my confessions.

Mitard stared, a one-man senate, Rubio felt trapped, snared as if this anti-theorist had been waiting for an audience for many years.

Your Confessions? said Rubio. That's very worthwhile.

If put squarely by one person, said Mitard, then the realities that I have known here will likely pertain to more than just myself. What is right for me in these conditions will certainly be right for an entire body of people in less material comfort, which is why what I've written is obliged to take on the tone of a confession.

I see, said Rubio.

He looked into the tea, dark liquid in a ring of white, he calculated a response and watched a drift of hot water submerge several leaves as they sweated out their flavour.

That is why I am here, said Mitard, and it may be why you are here as well. We may all be here to confess.

Rubio straightened. He went for a cigarette from his top pocket and pressed it to his lip. Mitard sat like a volcano, a white square in a field of browns and black, forward-looking from a deep eye that abolished the man within.

Think about it in these terms, said Mitard. Everything is addiction, the foundation, every father and mother, every teacher, promoting the same hope, every child betrayed by the same lie. Every mother a tyrant, every father a bastion of the values of oppression, yours a land of soft voices and soft lighting, mine a land of hard sunlight, flights of. . .

Rubio's lighter sparked a flame that struggled before he was able to smoke. He cast a glance at the wall above the desk, the slogans and faces of reaction, the sounds, voices and dances, all evident in the branch of revolution that encircled the consumer object with the spirit of anarchy.

. . . flights of what? he said.

Mitard's eyes were closed, his smile an effort to add sanction to his speech.

Once you are removed from the culture of excess, he said, you don't have to play its rules.

Mitard looked at his feet which poked from the crossed-up folds of his frock-coat while Rubio blew smoke in an irritated stream towards the floor. A cramp rose in Rubio's leg, and the cushion only made it worse. To divert himself he concentrated on pulling his facial muscles into an expression of interest.

I know what you are thinking, said Mitard. He looked to Rubio with an affected wisdom, a vulgar display of mystic traits. You are thinking of my wife and what happened to her. Then you think about Daniel and about what you can do for him.

Are you going to Mersa to collect her? said Rubio

I don't leave Siwa, said Mitard. I sent her to Alexandria to pick up some money and I hear she ended up in Cairo the worse for liquor. I heard she took a trip to Bur Said and undertook some business there. She was away for a long time.

You may have to go to Mersa for official reasons, said Rubio. I think she may be in trouble.

Mitard waved his hand and insects took off from the ground. They whispered in a cloud while he struck another pose in their contemplation.

I think she may be dead, he said. I think you may have been with her when she died.

Mitard's left arm formed a V while his right hand skimmed slowly through it towards Rubio. As this curious motion unfolded, Mitard made a whooshing noise as if to demonstrate his point, that here in Siwa, he was a sailor on an eternally motionless sea, an ocean where the waves were galvanised into one position, the very still present being.

I'm going nowhere, he said.

His arms broke from their painstaking pose and Rubio tapped his dead leg as the insects landed on the floor once more.

We can't talk of her here, said Mitard, and he held his hand in a fist. I've been informed that she is dead. I was worried about my son until this morning when he returned, but I won't thank you for bringing him here if that is what you've come for.

Mitard's hands stopped, stabilised as if at the centre point of a dance motion.

Daniel was returned to me by the same guides who brought you here, Mitard said. His means of transport are not as essential to me as the fact of his return. If he had not been brought by you then he would have been brought by someone else.

Shadows revealed plugs of wood holding the beams in place and a trickle of dust coughed out of the roof like a distant puff of cigarette smoke.

I wasn't looking for thanks, said Rubio. I merely wished to check that Daniel had reached home safely.

Mitard's disdain was obvious. He reached for his water bottle, a stage movement, and checking himself, he glanced at his decorative clippings. It almost fitted. The Situationist slogans on the academic's wall, Mitard forming a conception of what Europe was like as if by being in Egypt he could sum it up with one sly expression. The philosopher's first problem: how to make theoretical knowledge mean something useful when related to the real lives of the people you are describing? It was the opposite of what a doctor had to face. For the doctor nothing mattered but the material.

Daniel goes where he pleases, said Mitard. That's why it's best for him here in the oasis. Nobody can go through the desert, a person would be lucky to get five kilometres. The desert has a finality to it and she didn't like that either. She liked her freedom, whatever that was. She liked being told that she was free and she missed the television. She was a libertarian. Does that not make you sick? She was a libertarian which meant that she was a conservative. It meant that she spoke A and felt B. It was like political lip service listening to her.

Rubio looked at Mitard, morbidly unsure. Mitard paused and clicked his fingers in the air.

You like my cuttings then? he asked, and he stretched his hand towards the wall, while Rubio nodded and said, yes they're very interesting.

He fixed his eyes on the faded images and printouts, the shops burned out like the swept chambers of hell, the pictures of riots and clashing forces, the fists raised in accord with the polarisation of the rich and poor.

They can't have riots here, said Mitard, but at the same time I have these pictures to help me understand the varieties of social experience I want to describe. I used to think that it was the strength of the military that stopped revolution in the Near East but it's not. If people rioted in Cairo they would benefit nothing. Here a certain amount of anarchy prevails as it is. It's only human.

Rubio tapped his ash into the nearest receptacle. The dark broken ridges of Mitard's face watched, his elaborate Siwan clothes could ill disguise his ambition to deconstruct his homeland and his dead wife. The ringing was louder in Rubio's ear. The thump continued unswayed through Mitard's talk. It came from far away over the next dune and strangled him like an evil spirit. The noise was like an itch, but reaching it would be like trying to scratch your lungs, it just couldn't be done.

You need more to smoke? asked Mitard.

The head in the grey frock-coat looked at Rubio with the raised jaw of a dog. Rubio wondered if Mitard's knowing expression was a sign that he was stranded here too.
I'm okay, said Rubio.

Did she have any money with her when you found her? asked Mitard. I expected her to return with some of mine.

I'm not sure, said Rubio. There were bottles of spirits, the proper foreign bottles.

Indeed.

Mitard's former wife dead on a voluminous blanket, perhaps driven to insanity by the self-reflecting dictator, her husband.

I was just curious about my wife, said Mitard, and he blocked all light from the window as he stretched. Now standing, Mitard shook his frock coat free of dust and walked past Rubio to an improvised hall. From below the chambers came the cracked sound of a radio, brittle Arab music that created an odd background to the falling-down town.

There is a woman up there who is waiting for a dead husband, said Mitard. He went to Luxor where he was killed in a building accident. She believes that as long as she's here then he'll still come back.

Mitard turned to make himself mysteriously busy with a handful of pearly grey papers, perhaps evidence of the Confessions. He ran his fingers over a folded computer and picked at cushions in red weave, pillows which glanced away from each other at angles.

When I first occupied this house, said Mitard, a family stayed in this room. They used to keep their goats in that alcove that I now call a study.

A cable ran from the computer to the desk and printed sheets hung from the lip of a printer, settling in a tray. Above the desk, more cuttings, the desperate exertions of street protesters, vandal-ised movie stars, flags stabbed with paint and a Star of David tinted with stripes and stickers. Embroidery ran along the wall and from it hung bunches of silver chains and bells and when Mitard turned, Rubio sensed his host rear back like a snake.

I know you, said Mitard, and the many others like you.

His elbow jerked convulsively as he pointed at Rubio.

I wonder what you do for a living? he asked. I think possibly a teacher or a medical bureaucrat. I can see you administering healthcare initiatives, an ability to do nothing loudly. A pen-pusher with a computer and a car. A healthcare executive with a holiday to the Lakes. Maybe you are a dentist. You look like an unhappy dentist whose holiday has gone wrong.

Rubio looked in the crumpled packet of cigarettes, there were four left, jet white filters and loose tobacco.

Have you lost your luggage and your money? asked Mitard. What does Egypt look like from here?
I didn't bring any luggage, said Rubio.

He stared into the box of cigarettes as the room became colder. The walls glowered with the forsaken crumbs of paper pinned into the packed mud finish and Mitard leaned into the window frame as Rubio chewed on his cigarette and glanced at the Star of David on the wall, slender and blue, uncommonly defaced with slogans. Mitard had been waiting for this. He had lain in his spider's web for the fly, moving the great weights and levers of his opinion into position, and now Rubio had appeared within as the prey.

I know why you're in my house, said Mitard. It can't be a secret. Money? guessed Rubio.
That's right, said Mitard. I've been expecting you to ask for the

fare back to Alexandria at the very least. You are a man on hard times, it must be so difficult.

Rubio looked directly at the cigarette, his hand was like a chunk of wood and the smoke ran up his arm.

Giving me some money might be the decent thing to do, he ventured, and he wished to look at Mitard but it wasn't possible.

I don't think so, said his host. We've no ties here you and me. Look at this place. You are asking to be let out of here but I can't do it.

Rubio drew on the cigarette and stared onto the idleness of Mitard's desk. The man's bulk reclined, his eyes two dull slaves staring with dislike.

I can't give you money, said Mitard. If everyone else on this continent is stuck here then why shouldn't you be? You're a student of politics so you work it out. If you stay here it's bound to change the world, don't you think?

Rubio smoked and repeated the word *no*. The only word he could hear was *no*, it wasn't even his own word but a catch released in his feelings and he said it again.

I can give you cigarettes, said Mitard, she left all her cartons here so you can take as many as you like. We don't have much use for them so why not help yourself? They're in that drawer. Go on, she left them for you.

The drawer was near but Rubio did not move.

Go on, said Mitard. I really think you could help us out here. The cigarettes are going unsmoked.

134

Thanks, said Rubio and he disposed of his own cigarette in a tiny clay dustbin.

He glanced at the cigarette drawer while Mitard unscrewed a water bottle and began to drink, an unattractive sight, the gulping throat swelling and deflating. Mitard gave the bottle to Rubio and the taste was good.

My last job before I came to Egypt, said Mitard, was lecturing in Critical Studies. You wonder what it means, what advances we are making in vocabulary alone that keep the majority of the world living in disgrace. Half of Europe at a white-hot cash-register – and who but they could glorify poverty and turn it into a university course? A degree in diabolism, the escape routes from the down spiral, landlords versus landless, are you surprised I left and came here? Imagine scientising poor and rich in economic analysis.
  I don't know, said Rubio.

Mitard snorted and smiled.

You do know, he said. You'd better take those cigarettes and leave, and Rubio frowned, black-browed.
  Leave, said Mitard. Follow the back-packers out of here.

Rubio stared at his hellish host while Mitard stepped to the drawer and dragged it open revealing a treasury of foreign tobaccos. Coloured, ornamented boxes, a whole theatre of cigarettes, packs wrestling with the images of facts, contemplative and soul-mourning smokes in fine red, white and golden sleeves.

Take them and get out, said Mitard. Experience the oasis and leave me alone.

Rubio filled his pockets with the boxes of tobacco while Mitard stared into the border of the window. Forgetting his purpose Rubio seized as many of the boxes as he reasonably could and jammed them in his trouser until Mitard gave him a slight nod and said thanks.

He followed the grey frock coat to the door. The man stopped and pressed his hands to his temples as if trying to resolve some pain, before suddenly pushing the door open and coughing in reaction to the daylight.

Say hello to Daniel, said Rubio, but the man ignored the comment and pointed an arm towards the exit.

The door closed with the sullen diligence of its owner, scraping into place before being locked, and Rubio moved away into the old town of Siwa, listening finally to the repeated coughing from within.

•

As a doctor in the banlieue, Rubio had been obliged to take depression seriously from the off. Destouches, full name unknown, mumbled his symptoms wrapped in a warmish coat. He shuffled his finger along the edge of the desk and apologised if he were wasting the doctor's time. Rubio took the usual notes, the depressives had no idea what hurt them, they stared at their hands as if wondering what their fingers were for while the disease worked away, pulling their strings. The same pill was delivered for a range of maladies, a suggestion that the depressions were fabrications. It meant that those who could make it to their feet were marched off to medicine and encouraged back to work.

Destouches dropped his hand to his lap, a sandbag of a man with a chipped tooth. Rubio waited as Destouches dragged his hands from his knees to his waist, where they held on to his shirt as if he were about to tear it away.

How long do you think you've been depressed? asked Rubio.

Many of the patients disliked the word *depressed* and would not admit to it at all. Others realised that since the speed of consultation was the primary point of social healthcare, then *depressed* was the best they could get from the system. Some waited until the word *depression* had been suggested to them as a final possibility while those like Destouches had a rehearsed speech which they were going to perform regardless.

I don't know if you'd call it depression, said Destouches, and Rubio dropped his pen on the desk hoping for an impact leaden enough to wake them both.

You remember my wife, said Destouches, she came last year but I think she went to another doctor in Paris.

I remember her, said Rubio. Is she well these days?

She's better now, said Destouches. I had to go to work and I never knew what I was coming home to.

And you're still at work? asked Rubio.

I told you, said Destouches. I've been trying to go to work but it's difficult for me.

Destouches' jaw hung like a chop of meat. The room was so hot that Rubio felt he and the patient were in danger of sticking to their seats, like items on a cake about to find eternity as they welded into one.

I'm not at work any more, said Destouches. This all started when I finished work and now I can't get out of bed. She's not able to help. I can't even work if I want to. I couldn't manage to be there.

Destouches looked out Rubio's window where the sun dripped like glue. He spoke with the moody steadiness of a cloud, allowing Rubio to say *go on*, and wave his hand every minute.

She can't help me, said Destouches. I tried to volunteer but I couldn't make it. I tried to volunteer for charity because I thought I could give advice. There are people with problems and I thought since I had been through it then I could help.

Rubio nodded and wrote it down: The patient has tried to volunteer for charity but has not succeeded. Destouches scratched the desk with a finger paralysed like a pencil.

It sounds to me like you are depressed, said Rubio.
Destouches looked up when he heard the diagnosis, his brow hardened as if he were crushed by the word that he most longed to hear.

Yes, you are depressed, said Rubio. Certain symptoms are ambiguous but yours are clear. Having said that it seems to be fairly common. I sometimes think it's only a matter of time before we're all down with it.

Destouches mumbled beneath his breath, the light sank and his skin was the colour of cracked china, a quality most apt.

It's like I've fallen away, he said. The light had shaped his face into a simple and sad form.

Rubio stared. His patient had struggled a final poetic metaphor out of his catechism and had burst forth with a banality.

I'm sorry?

Look at it like this, said Destouches. It's like God has abandoned me, but I don't believe in God.

Rubio tapped his prescription pad and wondered at the possibility of a man falling way from atheism. He coughed and apologised while Destouches looked across the desk for support. Taking the pen from where it had fallen, Rubio scribbled on his pad: *Depression as an atheism, moderns proud of their lack of belief. Their denial of the transcendent.*

Perhaps, thought Rubio, their atheism is a pre-disposition in the same way that some realise they are naturally chosen. The atheists must have their devout, the heathens must have their rituals, consider immediately the implausible image of the worship of money, anything material on the altar of Man's Complaint!

If you're an atheist, said Rubio, you wouldn't worry about any of these questions.

What? said Destouches.

He was typical of Rubio's patients, unable to work it out for himself. One after another, the patients droned their lack of faith like crowing roosters, they sat before Rubio as victims of inactivity, an audience with nothing to do but clap and boo. Rubio sensed that Destouches was angling for drugs, that he was stuck in a hopeless pattern of repetition.

Have you noticed any physical symptoms? asked Rubio.

Destouches looked into his hands.

I was crying, he said, and I noticed that my hands were swollen. They had blown up. They were puffy and it was horrible.

And anything else?

Not apart from the dreams. In one an insect has claws that I can't unhook from my skin and it starts to suck me. It's a big insect.

It would have to be, said Rubio.

Destouches shifted, his face opened wide to garner sympathy. Rubio pretended to write some more, but he had himself to blame. Every last aspect of diagnosis had left his mind. He knew a bad jake from a healthy stream of urine, and could identify a stomach ulcer from the next room. Destouches was bearing into the chair and Rubio began to wonder why he had become a doctor.

That's not the worst dream, said Destouches, and Rubio nodded.

The flu patients, Rubio's one-time staple, went elsewhere now. Wearing a hairshirt of tissues and bad feeling they sectioned themselves in a special flu clinic nicknamed the Ice Cream Parlour, a silver block with over forty flavours of virus, a real holiday atmosphere. It leaves nothing for me, thought Rubio, but the life stories and the misery, this accidic binge.

I'm going to ask you to come back in two weeks, said Rubio. In the meantime I want you to keep the following diary.

Rubio pulled a roll of paper from his drawer.

There are questions on this sheet, he said. You'll need to invest in a notebook so you can monitor how you feel. There's a lot to write down to begin with but you'll get into the swing of it.

Destouches stared as if this solution were too childish an answer to his misery.

This method helps us both, said Rubio. As it is I can't put you straight on to drugs.

My wife was on anti-depressants, said Destouches and he stared in disappointment at the questionnaire. It had calcified in the light before him and its edges looked sharp enough to cut a wrist. It was Dymphna, said Destouches, I was hoping for some of that.

Destouches was now an expert in medicine, as if 20mg Dymphna could cure him of the cloud of bleach engrossing him. What a fix that would be, one whitewash replacing another, the colour grey obscured by another equally neutral tint. The sun held its breath as if waiting to see if Destouches would oblige Rubio by losing his mind there and then. Rubio was like the surviving madman after the flood, the last one left after the sun had darkened every heart. Fear had won and people were exhausted, too tired to care, too tired to volunteer for charity.

Rubio thought that he heard Destouches whimper as he took the sheet of paper with the diary questions on it. Am I the only one left? thought Rubio as Destouches stared in unhappiness at the questionnaire.

Write down everything that you know about your family medical history, said Rubio.

Quaker-coloured misery burned on Destouches' face. Sunlight spotted his chipped tooth and he held the sheet of paper, truly helpless, without doubt depressed, just as the doctor had diagnosed.

Is your wife really not able to help? asked Rubio.

I don't even know if she's healed, came the reply. I still don't think she can do anything.

Destouches had the picture at last. His wife had gone through it with the help of drugs and now it was his turn. The man needed to accept the life he'd chosen instead of fighting the taunts of his unconscious. Destouches folded the paper and placed it with the other archaeological remains in his pocket.

I've got so much time, said Destouches looking far away.

His eyes were of considerable size, cubical niches serving as the nesting place for tears. Every visit like this was another reminder that one day the depression would visit Rubio personally, with its black-locked promise of endless guilt.

I have to see another patient now, thought Rubio, but he was unable to say it.

He resisted the thought that the merest fact of physical contact with this depressive would be enough for him to contract the illness, and he leaned back with a professional hand clasp. In his filing cabinet there was a list of analysts that he kept for situations such as this, and he toyed with its removal.

Don't blame your wife, he said. If you don't feel better in two weeks I'll maybe help you find an analyst, it may be better for you. I have another patient now, but I'll see you soon.

Rubio looked into the ashen face of Destouches. Destouches stood up with his questionnaire, the sunlight dripped on to his jacket, folded inside his collar and jabbed him in the side. He mumbled *thank you doctor* and Rubio was now rid of him for two weeks.

From his window Rubio saw Detouches cross the street and push his way into the bus queue. Destouches was sadness's flea, a carrier oblivious, and Rubio smoked a cigarette out of the surgery window, as he had got into the habit of doing at lunchtimes.

•

Virginie has learned to weep, thought Rubio, unsure why his wife could cry for his mother and he could not. She has learned from the cinema how to make a crossroads of her eyes and express her sympathy by letting her nose run while her hands pull at her ears. She has achieved a redness in the roots of her eyes that makes a crucible of her face, she has formed an arc with her brow that gives her the look of a sea creature. When she is tired of that she then produces her master-stroke and commences her hand shaking and speechmaking with a delicate female handkerchief near and ready.

The funeral was decisive and irrevocable. It was hard on Rubio's nerves although absurdly easy. A bewildering process packed with dizzying paradox, with the strangest sensation coming during the ceremony itself. The coffin, the most indispensable prop, sat like a brick before the oven. The priest talked confusedly of the afterlife, as if out of a nightmare, and he asked Rubio to say a few words, some reflections on how kind his mother had been and on how greatly appreciated her cooking was. There appeared to be a unique compression in the atmosphere of time while Rubio spoke, a stuttering dislocation in the quantity of his speech with past and future rushing away at speed only to collapse to an utter stasis so that he had great difficulty spacing his words. Rubio had the impression that he was repeating the formula that severed him and his mother with terrifying speed in an increasingly high-pitched gabble, as if his voice were coming to him from the deepest anaesthesia yet was clear and hard as a peal of bells jangling the rawest, most sensitive nerve endings.

His speech was over and he sat down. It had been flowery rubbish about another woman. The priest appeared again and the mourners watched the coffin go into the oven.

The colleagues made a café of the wake by sitting cross-legged with wine, black side-burns and flashes of gold. The white flowers were as bright as ice cream and Burneto shifted them from table to table in Rubio's mother's house, making a third and fourth attempt at rearrangement.

I'm living at Neuilly, said Virginie to one of the colleagues.
The others nodded, they were virtually napping.
Life goes on with apparent normality! she said.

Rubio's anger burned low as his one-time wife worked the room, impressing that selection of his mother's friends that had risen out of Limbo for the day. The cabinet had not been cleared and Burneto's tiny lady figurine swayed with her parasol before plates with faded gold stars.

I enjoyed your speech, said Burneto.

His statement was typical of the featureless continuum that seemed to Rubio at that time to be almost bovine. Rubio found himself in welcome solidarity with the china figure of the lady who said nothing, did nothing, and only waited in the nothingness of her yogidom for the day when she would be shattered.

The speech was not to be enjoyed, said Rubio to his friend, who blushed at the thought and drank quickly from his glass.
I merely meant that it was apt, said Burneto.
Whatever, said Rubio.

Burneto, prone to sloth, reached out and said, *don't worry old man*, but Rubio avoided his hand as if it might damage him.

He lit a cigarette and let go of the smoke in Burneto's direction. Soon I won't even need these, he repeated to himself as Burneto's face was blurred, and another cloud of smoke flowed out his mouth and hung in the room.

The mourners appeared as in an uneasy dream and Rubio concentrated on the fortune that had brought all of these people to his old mother's house. Time was always doing this, providing great pauses when Rubio thought there was something he was supposed to be saying. Several figures forgotten from his youth had appeared for the funeral, a mocking court of Gallic incomers that were old and past, elders who only appeared for funerals when they weren't visiting churches and keeping a long-watch on the graveyards. Each in turn, their grimy ashes would be scattered at their favourite haunts, the river, the park, the café.

I liked your speech, said Virginie, and Rubio rested his drooping head in his hands.

What is it? she asked. Are you all right?

My speech was not to be enjoyed, said Rubio to his wife, who offered him her kerchief as if she were being gentle.

I meant that it was appropriate, she said.

Whatever, said Rubio. Who can tell the difference?

She would have liked it, said Virginie.

I didn't want to speak, he said.

He heard the colleagues in the corridor and noticed Burneto had returned to admiring the inmates of the cabinet. Again the opportunity. They were all here, like the marrow of his unhappines, they could all be theoretically cut out in one swift operation. To interrupt their mourning with the clearing of his throat, the tapping of a spoon upon a glass, or better still a hammer upon a china figure. . .

My friends and relatives.

Unless we retreat inwards to fantasy and create languages, he said, we run the risk of esotericising ourselves into nothingness. Look at my wife here, look at my colleagues. If I were to obey my first impulse I should tell you all now that I am sick of every one of you. If I were to obey my first impulse I should take this opportunity to damn you all. Your childish appreciation of each other is a kind of quarantine to communally protect your personalities against philosophy, authenticity, but hubris is like mumps, everybody, it's best to get it over with young.

Have a drink, said Virginie, you're among friends, and she took Rubio's arm and led him towards the colleagues who were doubtfully involved in a conversation about football.

●

A magazine photograph in his drawer, 'Sand Dunes in the Desert', a place where he had longed to walk. Rubio stumbled at a wedge of sand that became taller as he neared, the sand and its salt thickened into plates that spilled over his footsteps. The sun hung level with the town of Siwa, around its concrete fangs, the roofs of houses underground, the palm trees in between. Sand shadowed sand and Rubio wondered if there was a direction he should take, he kicked a stone and released a cigarette from the cluster in his top pocket.

Here was a postcard, the image of the sphinx, pert with a secret message for someone unknown to him.

Sand turned under and round the ankle, near dead, soft and moving forward on Rubio's effort, veering endlessly round.

His foot slipped and he found a pen, glared into the sun and netted a few insults to the colleagues.

the sand and Rubio crawled to face the other way. The sand swelled in the silence and he felt the jeep driver's hand grab him and begin to pull. The man shouted to the jeep for water and the passengers shivered as their depressions hustled back upon them.

Rubio listened to a second set of beats on the sand which indicated that someone else was approaching. Dismal sadness was heard in those footsteps, they echoed like the footsteps of patients on his stairs, trying to thump their illness out on the steps. The jeep driver took Rubio's collar and Rubio felt the hand throttle him, the glowing brand of the man's fist burned into his neck. The third party arrived and spoke. It was one of the women from the jeep and Rubio heard her say, I'm a doctor.

. . . at least the word *doctor* was considered by Rubio in his available ear to be the correct interpretation of what she said.

Scrolls of sand turned, Rubio's chin was on the surface of the desert and when his eyes adjusted he was looking into the recently breakfasted face of a female English-speaking pain in the neck, her fingers like wands waving over him. Through the sand in his ear, Rubio heard the woman begin the sublime procedure of surgical examination as she groped behind his neck.

Take it easy now, he heard, I'm just going to feel this.

Rubio attempted to locate the request in the inventory of his own medicine but found himself more entertained by the theatrical chit-chat of the examination. He tried to move but the jeep driver held him down, grinning as if he had caught a rare animal.

Where have you been? asked the desert doctor, a glossy coat of sweat on her forehead.
How long have you been out? she asked.

Rubio could not reply but smiled when he remembered that patients were always stupid and could never answer straight. It's the doctor's first defence, he thought, the assumption that the ill have been so stupid as to enter these cul de sacs of ill health from which they can't back out. His eyes felt like bursting. He had always believed that patients were at least in part stupid and this unofficial appointment proved to him that the theory still held good. It had been his fault, everything from the distortions created by his mother's death to his wandering in the Libyan desert. Everything from his marriage to Virginie to the godawful Burneto, those colleagues whose ennui found its tortured expression in the hunt for the perfect liver paté, the darkest coffee, the mot juste and the sentence with the neatest ankles.

. . . it had been. . .

All my fault, said Rubio unable to withhold the conviction any longer.

His words were a shrill squeak, not his own, and he tried to speak again to readjust them. The jeep driver bent down to look but the doctor shooed him away.

Time to get him to the jeep, she said.

The jeep and then what? thought Rubio. The pharmacy, the hospital and the grave? He struggled under the grip of the jeep driver who began to help him to his feet.

Please, out of the way, said Rubio but the doctor supported his neck as if it had been broken, while her other hand slid around his shoulder like the strap of a straitjacket.

A flame lit in the doctor's eye, her sturdy English accent mumbled a ritual phrase and ash from the jeep driver's cigarette fell, a lump like the slag from a volcano, spinning through the air towards the earth. The doctor insulted the driver for his carelessness. She was a doctor just like Rubio, her personality was a dead core calibrated to resonate with the miseries of her patients, each with their own states of distraction. The jeep driver shrugged and addressed her casually in Arabic, somebody else shouted something but Rubio was running for the sombre form of the next dune. The doctor shouted behind him, her voice a primitive yell but Rubio tore fearfully up the sand.

The fastest way down the next slope is to fall, thought Rubio, to take a jump and hope for gravity. Ahead of him were the palm trees of the oasis, behind were a congregation of French and English tourists calling for his return, their voices like the banal forms of the desert itself. Rubio rolled down the dune into deeper and heavier sand, kicking his legs in order to reach the bottom. Behind him, the doctor and the jeep driver shouted like fools glued to the palate of the dune. Rubio waved and jogged towards the oasis of Siwa, now visible a mile ahead, just the way that he had left it, through the salt flats, the dirty palms, up the track where the piles of rubble indicated the possibility of future building projects.

Picturing the queue of patients in his surgery, Rubio realised that he could refer them all to the desert doctor. She can sort them out, he thought, all of the modern problems in a one-stop desert shop, financial, medical, hopeful.

The jeep driver and the doctor were joined by another tourist in a baseball cap and they all watched Rubio leave.

Form an orderly line, he thought, everyone for the sand!

Nobody should fear that they'll go mad in the desert because there are doctors at every sand dune, down every crevice and under every rock.

He jogged towards the oasis and when he turned around, the spectators on the dunes had trailed away. The last to leave the crest of the dune was the jeep driver, stranded with his water-swollen tourists.

•

As ill luck would have it, Rubio stumbled in the remotest possible corner of Siwa, snagged his trouser and scratched his knee as he climbed towards his goal. Behind the dust and timber, goats were scraping, radios were whistling pity, and Rubio moved by the remains of houses until he arrived at two broken grinding stones. The hot air disturbed his touch and he thought of the word *water*, the position of the arms and hands while asking for water, and he said the word again before he observed the academic Mitard, his frock-coat open wide.

It's the dentist, said Mitard as Rubio collected his breath. Are you back for money?

Rubio stood against the wall opposite Mitard's burned brick house and thought out the word *water*, as if rehearsing how to say it.

Money, repeated the academic. I'd like to hear you ask for the money.

I'm a doctor, said Rubio with a certain recoil. If it makes any difference to you, I'm a doctor.

That computes, said Mitard.

Mitard's face was crimson. He scowled as if in preparation for a lynching. Above him were the ruins of a tower of clay studded with flies which reacted to his arrival by turning and facing the other way. Mitard picked at the wall with his finger finding the eroded remnants of a tiny hole.

I need your help, said Rubio. He panted out the words more fitfully than was required. He rested on a wall and looked at the ground, too weak to resist the other man's eyes.

The fact is, said Mitard, you have come to ask for money but only because you believe we share something. Sadly you and I have nothing in common and your reappearing here is either an example of terrible judgement or a blatant attempt to provoke my wrath.

Mitard gazed as if to make his point, insistent on the gravity of his argument.

I need some water, said Rubio.

Mitard held up his hand and Rubio looked along it and into the blue sky over the desert. The same glass bowl which covered the rest of the world was clear in Siwa and could reveal the light of the heavens to anyone who wished to look.

Deterritorialisation is taking place said Mitard proudly. In other words, so long as your needs are not met your re-organising of social relations inevitably leads to your trying to ally with me in favour of the Siwans here who may be willing to help you.

Rubio stared into the eliminating logic of Mitard's brow, the academic had already transformed their meeting into a teaching project.

Infinite justice constitutes a distillate of human relations, said Mitard as his hands dug into the frock coat and swung it merrily in time. You're quick to confuse need with exploitation to get what you require, and this writ large has given birth to the virtual multiplicities of Europe and America, meaning that social explanations of everything precede actions.

154

I don't understand, said Rubio, it's just a drink and some money that I need to get out of here. Don't you know that I was robbed?

You've all been robbed, said Mitard, robbed of conclusion and conviction, your only final certitude is the violence that you do against these people here, those whose water you are effectively asking me to share with you. . .

I think I have the right to ask, said Rubio, and he lit a cigarette and let his hand fall back into place. The smoke struck deep into the dry soil of his stomach and he coughed it out while the grey coat watched with a strange look of pleasure.

It's your asking that drags everything into international crisis, said Mitard. If you told me that you were innocent of the crimes of this world and that your privileges had nothing to do with the depredations of this and other countries, why should I believe you and not the next man?

The question appeared to Rubio as a dull pain immediately under the ribs, a slight inclination to cough again. His gums were spongy and his legs had swelled, he felt something in his throat and wished that he had asked for a bed instead of water, water instead of money, money instead of cigarettes.

Mitard's robust organism expelled a flow of gas in a burp and the razor sensation in Rubio's throat increased. Mitard burped again and held himself as if in epigastric pain, as if fearing the existence of some infection in his stomach.

I wouldn't believe you Doctor, he said. Empire builds the walls of human misery and what you do at home reflects that. What you eat every morning reflects that. Can you understand? The liberation of Africa would be dangerous to France. It may be true that in a moment of enthusiasm you felt empathy with the people of this country but you'll return to the weaknesses and prejudices of home. This water is ours and we are not going to share it with you.

Even as a man? asked Rubio, unsure of his intention.

You're going it alone, said Mitard, and he admitted a sorrowful sigh.

Rubio cast his eyes down to the dirt, water trickled somewhere in the ruin of the old town and he looked as if there was a source of it that he had missed. Mitard smiled in enjoyment of his superior abilities.

When I taught the students in Paris, said Mitard, I used to issue the old lies every day. I used to say: Poor nutrition in the Third World contributes to disease, but no one eats badly out of choice. When I said that my gesture and my manner filled the students with excitement, they became passionately attached to this cause but it was not a passion that inspired action. Their ambitions were for change, they wrote essays about the judicious organisation of the poor, and I taught them every year about economic organisation and global rights. Now of course my students have families and enjoy the opportunity of credit under the protection of planes and bombs, secure against imaginary assault. Some have been brave enough to follow me, some don't believe that the study of global relationships involves working in a European library and fantasising political solutions. I have some students in this country now but we have no formal lesson plan. They come, I teach, they go.

Rubio hunched his shoulders as though from cold and flicked at his cigarette.

You absolutely will not help? he asked

I absolutely will not, said Mitard, not until all of Africa has moved to France or until all of France has moved to Africa.

A thought, said Rubio, and his throat agitated for a drink.

Mitard smiled impertinently as Rubio's hope drained away, the academic amply filled his frock-coat which held his weight like an iron bracket. Rubio squeezed the cigarettes in his pocket while Mitard spoke again with a certain dreamlike quality.

The conversion of the world to what we term as fair and equal is well nigh insoluble, said Mitard. It can however be begun with action, the dissolution of nation state boundaries and an end to the tyranny of the ever-present consumer. As it stands the practices of imperial constitution allow us the power to do anything we wish in Africa, so simply withholding water from you for an hour is as good as it gets.

It's the way the world is, said Rubio. People do their best and I'm all for the liberty of anyone who is poor. Are you not?

Mitard scowled like a wolf and scratched a rash on his neck. An ice cold pain was spreading from Rubio's throat down into his chest.

The world is more moral than it has ever been, said Mitard, mass murder is more common but it has never been more moral. One moment it's nothing to do with you but the next the opposite seems to be the case and good intentions reign supreme. For each increase in the standard of living we take on a new differently packaged scapegoat. Drug dealers, youth gangs, child molesters and immigrants have all had their day. Science teaches us that matter is composed of atoms, that human life is created from chemicals. The earth, the air, the oceans all have prices fixed by mining rights, pollution rights, all of which are guarded by the force you name as peace. Do you think that existentialism has come to Egypt? Does the desert have time to analyse your academic debates on fair trade?

Everywhere Rubio squinted, there stood Mitard's bulk against the wall. Mitard stepped forward and Rubio noticed a curl of dust rising from the pit. Below them was a ton of dried matter organised into a magnitude of broken brick. The sun made little impact on Mitard's white hair, darted over it, showed a block of wisely brushed strands woven into the shape of an eagle's crown. Smoke projected from Rubio's mouth and his hand throbbed with the cigarette. His heart beat time with his feelings towards the man he hated.

You're stuck in your ways, said Mitard. In fact you've made an art of it.

Rubio's neck was sore and he needed water, just a glass to torch the hard sensation in his throat. The last of the smoke came free from his mouth and he looked at his hand where the cigarette hovered in wait. He heard a noise at the door of the house and Daniel stepped through the wooden frame and joined them on the porch. Rubio smoked the cigarette and as the filter reached his teeth, so Mitard's finger pointed at him. Daniel stood on the edge of the porch as if he were waiting to ask for something and Mitard looked to where the ground had fallen through into the pits caused by the collapsing sand. In a stack of dust the ground gave way and sand blew into the air, Mitard vanished into the shaft that had opened up and a mass of rock fell after him. A wedge-shaped channel appeared where Mitard had been and Rubio picked himself up to see if the kid was safe.

Daniel? he asked.

Dust hung in a yellow puff, neither rising nor falling, merely concealing the rubble of Mitard's body. From a nearby walkway Rubio heard a door and a man's voice. Daniel's face was the colour of the stone – he had blended in to the town as a fixture on the paper-stale wall. The dust quickened as if somebody had breathed through it and Rubio turned to the kid again who had frozen, awaiting a response.

Hold on Daniel, he said.

Two men approached and the goat looked out of its hole and smiled. Rubio's heart turned and he took a step away from the gap and lowered himself to the ground. Silence filled Rubio as his hearing ceased. It was a heart attack at last, silence but for the beating heart, not full of blood so much as air. The heart relied on the greater electrical charge of its heavier components, its hydrogen fusion, the monstrous temperatures of its cores. Rubio tried to recall a patient that had experienced something similar but past images escaped like dividing cells. Blood masses drove the tubes and looms to the heart's next beat, the sky gushed in violet for a moment and Rubio recalled medical articles and descriptions. The sky returned to an aimless blue and men in white robes drew along the tunnel of the walls to see the hole. The root sound of conversation from the men was a mutter of words that blurred in the lower registers of misfortune. The chamber of the heart filled with blood returning and the movement repeated in a burst. The pump closed again, clouds passed before Rubio's eyes and he felt an insect land on his face. His heart flexed in irritation while the insect tickled his cheek, a tear shaved from Rubio's eye and stopped just north of where the insect made its belfry. Finally the tear fell into the mosquito and together they rolled onto the ground and Rubio's heart laughed once, reinstating the creaking gates of the coronary valves.

Daniel stood above him and said something but Rubio was unable to answer. Rubio's leg hurt and he remembered again what he had come for, water. The sun cast a patch of heat upon his chest while his middle finger found a crack in the ground. He tried see if feeling had returned.

Go into the house, said Rubio to Daniel.

The boy stared while Rubio made it to his knees. He gripped the wall with each muscle creaking as he began life afresh. He repeated his command and the boy walked inside, and once Rubio was on his feet and had checked his balance, he followed him in.

In the house, whispers ran through from the furniture into the rock, artefacts huddled on a cheap dresser and shone in the brilliance of the sun. He walked to the cooking area, pushed the screen aside and took a bottle of water. The hearth glowed, cinders in contact with red hot rocks, and even as the water ran inside him, even as he looked into the glassy surface of the plastic bottle Rubio couldn't help but think about Mitard, and wished that he could have done something. Instead, the university would arrive in the area and make their own report, retrieve Mitard's case notes and his essays, dig in the swamp of literature the man had produced, and take the Confessions back to France for publication. Rubio took the bottle and walked to the hall where Daniel waited.

I haven't had a drink since yesterday said Rubio, but the kid said nothing, the tip of his nose pointed arrogantly at Rubio's brow. As if to prove his thirst, Rubio drank again, cooling his heart which returned to its normal size. He looked into the plastic bottle and thought of water as a new universal prescription, the heart's aid and a summer flowering of ice.

Holding a curtain, Rubio felt his heart enlarge and wondered if Mitard had any aspirin, any small aid. The academic's laptop flashed, indicating that work had been interrupted, and Rubio walked towards it and sat, rummaging in a drawer for pills. He glanced at the table where the laptop hummed, the hard drive filtering the air in a desperate attempt to keep the machinery free of the dust that clogged the hearts of men. On the blue screen of the computer a report was underway and Rubio focused on the words which became blobs in their own bed of light. Rubio read from the computer screen and wondered if Mitard had really been an academic. He read the script and wondered for whom Mitard's prose was intended, to whom it would make any sense.

Yet, again in Siwa even the execution of ceremonies is not methodically ordered, even though it is taken up with a consistent tone, a laborious theatricalism that sees the diverse strands of the religion knot together the specific concerns of the Siwan people. In looking in particular at the marriage and death rituals, both of which have an oddly externalised air about the way they are dealt with, I have detected the similar and more restrained versions of the Islamic symbolism that I studied last year, when I concluded that the superstitious elements of their lives and sacramental ceremonies were heightened due to their proximity to the desert and their distance from any major centre of orthodoxy. Although demonstrating no spiritual superiority, I would yet hazard that the differentiation which exists in the ceremonies associated with marriage and death, offer an enhanced access to the symbolically assimilated practices I have already discussed, and over a considerable stretch of time these seem to have been preserved rather than is the case in a larger metropolis, corrupted or adapted depending on influence. Death in Siwa has fascinated me in particular, offering the regenerative potential essential to all desert ritual while being deeply rooted in the Islamic ideal of

Presumably, thought Rubio, this was the moment at which Mitard left his home for the last time, the moment when he walked outside to jeer at a stranger and die, when he decided to exercise his opinions concerning self-imposed exile.

Rubio knocked some papers away and thought of the sand. He

picked a bottle of water from the floor and carefully typed on the computer:

this is what M. Mitard was working on when he died

Rubio shut down the computer, saving the academic's last work. A moment later he stood in the hall where he could see Daniel outside, sitting by the hole into which his father had fallen. At least Mitard's own heart was in a worse state than Rubio's, squeezed in the rocks where there was no air or water to save it. A stone broke upon Mitard's heart and the blood mixed with dust. The dust was compacted over the centuries and then some people dug up the earth, looking for stones to build their civilisation. In the farthest future, once Siwa has been rebuilt, destroyed by America in a war, rebuilt again and lengthened to carry the freight out of the Libyan desert, once the Temple of Amun is encased in glass as the most graceful relic of the ancient world, only then will Mitard's stone be moved. This beige rock, soft enough for carving, a lintel-piece in the silver capital of the sand – Mitard's heart.

Rubio looked in the pit and thought he saw an arm, a part of Mitard not covered by masonry, and he stared at it, seeing both a limb and a hunk of wood at the same time.

He walked to Mitard's front door and rested against the nearest wall where he tapped the earth, superstitiously, as if it might give way.

•

While Rubio dressed, political commentators spoke on the radio, outdoing each other with their calls for more money, computers for nurses, nurses for offices, offices for doctors, doctors for government and government for re-election. The radio news was the daily resurrection of the juggernaut cadaver, everybody pushed the corpse and Rubio scraped his face with a razor and took a glass of orange in the kitchen. Wherever she was, Virginie was briefly focused on her newspaper. She was the world's greatest tutter and she could be seen on any day of the week looking at a magazine and saying how terrible it was between mouthfuls. Wherever he was, the god-awful Burneto was a sucker for it too. Burneto repeated everything he read, swinging the bovine tail of his coat and arguing for equality all round, as if agreement with his simple analysis would heal the world of its evils.

Rubio listened, unable to relinquish his attention to this appalling situation. Because illness had been moralised and was interpreted as an attack on lifestyle, the typical role of the doctor was to look at the patient with the eyes of policy, if such a thing were possible. So Rubio did what he could while the Health Minister took the credit. The Health Minister, it had to be said, was the biggest bitch on the planet. Her task was to reinforce the covenantal relationship she had with the government by visiting hospitals and encouraging children to hold carrots while she was photographed in her grinning bitch of a black suit. Indeed, the Health Minister had more in common with the Minster for Defence than she did with any doctor or nurse.

Rubio heard the Health Minister speak as he prepared for work. She made him feel so old, inhuman, as if he weren't a doctor but a medieval quack. She made of fitness a medical cult, she proclaimed the immediacy of problems faster than the interviewers could describe them and she reinforced how much her government had done so far. Immediacy was the message with everything graphically drawn up and then wiped aside, and at the end of every interview she liked to call her nurses wonderful.

I wouldn't want to be tied down to particulars, said the Health Minister, but what I can say is this. We are implementing strategies, creating strategic roles, determining the best way forward, because we have promised that we will offer the public the best of care that our modern state can offer. At the end of this month I want to see a report on my desk giving me the peace of mind to say to the public that, yes, we have achieved our targets.

From the tone of the interview Rubio could feel how bad things had become. The speed of the Health Minister's policy indicated that in her view, doctors were merely super-gadgets in her moralising machine. More was needed to improve the health of the banlieue, she said, and that the government had always been committed to this. The government's commitment extended to a fair society and healthcare initiatives, the best for the most people, something like that. What Rubio noticed however is that the Health Minister never once mentioned depression.

Rubio coughed and stood up.

Madam Minister. I have sent so many of my patients away with drugs and yet they do not appear to be getting any better. These drugs, I would like to say Madam Minister, when taken in conjunction with the televisions that were prescribed by this government, have caused permanent damage to those who have already been dismally forgotten by this administration. As a doctor, I can assure you all, that daily they sweat and choke before me. It is clear in my professional opinion that the work of one generation becomes the depression of the next, and I would therefore like to call upon this government to tackle the root of the depression that is occupying the outlying areas of Paris and treat the people as if . . .

Mr Speaker! shouted the Health Minister as she ate a pastry and text-messaged the police. There is no evidence for there being depression in the banlieue!

I tell you Madam Minister that depression is there, said Rubio, but many men and women in coats shook their papers while order was called.

I have been to the banlieue said the Health Minister (a monster of a lie) and I can reassure this meeting that there is no depression there whatsoever. These reports of mass misery are in fact exaggerated crime reports and the odd case of insanity pushed to severe conclusions!

Order!
Order!

Depression is in the bainlieu, said Rubio, and he waved his stethoscope at the Health Minister. In many cases it is not depression, he said, insofar as it has evolved into something much larger than its sufferers. The church becomes wider as more credit is issued, as more television channels are broadcast, as more chapels became night-clubs, as the pitch becomes greater. This is what I am telling you. It's happening!

Order!

First in the door of the surgery that morning was Baby Gerard, carried by his mother who drove her long nails into her hair like they were bared sabres. As Gerard's mother introduced herself again, her worn-out clothes reminiscent of lost street ends, Rubio felt that he was watching another world. A section of reality was breaking off unnoticed by the galaxy and was floating towards the evil light of hell. Baby Gerard and his mother were pushing it from the shore while the dying rays of light fluted from behind their faces. The symptoms were nominal forms of the same and Rubio barely listened.

I've tried what I can, said Baby Gerard's mother. I need my own prescription renewed and I need one for the baby. I don't know why the law says that he can't have anti-depressants because he needs them. I should know.

Rubio said nothing and listened to his patient's story. He gave retirement a thought, but sensed the child's unspeakable outrage at the idea. He tried to maintain his look of interest, remembering that he was depression's enemy and that he had to stand up for its sufferers. When a doctor complains to his patients after all, then it's getting near the end of the line. When a doctor places the stethoscope on his own heart, he's not just worried about his patients, he's feeling society as a whole.

We're supposed to get him baptised said the mother, but what's the point in that?

Rubio said nothing but wrote the word *Christians* on his pad and read it repeatedly while Baby Gerard's blond head considered the fat pupae of his own body. The child felt any visit to the surgery to be time wasted, time that could be better spent with a good selection of Loire wines, or arguing with a snail merchant.

You understand that we all wish to do the right thing, said the mother, trying not to tug at her hair, but the priority here is our happiness.

Rubio scored out the word *Christians* and pulled over a prescription.

You don't think that baptism is the answer? he asked.

Our happiness, she said. I want my child to be happy.

Baby Gerard agreed and he nodded as if commanding the doctor to finish up. The Polidor would be open soon, the only obvious restaurant for one born into the wrong class as he was. The banlieue may have gone the way of the burger but in Paris there was still solid meaty fare for an aspiring aristocrat, like calf's kidneys grilled in mustard. They had dreamed it up and Baby Gerard would eat it.

Could you recommend us both the same thing doctor? asked the mother. We need to be together in this.

I shall, said Rubio and he clicked his pen and bared his teeth.

Baby Gerard licked his lips and the mother perked up, seized as if with alarm.

The main thing I would advise for you, said Rubio, is to avoid the television at all costs. That is very important. If you must listen to the radio, then choose a classical station. Don't listen to any news and try to avoid the centre of Paris, especially the larger stores.

The mother stared across the desk at Rubio's judgement.

Could you be more specific? she asked.

You can start by getting rid of your television, said Rubio. Let Gerard be what he wants to be but avoid encouraging him to escapist behaviour. Give him as much meat as you think he can manage. It'll give him a taste for social life. Meat for the child early makes the adult able to compete.

Rubio held up the prescription.

Of course I'll give you something for yourself, but you'll have to do exactly as I say if you want to get better. If you want Gerard to have a happy life then you must do as I say.

The mother understood enough to remain silent.
Good, said Rubio, and he began to write.
Again the quiet voice from his patient.
My husband likes the television, she said, and so does Gerard.

Rubio considered the leaded glass of her eyes. She was quiet, more repentant in her depressed state then she had been before. Like many depressed, perhaps she felt the television was all that kept her sane, a neat irony, if ever there was.

I don't know what I'm doing, she said, and neither does Gerard. When I look at the clock I'm seeing the rest of my life and if I don't think about it then it's all right. I need something to get me to sleep and the television helps.

You know my advice, said Rubio, so I hope you can work on it. No newspapers, whatever you do. As for you, come back for a prescription in ten days and I'll see how you feel then.

What do we do with the television? was all that she could say.
Rubio shrugged.

I am now telling all my patients not to watch it. No game shows or police dramas.

The police are live on cable, she said, but Rubio shook his head.

Not any more, he said.

The mother took her prescription and stood up. Baby Gerard was carried from the surgery into the sunless corridor of the stairs and Rubio swore he heard the child breathe revenge. Baby Gerard would be back one day with a sharp implement. In the flickering light of a candlelit dinner he would skewer the doctor for attempting to deny him the natural violence of his favourite shows.

Rubio wanted to smoke but there was another patient on the way. The ever-delaying moment of the end of time was passing by his desk and a second depressive would be along in sixty seconds.

While it must be realised that we are dealing with an elusive illness rather than a recognised virus, thought Rubio, the conclusion is that everybody will suffer this complaint before long. There is a sense here that everything could end suddenly, so everybody's on edge, the depression is moving in, elusive and only vaguely defined by. . .

He shrugged the feeling away. The fact that his constituents were party to a system much greater than they knew was not concealed. The illusion that money was everywhere was well-founded. So many accepted it as their sheer bad luck to be poor. They dragged themselves down the umbilical cords of their unhappiness to the surgery and let rip until Rubio believed that there were no illnesses left that weren't expressed by means of depression. Sadness had attached itself to the commonest of colds, an ailment that he barely dealt with anymore. He met patients with viruses plated to their throats and eyes, but not one of them needed curing of these.

Two more drug-resistant mutants entered the surgery and Rubio listened with his pen hovering over the prescription pad. In his own heart, depression attacked causing a bulge as big as a plum. The aneurysm pressed on his windpipe and by 2.30 in the afternoon it was leaking. By 3 pm Rubio felt like he was coughing blood and at 4 he was so short of breath that he felt close to suffocation, only able to breath again when the door closed and the last of them had gone.

When the train rolled from the canopy of Masr station in Alexandria, Daniel crouched in the open doorway with his feet on the plate. Nearby passengers ate yellow fruit as they passed towards the Delta through jumbled residential quarters where the railway line was black in filth, scattered with orphaned litter and machinery. Rubio glanced along the carriage and pressed his foot into Daniel's back. A group of men played cards and a fiery vermin of insects floated in the carriage. The vehicle slowed at a junction, a row of squint telegraph poles, each with a mixed configuration of wires. The roadway was sunk with wooden shacks and sheds and in the irrigated fields people stood like fingers, working spades and rakes.

When the train gathered speed, Rubio gripped a vertical rail mesmerised by the flow of flat-roofed hamlets. Water lay in gutters between corrugated tin sheets. The towns they passed were made of tar paper and oil drums, broken by the unpleasant constructions of the waterlogged fields.

The sign for Tanta was the remnant of an explosion battered on to a wall, the word in Roman and in Arabic, cracked as if used for pistol practice. People waited beside the track with bags and boxes while others emerged from shoddily made homes. Tanta was a town of vacant lots worsened by uprooted cement and stone works. The buildings were a tangled smear of metal, their supporting lattices twisted into spirals where girders gaped out blindly. Rubio put his hand on Daniel's head.

Are you okay?

The question was all that Rubio could manage, the mind was drained, perhaps by age, perhaps by this exhausting journey. The

Delta was a monstrosity after the desert, never was there a view without a face staring back and everything took on a freshly bombed character. The train waited in Tanta and the carriage buzzed, punctuated by peculiar silences. A van rolled past carrying long sheaves of grass, a black faced child staring back. The ticking of the engine stopped and there was a racket from the other end of the carriage as a man boarded to sell drinks, squeezing into the crowd with a bronzed water pot.

Do you remember where your Dad took you in Cairo? asked Rubio.

Daniel paid no attention. The man at Rubio's side smoked a cigarette in a wooden holder and stared as if in challenge. Rubio shrugged and bent down to Daniel's ear.

Where did you go in Cairo? It would help us if we had a start.
We didn't go to Cairo, said Daniel.
Didn't go, said Rubio. That's not what you said before.

When the train moved away the water seller jumped off and stood on a concrete bank to watch it go. The carriage squeaked with fatigue through a railway graveyard, dark bottle-green trains lay wrecked in broken piles as sharp as tooth picks. Further along older wagons lay on their sides, rusty weapons part buried in the ground. The dead trains brought to mind the vehicles of the Paris Metro, pencilling down invisible inclines in the black, emerging every four minutes through an arch into a cream-tiled concourse. Rubio thought of the lightweight RER, Les Halles with its escalators and its shimmering caverns, advertising boards and the ghostly boatmen of the trains themselves. He thought of the TGV rolling into Paris every hour with such accuracy, the teams of men that worked on this train's preservation, cleaning the blackened engine parts, dropping oil along the underside, and the train itself

171

reloading for the south of France. All were coming to the same finale, their arrangement was perfected at the end of the line where everything was thrown out of employment and left for scrap.

Rubio's Egyptian train slugged up to its top speed again and he gripped the rail and felt the wind rise. Lorries and trailers sat in lonely bays of dust, some stacked with boxes, while sick white cows stood frozen on the land. The cigarette smoker stared at Rubio and Rubio looked away and he picked at a chunk of blue paint on the wall of the train. A minute later he found himself staring at the man's shoes and their eyes met again.

Cleopatras! said Rubio, but the man returned nothing.
Rubio found his own cigarettes and held them up.
Cleopatras! he said, the best cigarettes!

Rubio's neighbour flicked his cigarette holder and nodded. Rubio held his cigarettes and offered one of them to the man. All of life had been like this, a lack of comfort in human relations. He took one of his own cigarettes and showed them to the man again. The man indicated that he was already smoking, his eyes dark in the light of the train doorway

Cleopatras, the best cigarettes, said Rubio.

Rubio flicked his lighter and it scattered sparks in the heat. The train passed shanties of shacks and tenements of wood, some of which were supported by advertising hoarding. The advertising boards were of a single type and showed painted Arab faces, squint letters, all of which seemed to be from the past. The train slowed and Rubio noticed the rubbish by the track, black wood, mud packed and rusted, barrels and oil cans, spills of stone, children in groups. Daniel hadn't moved for hours, he sat with his feet on the plate.

Hold on, said Rubio, and he took his own advice and gripped the rail.

A row of cattle stood in a harbour of dried mud formed by a ring of destroyed cars, the collapsing houses passed from view, replaced by fields and water channels. From Alexandria to Cairo was a land of ditches – you could walk the ditches between the two cities, cross the divide without ever leaving a soaking ditch serviced by dank water. Smoke burned from under the train and for a second it choked Rubio and spoiled his cigarette. The train horn sounded and the smoke cleared.

Unexpectedly, the train approached Cairo. Concrete walls replaced the fields and another set of rails diverged into many sets of drier and older tracks. Ancient carriages sat like ingots of lead, glued by the sun to their final halt, and the rudimentary structures of the Delta tapered into towers which enclosed the train as the city appeared. The train rode at a whisper through an installation of cylindrical apartment blocks where vehicles ran along ramps. It was hotter in Cairo than it had been in the Delta and the train slowed as if it were coming to rest on a cushion of air itself. The train line was a concrete conduit along which this heat rolled, the warmth sludged against the buildings and dropped over the embankment into the concrete channel of the railway. As the train rocked Rubio wondered if he didn't hear an explosion in the distance – something seemed to shake amid the fumes and the slices of office building. Rubio turned to the cigarette holder man and cupped his ear.

Did you hear that? Rubio said, but this man did not respond.
Rubio cupped at his ear.
Did you hear it? What was it?
The others in the doorway looked into the architrave of Cairo.
I heard a noise, said Rubio cupping at his ear.

He noticed that Daniel had kicked his legs off the plate beneath the doorway and was swinging his feet out as the train moved lower into the city.

Stop that, said Rubio.

His eye fell on the minaret of a mosque with large spikes cutting at the sky, behind this was a cloud of dark smoke, turning. The cloud of smoke behind the minaret broke up swiftly and the minaret vanished behind the concrete walls of more housing blocks.

People crowded the platform of the station, high pyres of faces on a blotting pad of sunlight. A siren rang and hands reached past Rubio as a crowd assembled at the exits of the carriage. Passengers were already pushing before the train had stopped, throwing bags and boxes clear. Rubio fell directly into the crowd which held him for a second before he caught his bearings. He felt his pocket and looked for Daniel but the kid had gone, merged into the press. Rubio was pushed forward, rocked by the strange triangular gestures people were making above their voices.

Daniel, said Rubio, barely loud enough.

Rubio pushed towards the centre of the station where the crowd eddied more freely than on the platforms. He stared at the train that had carried them from Alexandria to Cairo, Engine Number III with a streak of Arabic, the paint had fallen away and a muddy river of oil ran from its iron nose. He walked towards the doors of the station, to the main concourse where the bags were kept. Again he turned on his heels and looked into the impressive maw of the train, its great front windows squandered with dirt, as if nobody here would take time to clean a train, the last thing on their minds. Another train arrived and a swarm gathered to move upon it when it stopped. Rubio tried to recall what the original idea had been, the reason he had left Paris and come to Egypt. His head rang and the tinnitus blended with the crowd. He remembered Daniel and turned around. His eyes scanned the crowd for the kid, his hand took the cigarettes and shook them. In seconds one of the cigarettes was lit and fumed outside his mouth, and Rubio searched for a moment to see if he could find anything familiar in the crowd, but Daniel stood beside him.

Where did you go? asked Rubio. He almost dropped the cigarette and it spun in his hand as if he were trying to juggle it between his fingers and his mouth. Rubio crouched to the kid's level and felt his knees crack, he supported himself with his hand on his hip, the other hand on Daniel's shoulder. I was worried about you, said Rubio, a statement from his adult bank of useless expressions.

I went in the crowd and got lost, said Daniel.

Don't do that, said Rubio, the tone of his reprimand was automatic. We have to stay together, he said. Don't leave my side for anything. We're going to go and eat and then we'll see.

Rubio's eye caught a passing policeman, speaking to his radio. Daniel's problems were going to be a lengthy bureaucratic adventure, interviews and waiting rooms, and too many people with too slippery a hold on the French language. In Cairo there were embassies, authorities and offices, all the urban universals in the regimented monotony of correct procedure. In Mersa they would have locked Rubio in goal but in Cairo there was a chance that both of them could be dealt with in consonance with the rules.

An Arab voice screeched through the station tannoy to no immediate effect on the masses.

Hold my hand, said Rubio.

He returned to his feet and blood rushed up, it washed into his head and he blinked while Daniel waited at his side.

I have to smoke a cigarette, said Rubio. A few puffs you know.

He let go of the kid's hand and organised another Cleopatra. Daniel looked away but didn't move. He had an ability to sulk like this, to make it known that he was not pleased.

I'm tired, he said.

Rubio clicked his fingers for the kid's hand and they walked to the narrow doorways of the station. Near the walls, people sat in a bitter, restless force against the wooden slats, the noise of the crowd beat louder and where the crowd parted, two open doors allowed Daniel and Rubio access to the daylight.

All that Rubio recalled of Cairo was present, cars jamming and drifting, the noise of horns, a shouting of sorts, nothing intelligible. Rubio stood with the child and immediately people petitioned him, offering taxis and hotels, money changing and sight-seeing. Bodies climbed to the roofs of the service taxis, tying at bundles of blankets or boxes, and Rubio peered at the skyline where smoke curved along the top of every block.

Are you going to do what I ask? said Rubio to the boy.

The kid mumbled another word – it may have been a yes, it didn't sound like a rebutting no.

Where did you go when you used to come to Cairo? asked Rubio, but Daniel said nothing. He picked a spot in the flow of cars and stared into it.

Tell me where you used to go?

Rubio bent down to place his ear next to Daniel's lips.

Come on now, I'm a little deaf.

A hotel, said Daniel. We went in a hotel.

Which one?

Rubio looked across the square again. He heard Daniel speak through the ringing, the boy had begun to whine the word *hungry* like a donkey.

A cardboard box fell from a van in the square and Rubio pointed to it and said, look! A moment later a truck ran into the box and split it. From under the wheels came many coloured clothes, torn and spinning, the box itself pushed along the road, knocked aside like a dead body between several other cars, none of which slowed as they ran over it. The clothes slammed and tore inside wheels, mouths in the fabric opened for second while others were crushed flat into various attitudes of roadkill. When the show was over, the drowsy skin of smoke returned to the roadway and Daniel tugged at Rubio's shirt.

I'm hungry! he said.

Rubio turned his head. The kid had practically shouted.

I think I know the place to go, said Rubio. We'll need to get some money first and then we'll go to a nice hotel.

I'm hungry now, said Daniel.

We can't get very much just now. When I get money then we'll be living properly at the Pizza Hut. Do you like that?

Daniel had no idea. The name Pizza Hut was an incentive, its sound enough to stimulate a craving. He liked the sound of the Pizza Hut but he had no idea what it was. Pizza Hut, in all its fulsomeness, was something quintessential for the appetite, benign and non-poisonous at the very least. Pizza Hut was a strange antidote to the city of Cairo which was unremitting and never gave up with its crowds of people, swathes of them bent into submission on mats and in every corner. Rubio stared across the smoking traffic to where the fat face of a mosque pared away above the opposite billboards. He tried to swallow the lump in his throat. The ringing was cleaner than it had been, a simple note through which all other sound passed.

Was Rubio crying?

Daniel looked up at him, sweet and sad, and Rubio put his hand to his eye and wiped what was there. Some dust caught up from the passing traffic, an unfortunate speck of dirt from somebody's exhaust that had brought a tear to the surface, that was all. Everything was fine and Rubio repeated that it was. He looked for the correct way through the crowd, towards the River Nile, away from the station and into the teeming noise.

Let's go, said Rubio, and he took Daniel's hand. Before the patch of blue sky at the end of the road was the word Ramses and Rubio stretched his arm in mounting excitement each new time he saw it. The sun glowed on workrooms, storerooms and markets, the light dissolved into canals of rubbish, the traffic split away from an open midan and a railway bridge ran towards the Nile.

We're going down here, said Rubio in deliberation of the foot traffic. We'll go as far as the River Nile and then the Hilton. We can get money sent to the Hilton and then it'll be the Pizza Hut.

Cars were swallowed by bridgesand tunnels, traffic with no discernible speed limit. A bus stricken low with passengers bounced the curb, the doors were open and the people looked like they had been stuffed on by a giant hand. At the carriageway people ran across while others waited for a more secure opportunity, some gathered on a traffic island under the arch of the railway and they waved and smiled when they thought that it was safe for the others to move.

I'm hungry, said Daniel. He spoke with the pleading tone of before.

Okay, said Rubio. Look over there.

He indicated a food outlet on the other side of the road, a smoking shack threatened by the chaos of the carriageway. The sign on the shelter was Fuul Ahmed Mohammed and Rubio felt the coins at the end of his pocket.

You like the look of that? he asked the child.

Fuul Ahmed Mohammed offered several rows of red tables. An effort had been made to draw the premises in line with the egalitarian plastic of international fast food outlets but the effect was of progress blocked rather than achieved.

No, said Daniel.

What is it then? said Rubio. Do you think you can wait until Pizza Hut?

It was not a foregone conclusion that Rubio would win some money from the wire at the Nile Hilton, a task involving the incorporation of both begging and politeness. The fact that he could phone his mother-nation to be rescued by his bank balance offered him a social status unheard of in Cairo, however, he had to try.

Go on, we'll eat something from Fuul Ahmed Mohammed, he said.

The pair of them dragged into the shop where Rubio's money

changed hands, three coins and his last surviving bank note. He picked up a streamlined cardboard dish and wondered whether it would have been more sensible to have bought something to drink.

You first, said Rubio to Daniel when they got the plate back on the street.

At the mouth of 26th July Street in a line of awnings, they found a hole in the wall where a tide of chickens roamed, their heads making jerky spasms at the traffic. Rubio and Daniel sat half in the shade of a van, near where older men sat in blankets and under turbans. Brown-boned jaws stared with the same craggy expression that Rubio had seen all over Egypt, the expression of a long-felt need for respite.

It's good, said Rubio eating the fuul.
The child Daniel stared at the plate, angered by the sight of the food.
You have to try some, said Rubio, and so Daniel took the plastic fork and sucked the most tiny amount he could into his mouth and grimaced.
I'm not hungry for this, he said after a moment.
I know, said Rubio. We'll get something soon.

Rubio pulled out the Cleopatras and sparked his lighter until a barely warm flare covered the end of the cigarette. Daniel leaned against the wall, eyes half-closed and Rubio dragged on the smoke, almost a pleasant moment. Like a record beginning, the tinnitus blended with the sounds of the traffic as if it were a layer of enamel dropping into the ear. Maybe it had always been there, maybe at times like this it rose. The tinnitus made him listen to the sucking he made on the cigarette as if he could hear the smoke descend, but more distant noises were a blur.

He produced a postcard from his shirt. The cars blasted down Ramses followed by a tram beneath the railway line, a dirty metal vacuum with people clinging to its body, a paint cracked and ancient tram transported from the dark ages and then set rolling in Cairo. The tram passed, replaced by an equally rowdy set of buses, several of which jammed together in the crevice of its wake where men tried to stroll across the carriageway with hands in their pockets. Rubio considered the picture of the sphinx and drew at the cigarette, the sphinx glared from the couch of its broken stone plinth and Rubio attempted several thoughts for Virginie.

> I cannot easily put my finger on the very thought that I require, but I hadn't I suppose fully sounded these depths until now. There is a strange worry, a mild disquiet in Egypt, as if one's honour had taken a slight flesh wound having been unable to track down the history I've been reading in those incarcerated volumes in Sarcelles. It's as if . . .

Rubio pocketed the card and stared at a second card, there was still a nagging in his conscience as to what he wished to say.

> I'm enjoying myself here as best as I can. With respect to the anxiety I was feeling at home, I can only say that the heat has burned it away like so much tissue. I cannot easily put my finger on the very thought that I require, but perhaps by the end of the holiday that will be mastered also. I haven't seen the sphinx or any pyramids, but neither of course have they seen (!) – R.

Rubio's eye wandered from the image of the sphinx into the traffic which continued its aggressive campaign. The kid looked up and kicked at the dust, a desire for attention.

Are you hungry? said Rubio, but the kid said nothing. He looked as if he might be about to cry.

I've got a plan, said Rubio. If we get to the Nile Hilton then we can find something nice for you to eat.

I'm not hungry, said the kid.

Rubio scratched his head and Daniel sulked, cemented on the rock of the ruined wall, eyes focused on the passing cars. Wheels rolled and Rubio looked away, the full tide of human life passed in the gesture of speed, as if part of an explosion. Rubio killed the cigarette by pressing its face into a slab of stone, the plate of rejected fuul laid before them like a prison meal.

Look, said Rubio. He was unsure if he was heard above the curling crash of the buildings which grated like scraping metal.

Look, he said, it's not far to the Hilton.

Daniel snapped out of his thoughts.

I'm not hungry, he said.

I thought you were, said Rubio but Daniel shook his head.

Three people jumped from a passing tram while others sprinted towards it at the correct angle at which to seize a rail. Rubio stared, unsure as to how these men had appeared from the sixteen million, perfected their action and carried it out for his benefit. The kid hugged into Rubio's arm and began to cry. Rubio ruffled the child's hair and glanced towards the men at the wall as Daniel moaned. The men hunched on the ground in their blankets and stared as if the scene were natural.

Come on Daniel, what is it?

Rubio wiped Daniel's face with the end of his finger. He held the kid's face to his own and smiled. Daniel spoke, the traffic appeared from the flaming scrap-heap of the hill and people shouted over the street, the boy picked at a scab on his leg.

Have you been to France? asked Daniel with a frown in his eyes.

I was born in France, said Rubio. I haven't been anywhere except France. I've been to France and I've been to Egypt and that's all.

Where is France? asked the boy. He grew more lively.

It's in the North, said Rubio. Would you like to go there?

I was born in France, said Daniel.

The kid looked at Rubio as if waiting for an invitation. It crossed Rubio's mind that he should take him home instead of abandoning him. He smiled at the child as if in tactful appreciation of the problem. Taking Daniel to France meant weeks of custody and the unrealistic programme of the law.

We'll go to France, said Rubio.

He addressed the plate of fuul and felt the child's hand grip his shirt. A mess of passports and red tape materialised and Rubio shuddered, the cavernous spaces of waiting rooms appeared and he saw himself on chairs and benches for weeks as paper passed from palm to palm. He had no passport and the kid had no passport, the kid had no family and he had no money. It was an ominous although common prospect in Cairo.

As they moved on, the street narrowed into a union with the sky, the buildings were low near the river and water flowed in streams from muddy holes. At the Nile's bank were old car parts, small hummocks of them, and men walked amongst them picking at the rusted components. Other men carried the wings of old vehicles into alleys that vanished to black corners and Rubio let go of Daniel's hand, dried his own hand on his leg and then took the boy's hand again, this time more tightly.

The River Nile was sluggish, a transport of litter and beams had gathered at the wall and rats shivered past, beneath the water. The surface shone with the wet gleam of a meadow, the rats emerged from openings in the bank, some running for the water, others staring at the foot traffic like professors of hatred.

What do the rats eat? asked Daniel, and he pressed himself at the railings.
Rubbish, said Rubio. The rats eat rubbish.

Currents in the water collided, an iron bridge spanned the river, hammered with motor cars and pedestrians. Half a mile away was the main motorway-bridge and Rubio pointed.

We should go down that way, he said.

He let go of Daniel's hand and they walked together. He opened another box of cigarettes and while he lit one, Daniel stopped to look at the rats again. Homeless starvelings, heads angled out of the water like escaped criminals swimming for the shore, a mass of pent-up desire as if each rat knew its day would come.

I'll get some money sent, said Rubio, then we can go and buy some things. Would you like that?

Daniel jumped off the railing and continued down to the river, peering in.

I suppose, he said.

Block houses, river bus piers and balconies, everything square and rectangular, intersected with busy roads. The pavement beside the river was empty aside from a few dark-robed characters who seemed to be waiting for something. The island of Mohandissen in the central stream flowered with palms behind which was the suggestion of beautiful domed rooms. The mass motorisation continued, segregating everything, each vehicle with its own cubic metre of gas, each bucket of rust a challenge to the others.

If we go to the Hilton, said Rubio, I can get the money from the exchange there, and he pointed at the Nile Hilton, a hotel surrounded by flyovers. Daniel stared at the hotel which stood like a trap about to snap, it rose from the isolated ghetto of congested streets that formed the motorists' grid.

He led Daniel along the embankment. Rotten barges appeared on the edge of the water and with them more rats, wet and toothy. The barges were half sunk in the hard vinegar of the Nile, and Rubio looked directly into the sunken hold of the nearest one. The barge was clad with steel. It rested like an unhappy stile on the surface of the water and the rats docked where they were able, ducking under the refuse and oil.

•

Still Rubio took days off from the surgery. Patients groaned all week and Rubio played with a pen in the shape of a syringe, a gift from the company that manufactured Eleuthrotol.

Burneto brought many medical gifts from the United States. He had golf balls with sinister logos on them, writing pads in the shape of kidneys, hearts with the legend Treponema and thoraxes that read Pallidum. Every company and drug was represented. Burneto had brought a measure, a tiny wheel on a stick that read: *The Handles Can Be Embossed With Your Company or Product Name.* The syringe pen was a gift from Burneto and Rubio appreciated the humour of writing prescriptions from a vessel filled with a mild yellow syrup that oozed from one end to the other when he turned it down to write. Burneto succumbed to every snare with pleasure and negotiated Rubio's disdain but not acknowledging it in the slightest. When Rubio had planned a day in Paris, Burneto suggested that he come too, so they met at the station in the morning, Rubio smoking, Burneto saying that it was a bad example.

I don't smoke in front of the patients said Rubio, but Burneto was a physician of the human environment as much as its individuals.

The world itself is the sickness to be ministered to, said Burneto, I have a synoptic notion of doctoring.

Is that supposed to be Buddhist? asked Rubio with a flick of tobacco.

It's merely the holistic principle, said Burneto.

What's that? asked Rubio, bracing himself for the worst

It means that if the world can be cured then the body can be cured, said his friend. That's why we don't eat meat in our house, less suffering and better health means the furtherance of happiness – all our happiness!

For the love of God, swore Rubio and he looked down the moral rails in the dire hope of a train arriving.

Burneto extracted a banana from the murk of his pocket and held it up to Rubio who waved his cigarette to make him put it away. Together they looked over the rails, two iron tracks packed against stones, all but covering the sleepers. The line was a litter of cigarette ends and drinks cartons, chocolate papers and small rocks of gum, in short, the enemies of Burneto.

Surely, a doctor is the only person who can smoke? asked Rubio.
Burneto raised his eyes from the track.
How can that be?

Burneto asked the question with his habitual cheer and Rubio looked to where the rails curved between several housing blocks. The blocks looked empty, like they'd been bombed out, washing hung from windows in tatters, the wire aerials on the roof had been planted against the skyline at odd angles.

By your explanation the doctor's health doesn't matter, said Rubio. It matters only insofar as it affects his ability to cure. In general therefore, the rules need only apply to those for whom they are designed and not for those who made them.

Burneto thought about it, Rubio wished he could push him on to the rails for being such a logician, for obeying his fake supernatural ethic.

There can't be one rule for one and another for the rest, said Burneto. We can't dictate what people do and then live by a different code.
I disagree, said Rubio. I do exactly what the accountant says regarding my tax because I don't know what it all means. I know however that he won't give me the same advice that he would use in his own affairs.

Burneto dug his foot into the platform, an illustration of his childishness. He was a loyal customer of reasonableness and had doubtless forgotten that he must never disagree, that gainsaying Rubio was the most hellish crime of them all.

The train appeared and Rubio felt sick. In a flash, both he and Burneto would be gone and their bodies would be laid out in the morgue. Rubio had dreams about these trains, they were so like human bodies.

The train pulled in, as depressed a face on it as any resident of Garges Sarcelles. The vehicle moved so slowly in the heat that once it had stopped Rubio wondered if it could ever be persuaded to move again. The doors opened and the cabin seemed too steep for Rubio to climb inside. The light guillotined from the windows, cutting Burneto in two where he sat.

I know what you are thinking, said Burneto. You're looking at these people like prospective patients.

It worries me, said Rubio. One minute the world's building a Utopian future and the next everybody's feeling wretched.

Don't think about it, said Burneto. Even as a doctor, it's not your problem. Even if you can change the way it is today you can't change what has happened.

The train moved on and Rubio gazed on the yards and warehouses until the carriage rode through a cutting decorated with graffiti.

I have no wish to denigrate you in the slightest, said Rubio. All I wish to do is bring to your attention the ease with which even the highest of us can fall into a trap of self-aggrandisement, most particularly, when we are a little unhappy about our choices in life. Leaving aside the resentment we release on each other's heads, for actual and perceived neglect, all we encourage are the usual superlatives. Our stumbling into situations must be dressed up as moral courage, as in the case of every publicly avowed ex-addict that you treat. Without God – and I don't count the crystal genies of the New Age – we're left to fashion our own righteousness, and we unfailingly do so, personally and politically. May I ask you how many patients have recently come to you and condemned themselves? No one. Perhaps I have condemned myself? Tell me, have I?

Burneto stared at the banlieue as if in search of the population concealed behind. His smile was fastened by two supporting pins and Rubio listened for a reply, a sign that he had spoken.

As they reached Paris, Napoleonic structures rose from the trees. The train glided into Les Halles and Rubio wondered where next. Glass created a multi-tiered domain so that walking here with Burneto was like being on the surface of a giant television screen. Struts held the shape with good manners while prefabricated shops were slotted in an interchangeable fashion. The elevator carried Burneto and Rubio to the surface through a system of conditioned air until sunlight appeared behind smoked glass. A minute later, among the flower-beds and concrete basins of downtown Paris, Rubio took advantage of his escape with another cigarette.

Best if you leave me here, said Rubio, poorly disguising the ill will he had for his friend. Burneto looked surprised, his robustly modern clothes crisp and to attention, his mind working for the most hospitable reaction to Rubio's blatant rebuff.

Are you sure you'd like to be alone? he asked.
Absolutely, said Rubio
There's a great café I thought we should go to, tried his friend.
But Rubio said, no, and offered nothing more.

Rubio shook hands and withdrew for a coffee. The waiter that served him was perfect company, he didn't want to talk beyond a confirmation of the order and retreated to his kitchen from where he stared with satisfactory dislike. Nothing came to mind and Rubio recalled the captured hours he'd spent behind his desk. His afternoon walk in Paris emptied his mind of patients, of the godawful Burneto and his pathetic mapping of their friendship as a historical necessity. Instead, the spectre of his own stupid waste challenged him, the pathetic fumbling aggression he felt towards everybody, it bothered him and it did not. His blunderings, his information-clogged synapses, they drifted with him in the noon, oblivious to everything until he saw Virginie emerge from the wrangle of faces.

It wasn't at the department store but it was near, certainly one of the places typical to his ex-wife. The scene was obvious, a crowd goaded into slow motion by the sunshine. Of course, Rubio didn't recognise Virginie, not with the child in the push-chair – he might not even have stopped but it was too late – she was skilful with the pram, and Rubio watched her approach, felt a bus brush by and realised that his chance to flee had gone.

Look at you, he said.

Virginie was more attractive than ever whereas Rubio may well have been wearing the same clothes as the last time she had seen him. Rubio looked into the blankets of the pushchair where the baby was asleep.

Who's this then? he asked.

The question was faulted from its inception and now he was lost for words, for a cigarette and a tone of voice.

This is Liliane, said Virginie. She spoke into the pram and didn't even look at Rubio.
Very nice, he said. Very lovely.

Rubio looked in the pram at the absurdly pure baby and issued another congratulation with a little wavering in his voice. In his mind he was saved by a car crash, a bomb exploding, and then he remembered and pulled out a cigarette and thought, not in front of the baby.

Yes, so it's a girl, said Rubio.

He looked at his former wife who smiled into the pram.

Fifteen weeks, she said. We're just on our way to La Pause. We're going to meet daddy.

Virginie beamed into the pram. La Pause was the sort of place that Virginie and her husband might go, the very last place for a child.

Daddy's coming especially from work, said Virginie into the pram.

Rubio held the cigarettes and wished he'd had the nerve to avoid this encounter, step away from it with a polite shake of the hand and a wave. He could see himself doing it, looking at his watch, thinking, damn you, and smiling like an unhurried relative.

So where are you going? asked Virginie.

Rubio felt evil, he wasn't going anywhere.

I've a day off, he said. I might buy a few things.

A constant regression to a previous state of heartache, even at his age, Rubio had not yet mastered himself.

The surgery still in the same place? she asked.

An entire chamber of questions, but Rubio's lack of articulation was his own doing. He stared at Virginie's red jacket and brooch. He heard the dry rumble of the traffic and felt her ease with the city.

They're all depressed, he said. Depression's the growth illness in the banlieue. I don't think they've got it in Paris yet but they've certainly got it where I am.

Well it's catching, said Virginie, and she rearranged some baby blankets, perhaps to disguise the reprimand she'd just given him.

I haven't got it, said Rubio, and he put his cigarettes in his pocket, keeping his hand there, lending his posture an unreal casual air that would have made him sick in anyone else.

I'm just saying that it's infectious, that's all.

Virginie was still addressing the pram.

We had a friend who had it, she said. He was very depressed you know. Poor Pierre and his poetry, he had to go to hospital. I think he got it from his father, so you see it's catching.

Virginie made a velvety noise with her lips, something that attempted to appeal to the baby. She was telling the story of the depressed friend to her child, whispering the words into the cot. Rubio's former wife was a silly woman, telling her baby that depression was infectious, telling the infant Liliane that Poor Pierre had to stop his job and that he didn't like his baby any more.

Pierre caught depression like a cold, she said, and he was too sad to love his little baby. Isn't that a shame now? It's the worst thing for a baby if it doesn't get its lovie lovie.

Rubio leaned, assuming that the only way to maintain Virginie's attention was to join her, bent into the mouth of the push chair. He obliged and looked at the child, trying to avoid the image of the baby growing into a manicured and almost human life.

Are you going on holiday this year? asked Virginie. She pulled the question out of one of her jacket pockets, a reservoir of painless points to help you through the day.

I'm on holiday today, said Rubio.

Light ran over the surface of the car roofs and Rubio stared at the office windows. Of course people had to get away on holiday, of course their homes were rotten. Of course every person would be going on holiday this year, even the poorest and most depressed of Rubio's constituents would be rumbling off to the seaside in a sagging caravan. Even the worst of society had the decency of a holiday from society.

I'm going to Egypt, said Rubio, and he looked to see what had made him say it. Something in the road, a gap in the traffic and a clutch of people in suits. Rubio watched as more people landed on the near curb and Virginie restarted the conversation.

Michel's spent some time out there, she said.

Rubio nodded. He was sure that Michel was the new husband, and the kind of guy to have spent some time out everywhere. He looked towards the Opéra and remembered going there with her, the loathing he had felt, the slow pulse-beat of his anxiety as he tried to talk his wife out of the foyer and into a train home.

You've caught it, she said. Our friend caught it and all he could do was spread it.

I have a theory about that, said Rubio.

He got together some words but Virginie made the gibbering noise at the pram again, an otherwise sophisticated lady in a red coat, she had become something baby-like herself.

You have theories for everything, she said, and she looked at him like she used to, with all the powers of marriage.

I thought you never wanted to have babies, he told her.

I'm a woman, said Virginie as if Rubio didn't understand. I was young and I don't think young women should have children, not unless they are in an extremely loving relationship.

Rubio squinted as the sun peeked over the top of an apartment house and shone in his face. What was extreme love anyway? Clearly something alien to Rubio.

You're absolutely right, he said.

Rubio looked at the child and it glanced at him. Here he stood with Virginie, so many years after the offence of their relationship. He searched for a sentence or a phrase that would reduce her argument, bring her round to look at it his way. The traffic remained cheerful all the way towards the Opéra, the corner of which was visible. It was funny they should meet there, just where you could see it.

The Opéra, said Rubio. Have you been to the Opéra?

No, said Virginie. We sometimes go to the cinema or to see a band.

Rubio doubted all of it. Not in that red jacket, he thought, not with that lipstick and that haircut. Not with that pram and that shopping bag, there was no way that Virginie and Michel went to see rock bands or even classical concerts. The idea horrified Rubio as it was naturally intended to do.

Do you remember we used to go there? asked Rubio, and he looked in the direction of the Opéra. The scene repeated, just the way it had been before.

When Rubio and Virginie faced the pram again Michel had

appeared and put his hands on Virginie. At the sight of this fellow in a trimmed beard, Rubio wished only for invisibility. He had no idea how he had ever managed to woo Virginie in the first place, with men like this one in the world.

Michel this is Rubio.

They shook hands, Michel doing so long enough to show an appreciation of Rubio's discomfort. Michel's sports jacket however concealed its own host of anxieties. A growl in Rubio's stomach jumped into his throat and nearly popped out of his mouth. Michel didn't say anything, he looked at his baby and cooed instead. Burneto really should have been there. Virginie stood in good spirits at this most therapeutic meeting of souls and Rubio suddenly thought he should back off, but was anticipated.

Why don't you come round for dinner? asked Virginie.

Rubio sensed Michel's surprise also, but Virginie was ahead of the game. Parisians were infected with a chipper scientific expression, their nueroses made them experts and Virginie was on top of it.

I'd better not, said Rubio, and he shook hands again.

He watched them go and tried his cigarette.

So it's happening, he thought, there's nothing left for me to say, I've despaired of everything and everybody. In Paris a change of mood matters as much as a change of display in a shop window, the lively atmosphere is nothing more than a seemingly endless series of loaded questions about what do with your free time. The answer is always the same. Stick on another video, electrify the night, raid the mini-bar, or shop.

Virginie and her family disappeared into the long-faced army of pedestrians, and Rubio moved straight for the station. He would never have known the sun was out, and underground again and on the platform, it was all the same, the way he realised he liked it.

•

Rubio pretended to tie a shoe-lace while Cairo's tourists passed nearby, under guard. Parties gathered outside the Museum of Egypt and gawped into traffic, while an army of military youth slanted their weapons in complete silence. A young Cairene in a brown suit approached Rubio, offering in English a good hotel. He pointed across the square with a cavalcade of promises in speedy syllables.

La shokran, said Rubio, no thank you.
The man lifted his arms as if to embrace Rubio.
So you speak Arabic beautifully, he said, and he bowed mild and dutiful, determined to labour his politeness.

Rubio kicked a stone towards the gate of the Nile Hilton. It glanced across the thousands of white tiles which led to the River Nile. He wiped his eyes. There was something in there, the breath of bones solidified into dust and cast into collision with him. From the scruple of the sun's glare the museum was an urn behind a solid arch of marble in the west of the Midan Tahrir, monogrammed with the word EGYPT.

Let's go and get the money, said Rubio and he clicked his fingers for Daniel's hand to hold.

The two approached the garden of the Hilton where two Arabs in blue suits smiled vaguely. Rubio straightened and took Daniel through the plastic arch of the metal detector, a pearly gate on the marble white pavement.

Have a nice day, said one of the suited men at the gate. He spoke in English and motioned through the plastic archway, allowing them admission to the Hilton gardens.

Thank you, said Rubio, and he scratched at his eye but a tear would not come, the speck that jammed there was absorbed and beyond his reach.

In the grounds of the Hilton were trees and tables, a fountain and a row of bars and shops. Rubio and Daniel walked the coral white path to a dining area where women with pointed hats and sunglasses sat in appreciation of the waiters who smoothed their way between the tables. Men and women in colonial colours seemed timid beneath a row of potted palms, the curl in their voices and the vapour of their skin showed them up as the rulers of the planet. The capsized sun of all Africa was filtered through the green columns of a simple hedge and waiters approached with cocktails of the most bizarre origin. Daniel was also moved. The diners talked at a quiet click while in the background a laugh rose up. Under an umbrella a white muster of Britons twittered while at another table a woman with long bare arms cupped the head of her lover as she blew a kiss.

Daniel and Rubio slouched towards the Hilton and the doors slid open to the air-cool foyer. Stone floor changed to blue carpet and a round glass elevator ascended from a mall which offered more shops, a kingdom of retail in the transparent body of space. Diamonds turned in the roof where the light jagged hard at the misted glass, and a man with a bag of cameras lowered his spectacles and stared.

Let's go to the toilets, said Rubio as they passed into this mall.

In a minute, Rubio and Daniel were safe inside a cloister of sinks and mirrors. Dust had formed a rim across Rubio's head and his lips were cracked. When he unrolled his tongue to lick his lips it appeared as a sickly brown carpet, like something from inside a dead face. He ran the tap at its fullest force and water emerged, the clean white colour of the master race itself. He stopped the tap and looked into the water as the room became silent.

Daniel, are you okay? he asked.
He heard Daniel move inside a cubicle.
Uhu, said the little voice.

Rubio pulled water across his head, pressing his hands to his scalp through the thin hair. The door opened and a member of hotel staff entered, a dark and shaven Arab wearing the same customary blue suit as the others. The man's shoes knocked out time on the floor tiles as he walked to one of towels.

Yes, how are you doing? he said, in English.
Rubio nodded and said, fine thank you.
Very good, said the man, and he picked up one of the towels and shook it out. His smile dipped up at the ends and he carried on shaking out the towel while Rubio rubbed the soap into his hands.

You are staying long? asked the man in the blue suit. He was still shaking this towel, fanning air across the room.
No not long, said Rubio.

The soap lather released a season of grit from Rubio's pores, dust and sand dropped from between the marks and ridges into the basin of the sink.

We came to use the bureau of exchange, said Rubio, chastened by a possible expulsion.

The man stopped flapping his towel and laid it out to fold.

What? he asked.

The word flipped through the air and the ringing in Rubio's ear kicked in.

We came to get some money, said Rubio, shaking his hands.

The man folded the towel and replaced it exactly as he had found it.

Have you seen pyramids? he asked.

From the distance, said Rubio. I saw them in the distance from Mohandissen.

You must see the pyramids, said the man.

He left the towels to gave his full attention to Rubio.

Everyone has to see the pyramids, he said. They are magnificent.

Yes, said Rubio, we've just been too busy.

The man offered a hand to shake so Rubio dried his right hand on his trouser and touched him in the palm.

You should see the pyramids, said the man.

Yes, I will, said Rubio, formalising the agreement proper. I will definitely go to see the pyramids.

The man walked smartly away and pushed the light wooden exit door, leaving Rubio with his sink of water and the faint smell of cologne in his trail.

Are you okay Danni? asked Rubio and he heard the kid mumble *uhu* again.

The water in the basin was dirty from Rubio's face, so he expelled it and took the towel recently refolded by the Egyptian. A minute later he had filled the sink again and was drinking from it like a dog. Rubio's hands pressed into the bowl and his jaw bumped against the porcelain so that the ringing in his ears took to a lower note. He found that he couldn't get enough water and took a breath to see what he was drinking, this clear water, overcharged with health.

Daniel you should have a drink, he said.

You're not supposed to drink the water, came the petulant voice from the toilet cubicle.

Rubio stuck his head in and lapped. The water trickled off his face and rolled into the sink. This is Hilton water, he said, of course you can drink it. It's the best water in the world.

Rubio's voice faded as the noise came on stronger in his ear. The scraps of tissue in his eardrums were hurting, sounding with the long pain that he bore, and Rubio saw to the bottom of the basin where undisturbed, the rocks glowed, some of them with strings of algae, some with the silver light of the sun. It's the best water in the world, he repeated.

The cubicle opened and the kid marched to the sinks. He reached for a tap and began to fill a basin with his own cold water.

Would you like a hand? asked Rubio, his face dripping wet.

The kid said nothing and plugged his sink.

I could give you a hand washing, offered Rubio but Daniel shook his head.

No, he said, I don't want you.

Rubio tapped a cigarette from the packet and dried behind his ear with his cuff. The shirt was useless with a tear across the left shoulder and one loose sleeve. He rolled up the cuffs as profession-ally as he could and prepared himself for his meeting at the bureau of exchange. Daniel threw water over his face in an attempt to wash and Rubio stuck the cigarette in his mouth and took the kid's hand.

Let's go and get the money, he said.

He followed Daniel to the door, lighting the cigarette. In the foyer they stood outside a French-themed pub and looked into the small arcade where the diners from overseas formed their own boulevard in the heat. Here they stayed within the girdle of the Nile Hilton's fence, licking their dainty skin and uplifting their weary hands against the sun. The sun crushed into the Hilton's blue umbrellas and two armed guards stood chewing gum with their guns pointed towards the city. A woman turned to look at Rubio, her mask was already set. Rubio smiled but she looked away again, she sat with a tall green drink, looking through the potted palms at nothing.

We need to get the money now, said Rubio and he reached for Daniel's hand.

The kid pushed him away and Rubio grabbed at him as a disagreeable reminder as to who was in charge.

Behind a heavy glass door was the bureau of exchange. The walls were decorated with travel pictures, a map of the world, with credit card adverts and a row of seats.

Hello, said Rubio in English, I have to tell you first that I have been robbed and I need to ask a favour.

At the counter an American woman with a whip of blonde hair

listened to Rubio through an excommunicating glass panel. She interrupted him and said the word *embassy* several times until Rubio stabbed his cigarette into the sober ring of a nearby ashtray.

This is very simple, he said. I need to make a phone call for some money.

Have you called from the hotel?

I am asking you if I may call from here.

Have you reported this theft?

The fact is that just now, I need the money.

The hotel cannot be expected to meet the cost of such a call.

My son needs something to eat.

When Rubio said the words *my son*, he turned his palm to Daniel who was pressed to the glass, chin uppermost. Quiet came to the woman's eyes and she touched her hair with a hand that suddenly made a little fist.

You should call from the embassy or from your own hotel, she said.

I have no money.

Rubio pleaded his case while still demonstrating the kid.

Take a seat, she said and in an agonising slowness she departed from her chair to a nearby office.

Rubio smelled his cigarette breath and stepped back. Daniel was at the door, leaning into the glass, facing the dried-up concourse of the hotel.

Soon the woman behind the glass panel returned with a man in a white tie.

Yes sir, may I help you?

A fan spun in the roof, pulling air into the dullness of another question. Rubio looked along the counter to where the light approached the cash registers and a glass globe. He began the story a second time, attempting to paint himself as a hapless tourist. I'm a doctor, he said at one moment, as if his professional status would help, but the gentleman in the tie held his hand up as if Rubio were an item of traffic.

You are a patron of the hotel? he asked.

The tie man didn't miss a syllable, everything stressed so that there could be no mistake.

Not at all, said Rubio. I need to call for money to be sent to this office.
Are there phones in the hotel? asked the man.

He meant to direct Rubio out of his office and point him to a payphone, but Rubio shrugged and let his arms drop with the load of this suggestion. As the sun puzzled at the glass and the fan blades spun in time with the ringing in Rubio's ear, the fleeting image of the man and woman's stare broke apart. The dry dust of the world had solidified into the chemistry of two people in suits who were by their very occupation stubborn, things among things, components to Rubio's request.

Ten minutes later the phone was ringing in Virginie's home at Neuilly and Rubio was smiling apologetically. It had taken ten minutes to establish contact, to fly his voice out of Egypt and back to Europe, to have the call accepted, the charges reversed, the suspicions allayed and the present moment of his Egyptian disaster reintegrated into the unity of France. After clicks and hums he heard the voice of Michel and Rubio spoke as if he were making a social call, a strange register in the climate of Egypt.

Michel, he said. I have a terrible favour to ask of Virginie. I'm afraid that I've been robbed.

Where are you? said the new husband. His voice was a distant crackle, the line precarious.

I'm in Egypt, said Rubio. I'm at the Nile Hilton Hotel in Cairo. I'm at the Hilton and that's where she'll have to send the money.

Money? said Michel. The word was an abrupt full stop.

Virginie will know what to do, said Rubio. She can send me money from the bank.

Rubio raised his voice. He had the awful idea that he was not getting through to Michel.

She'll have to send it to the Hilton, he said. I'm at the Hilton you see.

I'll just go and get her, said Michel.

The phone dropped and Rubio looked at the bureau staff who were watching him, neither much pleased. He turned to see if Daniel was there and saw the exit swing closed. Daniel had pushed the door with its mosaic of travel stickers and he now stood looking to where the escalator rose to the first floor mezzanine.

Daniel, Rubio shouted, but the kid acted as if he hadn't heard. He was about to speak again when he heard Virginie.
Hello? she asked.

Virginie's voice was more distant than her husband's, the stopwatch technique of satellite communication projected an unlikely and nervous representation of her neat Parisian self.

Yes it's me, said Rubio. How are you doing?
I'm doing fine, she said. Where are you?

I'm in Egypt, I've been robbed and I'm sorry to call you like this. I'm staying at the Nile Hilton but I really need some help.

It's okay, said Virginie.

Rubio heard a whistle in the background as Virginie covered the receiver with her hand and said something.

I'm really sorry to call like this but I was attacked and robbed.

All you all right? asked Virginie.

Rubio fingered a rip in his shirt and wondered what Virginie was wearing, imagined her body clothed in the anatomical entities of the free market, the soft fabric goods and dynamic colours of the forever young.

I'm okay now, he said, but you'll need to send me some money. I've got the number here and if you could do it today that would be great. We don't have anywhere to stay.

We? asked Virginie,

Daniel was tracing his finger around one of the advertisements printed on the glass.

I mean I'm alone, he said. It was some days ago and I haven't been surviving very well.

A scudding and scratching noise from the earpiece and Virginie sighed. Rubio dimly realised that he may have destroyed a Paris Saturday, her most precious day, the day of shopping, the day of food and foolery.

I'm sorry it's a Saturday, said Rubio, but the apology was like a venomed dart. His voice descended into Europe over the chlorine grey of the Alps and straight into Paris where Virginie's husband stared at his wife, thinking about Rubio, the liability doctor.

I'm just going out now, said Virginie. Do I have to go to the bank?

Yes, said Rubio, you have to go to your own branch before it closes.

Virginie paused and Rubio asked her if she had a pen. Again a delay, a crackle and the pen passed over from the arms-folded sensory cortex of gluttony she called a husband and Virginie asked for the relevant numbers which Rubio dictated slowly. She read the numbers back to him and he quickly said how much he wanted.

That sounds a lot, she said.

I'm coming straight back, said Rubio. I should see you next week.

You don't need to come here.

Rubio could hear the husband straightening up, readying for a confrontation, the defence of his spouse's rights.

Whatever you like, said Rubio, we'll talk about it. I'm sorry about this but I'm in a fix.

It's nothing, said Virginie, words designed to cause discomfort. We're taking Liliane for her walk.

The child again, the peering baby in the pushchair. Virginie had to remind Rubio that whatever problems he had, none compared to the twenty four hour regulation of this fat parcel of fun, the newest of all Europeans.

Rubio interrupted.

That's great. Can I expect to hear something in the next two hours?

A pause and further rustling. The husband's moustaches were pointing up like two tiny chimneys about to blow, and Virginie agreed that an hour or so would be adequate.

Rubio stared along the counter to where the bureau staff watched. The man in the white tie took the receiver from Rubio's hand as if it were a sharp knife, and he placed it in the cradle once again. Rubio stared at the phone, the sort they used to have back in France, the plastic mass-produced phones that were made for the obscure proletarians to transform themselves.

About two hours, said Rubio and the man nodded.

He looked towards the door for Daniel. The paved foyer of the hotel was empty save for tiny figures at the desk. When he said Daniel's name to himself, it meddled with memories of his own childhood. It could all be counted, like steps along a causeway to where his own parents stood like statues.

I'm sorry, said Rubio and he drifted away from the desk, finding the door heavier than before.

The lift doors chimed and the escalator rose. Rubio walked to the main door but there was no sign of the kid. He looked past the terrace where the diners stared flinty-hard at their cold drinks and where men with white trays brought more from a secret location within. He walked the white tiles to the bronze arch of the garden where he was pestered by a butterfly, his eyes met with one great palm after another until they rested on a fountain where gummy water shot into the air. He blinked when he saw Daniel, the kid was speaking to a teenager with a black tattoo on his arm, their laughter reached Rubio like a contented smack. Rubio walked over, the teenager flexed his arms, a dark beard on his pale face. He had his hand on Daniel's shoulder and Rubio dragged himself up and interrupted.

I'm glad I found you, said Rubio as he walked up to Daniel.

The teenager stared, carelessly nursing a cigarette, a self-rolled stub of a smoke that spilled wet tobacco near his mouth. The boy was French, a plodder from the terminal planets of the North, a type of person that Rubio recognised with a deepening sense of disaster. A silver chain hung from his waist much like the phone on a string around his neck.

Are you Mr Rubio? he asked. His accent pierced to the depths of a class consciousness that Rubio had not been aware of since leaving France a month ago.

That's me, he said, and he offered his hand. As soon as it was released the hand went directly for the cigarettes.

Cool said the teenager, and as an afterthought he drew on his own loose cigarette before he dropped it in appreciation. Rubio peered at the young man's phone, the order and position of its buttons, its expressive screen and plastic garment. The cigarettes were fumbled aside as Rubio flicked at his lighter which failed to produce even the most trivial of flames.

You don't have a match? he asked the teenager, but the black and scrappy beard shook its head and said, Hey I'm afraid not.

Rubio struck at the lighter while the two watched. The plastic cell of gas produced its last ever flame, enough to circle the end of Rubio's Cleopatra, and he drew on the smoke to make sure that everything was properly lit. When Rubio had finished, the teenager said abruptly, Where d'you meet this boy?

Rubio glanced at Daniel and the child froze.

Do you two know each other? asked Rubio.

Course we do, said the black beard. He said his dad's had an accident.

Rubio looked at Daniel. The kid's eyes were wet, the whites brimming with emotion. Rubio felt drowsy and stepped across the fringe of light into the nearest shade, out of the sun's influence.

It would be better if we could speak alone, he said. I shouldn't explain it here.

The black beard clapped his hand and issued a word in Arabic to a waiter. Rubio felt the warmth of the cigarette as he tried to conceal it in his palm and the beard pointed his tattooed arm to the kid and watched the waiter fade into the brilliance of the hotel.

We're all students of the man, he said. My name's Daniel, same as his.

The teenager squinted at the kid. He reached for the boy and pushed his head fondly, his smile an odorous fluid of familiarity.

That kid's a genius, he said.

A glass of cola arrived, a drink with ice and an umbrella, as if it had been carried from Paris like this. The kid locked his lips to the straw and the ice rattled, the older boy pushed him once again and gave his arm a gentle squeeze.

Go to the wall while I speak to the man, he said.

Rubio smiled at the kid but it was a seedy effort, useless in the circumstances.

I'll see you in a minute Danni, he said and motioned the kid to go.

Daniel walked to the flower-bed with his glass of cola. He sat on the wall and drank. Rubio shuddered, searching through the rough face before him for any sign that the encounter may be over soon.

You're students? he asked, and he watched the boy examine his mobile phone.

We're the Professor's doctoral students, said the black beard. We were working on Siwa and studying the folks there. They have a festival in August where they have to make up if they've had arguments during the year.

They're both dead you know, whispered Rubio as the mobile phone shifted from the neck loop to the palm.

The student stopped and the substance of his face changed as if in the digestion of a nasty piece of meat.

I saw them both die, said Rubio.

The idea organised itself on the student's face in a muscular contraction, his eyes widened to show two burning centres where the lazy white had been before.

Both of them? he said, after a moment.
Yes, that's right.

The student unloosed the mobile phone and stepped to Rubio, almost touching him, the phone aimed at his chin.

I don't like this, he said. What are we supposed to do about that? There are four of us here on a project. This is like our dissertation year.

The student's voice lowered to a snarl and his threat launched Rubio's forehead into a ring of sweat as he stepped away.

Can we not have a drink? said Rubio, and the teenager stepped closer to him once again.

We're all working with the Professor, he said. You had better sort this out.

Come on, said Rubio and he pointed to the terraced garden where the drinkers waited.

They walked the terrace to where its kerbs and sculptures formed a separate garden. Faces rested in clumps of pale light and jawbones moved as conversation emerged. There were drinks too, the tinkling of ice and the subtle shades of bubbles from the bottom of each glass. Rubio followed the student beneath blue umbrellas while above them the face of the hotel gleamed, a symmetrical composition of vertical flanks slowing to meet the engraved word *Hilton* half a mile above them. An ample galleria of space stretched into the awnings of the building, interwoven with potted palms and the silver capsule of a bar. Rubio and the student sat beneath an umbrella that protected them, not from the light but from the idea that they were in such a brutal city as Cairo.

Drinks, said the student.

The word was slow as if he were slaking his thirst for silence, the syllable rolled out as if on to a bed of ice where it lay waiting for an axe.

Anything, said Rubio,

In the moment during which they waited, Rubio's eye caught Daniel on the other side of the hedge. He sat with the straw of the cola in his mouth, not drinking, just resting in the rarefied attitude of boredom, his constant indifference. The waiter bent under the bow of the umbrella and the student asked for two beers. The waiter wrote thinly on his pad and walked off as if not wishing to disturb anybody.

A crazy city, said the student. We've been here for six months so I don't care much for the hawkers any more. They'll follow you right to the hotel but thank Christ they can't come in.

Rubio sank into the seat. The noise of Cairo was replaced by the consoling sound of Europe which was being accurately piped across the terrace. From under the palms, the sound of newspapers, a teaspoon applied to a cup and saucer, a lady's voice and a laugh.

Yeah it's a crazy place all right, said the student, and they both stared at the next table where flies had halted on an empty plate. The drinks were brought forward, stewed in their glasses and were placed down with tiny mats.

Santé, said the student applying his lip to the flossy head of the beer.
Yes, santé, said Rubio and he did the same.

The keen ceremony of another crisp beer; the cold shivers on the roof of the mouth; the student burped and hissed as if the beer had released pressure from within him and Rubio felt the chill of the liquid in his lungs.

You in Egypt on your own? asked the student as he checked the mobile phone. His voice had relaxed into the leisurely façade of the terrace, the articulation of its parts.
Yes, said Rubio. I was until I met the kid. He shook another cigarette free.
You are married though? asked the student.

212

Rubio glanced across his fingers. Why did the boy assume what he could not know?

My wife left me, said Rubio. He spoke past the boy into a depopulated distance where his words would lodge into the sand and dissolve. Virginie was at the edge of his thinking, her lips were pursed as if she were about to tell him something, she was about to say how much she loved it here in this stunning hotel, exactly her type of place.

Virginie, said Rubio, but when he stared into the spectral conformity of the crowd, he realised that she was nowhere near him.

That was her name? said the student and Rubio nodded.

A tear cupped Rubio's eye and he felt the whine of a mosquito at his ear. He slapped at his head and dropped the cigarette, as it rolled under the table he bent to catch it and wiped in his eye where nobody could see him. Something was coming, he felt it in the heat, a wave behind the hotel, a memory as big as the city was going to carry him away, maybe over the land and into the sands again.

How long have you known Danni? asked Rubio

Rubio held his hand in his eye as he sat up straight. Between the crack in his fingers he saw the student's beard begin to chew upon its answer.

I've known them since I moved here, said the student. I met the Professor at the university. Is he really dead?

Yes, said Rubio. I'm afraid a part of the old town of Siwa collapsed. I sent a cable but I don't know if it got anywhere. I wrote to the embassy and then I cleared out. Danni and I didn't have any money so I thought I'd take him here. I haven't even found where the French Embassy is yet. Do you know where it is?

It's a shit hole, said the student and he stared over the hedge at Daniel who was watching them both, still ignoring his drink. The kid's face was a cut-out of several expressions, an unfinished puzzle.

I think maybe the kid could go to the embassy, said Rubio. I don't know after that.

The Professor's got no parents before you ask, said the student, I've no idea how you'll find out who his guardian is.

The student finished his beer, puffed and pleased, smothering his head with a handkerchief, checking the mobile phone for missed messages.

It's a shit of a mess, he said to Rubio.

What about the Embassy? asked Rubio.

What about it? asked the student. His finger came close to Rubio's cheek and he pointed, then clicked and said, you're running the show old man.

Rubio glanced sharply at him, the very sinking thought that this boy had just expressed, the idea that none of this was going to be easy.

I saw them both die, said Rubio. She was poisoned by alcohol and Mitard took a wrong footing. The town's collapsing, it's all in cross-sections. Have you been to Siwa?

Don't sweat it with me, said the student, and the finger withdrew and clicked at the empty beer glass. He spoke like a Parisian, an over-developed expert who knows the answer all along.

I think you should take Daniel, said Rubio.

The student opened his mouth in clownish horror.

I mean it, said Rubio. You know the parents and you stay here. I can't take him out of the country and I have to be at work shortly. I'm a doctor and I can't stay on holiday forever.

I'm at work too you asshole, said the student. Me and the guys are doing a photo-shoot. That's what we're doing in this dump. The guys'll shit it when they hear about this.

Rubio stared up the terrible left arm of the student into a knot of skulls and blue lines that spelled an unknown word. The student silenced Rubio before he spoke, he shook his head and he stared over the hedge at Daniel.

We're shooting in about ten minutes, he said. How can you expect us to look after a little kid when we're shooting?

You're maybe the closest he's got to a friend, said Rubio. I think he would have come to you anyway. Maybe the university will get in touch until they can organise something?

The university? asked the student, and he put down his glass. I'm not his relative and I don't work for the university. We're students and we're only here to model these shirts.

What then? asked Rubio, but the student wouldn't be led.

What then indeed, he said, and he stood up. You better take him to some place or something. I've got to go and do this shoot now. Take my number and get in touch if you can.

The student scribbled out a number on a ticket and handed it over.

Thanks, said Rubio, I'll call.

Rubio watched the student join his friends under the white hotel. They seemed at first to find something funny, but a moment later the student must have told them his new story, because they turned to stare at Rubio, four mouths open. Their faces were obscured by the light but Rubio could feel them watching. He was clear about his guilt concerning the two deaths, the man and wife, the unknown woman and the unkind man, the two dead bodies in the desert that for several seconds worked up a hectic interest among these glorified holidaymakers.

•

The stiff folds of the curtains in the medical surgery, silence punctured by the ringing telephone. A body of visitors in the waiting room, the assembly seated without courage or religious soul. Plain posters advertising caring agencies and alternate therapies as if Rubio hoped that the patients may change their minds at the last hurdle. Consultation time of seven minutes with a backlog forming.

When Rubio was a student, depression was a myth, a book-plate, an intellectual activity, at worst the inevitable burden of material culture. Rubio would hear that somebody had killed themselves and it would be made known that the person had been depressed. Those who survived depression took for the cover of alcohol or else feigned conformity for forty years, a very common tactic during the mid-century.

The first official cases of depression were curiosities and were determined by lengthy medical interrogation. Blood was taken, units of alcohol were counted, the glands were felt and the checklist of habits and allergies was read out. By the time the disease had become epidemic, the depressives were already there. Rubio had noticed them at the periphery of his waiting room and had seen them move to the centre of his attention until such time as he opened the door and they were all he saw. Their coats flapped in the wind like flags, their shopping bags formed a line at the bus stop, and the revolutionary magic of their credit cards continued at the retail park.

Ultimately the only assembly which catered for these invalids were the drugs companies who offered an always-moving schedule of psychotropics, as explosive in colour and effect as any other product of consumption. The drugs were designed in airy towns in England and America and advertised to the doctors by a salesforce that wished only to pin down a surgical alliance. Rubio began to prescribe the drugs to the depressives who knew more about their effect than any doctor did, their requests increased and their *taedium vitae* became well-known to him. Depression tore itself out of the buildings and appropriated the desires of the people and as a decisive nail between the ears, the steady eye of the television overwhelmed them. They were darkened people, caught in the dirt clods of their desires, trapped by the sexual nuance of advertising, always believing in someone else's happiness.

To the progress of this, the drugs companies intervened with a selection of seminars intended to help the doctors with the obvious path from illness to cure. Nothing solid had come of a seminar however, leaving as the basis for Rubio's training in depression a stretch of magazine articles that he hadn't read. Consultation time was still seven minutes and the range of cures was markedly smaller every month, dietary problems were dealt with by reference to the drugs manual just as depression was nudged towards the same satisfaction. Rubio made the same speech each time, in the vital minimum of the seven-minute consultation, and each patient sat in silence, playing thoughtfully with the buttons on their jackets.

If you stop taking these let me know, you may become dizzy.

Please don't drink while you're taking these, you'll find the effects adverse.

If you lose them, call the surgery and the nurse will make an appointment.

If you forget to take them don't make up for it by taking more.

Don't let anyone else take them.

You'd be better off not driving for the first week.

Don't drink please.

And try and relax, enjoy being yourself.

Doctors could make free with the decision-making plastic bottles, and Rubio offered each visitor seven minutes and heard as much of the story as he could. His notes for the year read like the description of a city silenced where the landlords stood like theatrical scum in the sudden unexpected pleasure they derived from owning a slum. The motorways were vibrant but the pavements were at a standstill but for the pronounced faces of the depressed, viewless and with pockets full of tranqs and anti-d's. They spoke to Rubio in their drugged magic and he looked at his case notes, although there was nothing that would access this disease for him. All of my colleagues from the medical faculty have became surgeons, or specialists in kneecap reduction, thought Rubio, except one interminable clinging dog of an annoyance called Burneto – and it was Burneto who attempted to keep Rubio up to date, constantly inviting him to medical meetings, pharmaceutical exchanges, any of the in-service events that Rubio detested. Burneto ensured that Rubio received every invitation however, including those to the seminars in Paris where pharmacists talked of the newest remèdes prophalactiques contra la depression and more often than he wished, Rubio was led to a conference suite with a hundred other doctors and offered coffee and wine by a team of entertaining salesmen.

It was the same drill each seminar. The doctors were shown a film in which popular methods for eradicating troubled mental states were discussed in the light of some brand new pills, and then the sales reps circulated while the doctors attempted to catch up with each other. Rubio mingled in these crowds, dutiful and polite, haunted by the anecdotes of his colleagues. A trail of grey poison happened up from the cigarette at his wrist, but nobody paid any note, the hotels never even put out ashtrays. The doctors talked brutally of their patients, the universe speculated upon by the physicians was a sick one, their habitually abstemious minds couldn't see it any other way.

Have you noticed that people are becoming progressively more ill? said such a doctor
Yes I have, said Rubio.
Everybody seems to be down with something. They're depressed or hyperactive, ignorant or lazy, it makes no difference.
They're all the same, said Rubio.

Rubio talked with the colleagues, observing a variety of recondite protocols and smiling at the ladies. He spoke to an analyst who was visiting the same hotel on the same invitation.

I'm retiring, she said.
Why invite analysts? whispered Burneto, while the others tried to disguise their interest.

Rubio said nothing but the colleagues hummed in disapproval because they all wished to retire also. Someone returned to the usual theme, the fact their patients were not only ill, but they weren't what they used to be.

What did they used to be? asked Rubio.
They used to be polite, said one.
They used to be grateful, said another.
They used to be curable, said a third.

Rubio collected the ash from the cigarette in his hand until he gave up and let it drop on the floor. An insuperable barrier had appeared between him and his colleagues and Rubio had missed it.

Curable? he asked.

Joke, the speaker said.

They aren't grateful though, said the analyst, and it's correct that our conditions have become intolerable.

Every colleague agreed with the analyst, although Rubio sensed their annoyance. The analysts earned criminal money and their offices were the epitome of chic, as holy as empty prayer rooms. General Practitioners could only dream of that level of ease, soothing the mountain of cabbage and buttermilk that constituted the brains of mid-town Paris, a city unhappy in its job, unhappy in its lifestyle choices, unhappy with its children, its neighbours, its tattoos, the state of cinema and the next ambiguous war. That was the analyst's job. They took the square peg of the demanding professional and brilliantly introduced it to the round hole of happiness. They were in general, the very bald goats that controlled international depression.

I'm jealous, thought Rubio as he listened to the retiring analyst. I want to be analysed too, he thought.

That's why I'm retiring, she said.

The analyst's professional piety was impressive.

It's awful the way folks live, she said, working all hours, then trapped by their leisure time.

There was agreement, and yet when Rubio saw the analyst's smart and unsexual face it seemed to him that it was her attitude, her race and nation that were the cause of the complaint.

Rubio took the train back to Sarcelles and walked from the

station, down one street end after another. Finally he arrived by the motorway and found the high rise coffin in the park that passed for the recuperative care home. There in the window were the patients, a row of them overlooking the motorway, the most favoured view in the hospital. Up there were patients of his own and Rubio liked them being there. Better there than on the streets, he thought, picked on by the wantonness of a world that needed everybody strong and ready to fight. A secret senate had met and decided that there were people who didn't fit into society, a kingdom of departed peoples who were crazy, jobless, rootless, too unhappy for the unpleasant trammels of wage labour. The atmosphere in this wing of the hospital was that of a search completed and people cried in a way not permitted outwith the walls.

I'm jealous, thought Rubio, as he watched the care home and the motorway. I want to be analysed too, he thought.

The patients stared at the motorway and didn't see him. Paris was almost visible from there, a sculptured architectural vanity that was its own message. Paris was a world of Greek metre, a mountain-chain of cash and plats chauds, it was the uncouth stock of art, blood strange and present for the pleasure of the nice, the motorised and sane. Rubio stared at the care home which sent no messages back but which faded into the twilight as he smoked and contemplated his retirement.

•

Another aeroplane thrilled the sky and the patrons of the Nile Hilton watched as if for one more chance at happiness. A mile below the charge of the jet engine, their hearts obeyed their eyes and they were awakened to the possibility of other lives. The aeroplane vanished into the clouds and the people returned to their drinks and newspapers, extended legs crossed below tables and the shutters closed on the pathless swell of Cairo.

At the door of the Hilton, the teenager Daniel stood with three other boys while the photographers assembled equipment and posed them in a nightmare somewhat similar to the grandiose statuary that rose above the Champs Elysées. The models stared with serious expressions into the distance, while the photographers pressed at their frightful cameras and said *hold it!* The bearded boy stood with self-commitment – he looked as if he may be wetting himself. And who knows, thought Rubio – how many Gulf princesses are on their way to Paris right now to wrap themselves in haute couture collections as inspired by these indulgences at the Nile Hilton?

Rubio walked to where Daniel was sitting on a wall. Beyond him was the security gate that separated the Hilton from the world of Cairo. He took Daniel's hand and led him to the metal detector, Daniel facing into the tiles as they walked.

You wanted me to go with him, said Daniel.
It was an idea, said Rubio. Would you like that?
Not after you promised, said Daniel.
We'll stay together, said Rubio – and he glanced back at the models who smiled into the various camera lenses present. The student Rubio had spoken to had lolled his way out of an unsettling situation using old-fashioned French cowardice.

We can eat soon, said Rubio, I've got money and I've bought two tickets for us to fly to Paris.

The marble temple of the Hilton passed from view and they walked through the metal detector into Cairo. It was like re-entering a prison. The sound in Rubio's head swelled as he met the chaos of the roads, the forever colliding materials of the city. Behind them the diners were in the same light poses as before. They would be there every day that Rubio scraped over the streets in Cairo, every minute until the sun burned the bedrock of the world and their drinks exploded in their hands, melted their sunglasses to their eyes. Rubio felt his chest tighten. He went for his cigarettes and passed with Daniel towards the traffic. More tourists stepped from a dark coach, guided to the ground by a handrail, and Rubio realised that this vehicle had travelled from the museum, across Liberation Square. He bent to Daniel who was staring across the square to where the Pizza Hut was now visible on the other side.

Look at those people, said Rubio. They take a bus across the square from the museum. Isn't that funny?

Muh? said the kid and he pressed into Rubio's leg.

Street hawkers approached, liver-coloured faces, characters elusive in their requests. Rubio felt the money emboxed in the side of his trousers. He slipped his hand in and squeezed. It had the texture of good bedding. He twisted a foot into the tarmac and looked at where the clouds laid on the towers of Cairo, he studied the sky beyond the black peaks of the city and counted three aeroplanes in various attitudes of everlastingness.

Where are we going? asked Daniel, and Rubio pointed across the square to where the Pizza Hut waited in a red plastic cuff against the sandstone. Daniel said nothing and Rubio wondered about how to take the child back to France. He took Daniel's hand and started on the pavement that circled the square. The traffic galvanised everything into one ringing noise that he had to speak above.

Do you think you'd like to come back to France with me? he asked.

Maybe, said the child, and he looked away.

You can't stay in Egypt by yourself, said Rubio, but Daniel said nothing.

They walked the golden circlet of the pavement from one traffic island to the next, through wings of smoke and across the flashing storm of traffic until they arrived at Pizza Hut, a precious stone set in the throne of buildings that overlooked the square. The city pressed close as if it to oppress the moulded shack of Americana before them, the rounded croft of colour with an armed guard and never ending sets of double glass doors. American students gathered outside, amorous and cavalier, a small denomination that were passing through for academic reasons as perhaps Mitard had been.

As one academic falls to his death, thought Rubio, so there others willing to commence where he left off. He wondered if the dead body had come from Siwa yet, if the French University had got round to digging out their greatest rogue.

He stared across the road while people brushed against him, faces approached from the crowd, black eyes stared through ruddy light and Rubio stared back, his only credentials being his skin.

Now we can eat, he said.

They walked into the crowd that was making its way into the Pizza Hut, moody customers snapping into a fixed misery at the sight of the brightest eating house in Cairo. Those of the Cairenes who made a living enough to afford the spectacle of this culinary fad were moving in one herd, while against them students from the American University pushed and laughed, liberalising the air with their accents. This air was cold and it filled Rubio's ears with the deaf flounder of the tinnitus he had felt so painfully and so often. Air had never been considered a luxury until now and in the Pizza Hut the Europeans and Americans breathed it up their discreet white noses, while the glass doors closed and the smell of warm food allowed their lusts to engage.

It's cold, said Daniel.

Rubio took his hand and agreed.

Air conditioning, he said, but he wasn't sure if he'd heard himself.

Air conditioning, he said again, as if it was the first time that either of them had felt it.

What'll we do? asked Daniel.

Rubio looked to the counter and around the tables and wondered.

I don't know, he said. I can't see a space.

Customers hunted in coils at the salad counter, bravely working their way towards the checkout. Daniel tugged Rubio and pointed to the water dispenser. The water in the unit was crowned in light and upturned plastic tumblers nosed out of a serving tray. Like the air, the machine promised a relief that couldn't have been imagined outside.

Come on, said Rubio and he led Daniel to the water.

The cold air beat down, a normative force from above, Rubio had no idea where it came from, it could have been pumped in from the US. He pulled two cups and watched as the cold air propped the hairs up on his arms. The water squirted down, plops and bubbles rose, a group of Arab boys in suits had spotted them and were flicking up their chins. Rubio passed a cup of water to Daniel and they both drank, it tasted ridiculously good and Rubio spoke to the kid when he had finished.

The water in the water dispenser in Pizza Hut in Midan Tahrir, he said, is the best water in the world!

They smiled as if the rediscovery of water had prompted a revelation, a readable hope in their future together. The water possessed them both, the action on their bodies was final, the strength that it gave Rubio made him issue a lewd laugh, suddenly and without warning. He filled his plastic cup again, and one for Daniel.

Come on, said Rubio, we'll see what's on offer.
They inched into the crowd.

Again the faces of the young Arabs, closer than he would have liked – one held the bronzed crust of a pizza at an improper angle towards Rubio's face, others spoke a rambling harshness of words. The nearest young Arab restricted himself to digging into Rubio's rib cage with his finger.

Please, said Rubio.
He held his hands up as if he were being threatened with a gun.
We don't understand, he said.

More squabbling from the faces before him and a further rabble of boys joined the invective, boys in ties which they straightened while they spoke. Some of the boys were laughing but most lowered their looks to Rubio's shoes and shook their heads. Rubio offered his cup to the nearest of the young men who spoke at him in a staunch Quranic stream of words. The man held up his hands and Rubio offered the cup to another who snatched it and threw it down. Hand free, Rubio took Daniel's wrist and moved towards the counter. Two boys in caps, Americans with fair faces, stepped aside. The nearer one smiled.

They're just jerks, he said.

Rubio smiled and led Daniel through while the party of Arab youth cussed out behind him.

The American kid spoke again.

Jerks, he said.

A laugh rose from the Americans, but Rubio kept his head down. A young Arab in Pizza Hut livery guided the crowd upstairs calling out in English that there were seats available elsewhere. He was a hybrid beast, a desert animal with a Christian training in the arts of service, he was observed by a muscle of US youth on the upper level who sought to block him. The golden corner of a pizza crust was pointed like a bayonet and from beneath a baseball cap a finger was raised in return. Subtle Arabic poured from the boys at the foot of the stairs, while mockery beamed from the Americans who repeated the word *Jerks*, their smiles stretching greenly from wall to wall. The word *Jerks* dwelled in the air, ineffably sublime, and the Arabs stared back, a whiteness in their eyes.

Rubio held Daniel's hand, and for a moment before the food was thrown Rubio paused in unknown despair.

The first missiles were American, a rain of food from the Yanks, laughing at their hosts. Bread and salad patted down upon the Arab boys, and having cut off the enemy lines of supply to the salad counter, the students continued their bombardment. Crusts and croutons, drinks cartons and potato fries all wreaked havoc on the Arab defences, and realising that resistance was to no avail, the Egyptian forces resorted to grabbing one of the smaller students as a human shield.

Come on, said Rubio and he ducked Daniel to one side as the

chemical weaponry of ketchup was brought into play. The bombing of the Americans had become more precise, and the Arabs were more than adept with their burger buns than Rubio could have dreamed of.

The Arab boys gathered under fire and in an effort to demonstrate their own offensive capabilities, they launched an entire four cheese and ham. The US students responded with French Fries and battered chicken until the Arab threat was secured and they had claimed the territory around the water cooler.

Rubio held his hands up as if a casualty and a cardboard box knocked him in the eye. A moment later he was able to see again and noticed Daniel eating from the floor, scraping at the remains of a deep fried apple dessert.

Jerks! the same word as before, the Egyptians goaded into regrouping. Calls rose for a flanking manoeuvre at a vulnerable point where one Arab teenager was attempting to scoop up sticky particles of chicken for re-use, and while boys with baseball caps and trays of salad circled the enemy on the left, a second party near the door cut off the avenues of retreat.

The leader of the US forces stood his ground with a drinks carton and the final and complete destruction of the enemy forces began as caramel-coloured cola began to pour on the Arab boys' pressed suits from the upper tier of the restaurant.

Later that day these scenes of destruction were flashed by news services around the world, footage which featured the Arab boys led with great speed into secure accommodation in an undisclosed Cairo prison and a man who said that America would rebuild a new and by this time, permanently occupied Pizza Hut in Midan Tahrir.

The trains of Garges Sarcelles skimmed the rails and appeared at five o'clock in symmetry beneath the housing. At home the passengers took quickly to the televisions, the dearest ornament of their possession, the last of them left the surgery and Rubio walked to the cigarette kiosk, seated in the corner of the square.

The man who served him did so from behind a wall of unsold newspapers tied in bonds and bails while the townspeople passed in an angry breeze.

At the surgery a man was looking through the shower of curled paper that Rubio called his notes. The man's glasses lay on the prescription pad and the shrivelled lump of Rubio's cigarette burned until he put it out against the sink.

Those are private files, said Rubio eventually.

The man looked up. The filing cabinet was open and folded leaves of paper had been removed and stacked to one side.

Those are the files of my patients, said Rubio.

The man looked on with the half-suppressed breath of an inquisitor, one come to pry by arrangement of a higher authority, but he was no state agent. His intensity and colour embodied a purpose far more sinister. He closed a file and made a note on the cover. Rubio tried to see which file the man was looking at and the man reached for his light-rimmed spectacles, the formulation of a new expression, that of the examiner.

You are the doctor then? he asked.

The word *doctor* was couched in as much remoteness as the man could muster. He began on the second file with his pen and Rubio tried to see what was going on. As Rubio bent forward, the man at his desk looked up, a substantive rebuke, the exact stare that one reserves for a child.

I won't be long, said the man.

Rubio sized up the chair normally used by the patients and took out his cigarettes. He reached for the waste-basket, today's ashtray, and lit up, glad to fill the surgery with a flagrant veil of white. Rubio peered to see if the man was looking to see what had been prescribed because that was normally it – a regulator flown in to catch doctors on the take. They had the powers of the police and hunted in the banlieue for mediciens who shared their patients' addictions. Maybe somebody had said something, referred to Rubio's bad mood, perhaps the bouderie and peevishness of the last twenty years had finally been attributed to a drug addiction – so Rubio settled his eyes on the year planner where he had placed an E above June, his trip to Egypt, only four months now, and he waited. The man at the desk took a file and pointed his pen at the cover.

Do you know this man?
If he's a patient I know him, said Rubio.

Rubio stared into the fudge of his own handwriting and the visitor looked frankly at him with unaffected dislike. There was something superior about the curt profile the guest offered. He resembled an ill-tempered egg.

Rubio looked at the file, it belonged to the man called Destouches that had arrived depressed and asked for pills, the same frozen orbs of chemicals that his wife had once tried out. Rubio recalled the last consultation. The case notes read of the patient's use of illegal drugs as a self-indulgence, so Rubio had eventually referred him to an analyst that he could afford.

I referred that man to an analyst, said Rubio. With analysts they come into their own, they share their anecdotes and guilty memories, all for a fee of course. Analysts encourage this, they sleep through it as far as I know.

The visitor was disappointed with this response and he put down the file.

I don't normally do that, said Rubio, but this patient could afford it. I have people here who need proper help. This man needed a good cry.

That was your diagnosis? asked the visitor and he held a hushing finger in the air.

There wasn't much that I could do, said Rubio. If a patient has an issue with their parents then this surgery can't help them.

So you refer them on, the man said.

Rubio dropped cigarette ash in the waste-basket and turned to the dead pan diatom that stared him down. As Rubio tapped his cigarette, red candles of ash dropped nimbly among the papers and he had to sift through parts unknown to ensure that they were dead. The circumspect investigator at the desk was naturally fascinated with this process and watched until Rubio had finished.

I knew this man too, said the visitor, and he closed the file and put it with the other ones.

The visitor reclined like a philosopher about to illuminate the waiting temple of his students, his hands folded like clamps and he stared, happy with the sizeable mystery that he had created. Again the man indicated the cabinet.

I shouldn't have come in like this, he said in a sudden spat of politeness. There are a few more files that I'd like to see however.

Rubio cleared his throat of smoke, a curving neck of grey relaxation in the watery world of his chest.

Have we met before? was all that Rubio could manage, but the man shook his head as if disappointed.

He pulled more files across the desk and straightened the glasses on his nose. His hands flicked through the dreary files and he spoke crisply in his pensive cadences.

Are all of these your client files?
What do you mean?
I mean, do you keep any at home?
Why would I do that?
Some doctors do.
They're all my files.
And you don't share them with anyone.
Of course not.

The visitor held a hand up, the signal to stop.

This man died last week and you weren't informed?

The visitor's fingers were pressed into a brown paper wallet which he offered to Rubio.

Nom Monr. Destouches, aged 38, unhappy as sin, was brought up in Germany and so spoke with the over-nice expression of the non-native speaker, wished to be a journalist and was last heard of writing his own reports on the housing projects. Destouches, Rubio recalled, had drug problems of his own and arrived in the surgery with eyelids hanging down to his chin.

I remember him, said Rubio. My opinion on this occasion was that prescription drugs would be of little use but I told him to come back if nothing changed. I can't prescribe Thelxepeia to someone who may be using amphetamines, or worse. We talked about the possibility of prescription, and I didn't see him again.

I wasn't informed of that, said the visitor and he closed the file.

Rubio stiffened. He took the file and saw that the man had pronounced the papers on this patient ended, the subject dead, apparently expired the week before. The cause was not described but in the scrawl the man had left Rubio sensed a boorish impatience, the loose circles he had made in random places on the page.

How did he die? asked Rubio.
How do you think? the man snapped. This man killed himself.

Rubio held the file. There was no factual basis for such a quick diagnosis – he wouldn't have expected that of Destouches – the patient seemed to be unhappy but most of them were. Wandering into the surgery and which is it? Are you depressed about your landlord or depressed about your tenants? Are you on drugs or do you want some? Perhaps all their diseases had agglomerated into one, their erratic thoughts sickening their weakened bodies. Destouches hadn't been the type, he'd enjoyed writing about the housing projects, prescription drugs had been a waste.

Are you from the police? asked Rubio.

The man shook his head at the stupid question and touched another file with a grimace.

This one too, he said.
Rubio looked down and remembered.
I know that one killed herself, he said.

The man rasped out the name of the Son and opened the file where he ran his pen down the column.

I need to see your list, he said. I would like to see the list of all these analysts you've been recommending.

Rubio didn't budge but looked at his undesired guest. The man was trouble palpable, a government officer come to root out the evils of old-fashioned medical practice.

Have you got the list? asked the visitor, anticipating Rubio's next claim, and he gave the pile of unopened papers a tentative poke.

Rubio walked to the filing cabinet and closed the open drawer, it squeaked like a tram. In the next drawer, he found the list of analysts and dropped it on the desk. The list seemed to have a stupefying effect on the visitor as he read it from top to bottom.

That's me, he said, and he ringed one of the names on the list and handed it back.

An analyst then, a psychoanalyst, the thickly woven mystery, the faint flame of evil and the casement of his spectacles, all typical of his trade. He was an analyst, a visitor from the high point on the medical chain, the collectors and the listeners. Rubio returned to the door and pulled the chair to the desk. The analyst's eyes formed

crosses under his spectacles and he shook his head and drew his
pen across the file.

There wasn't anything unusual about Destouches's depression,
said Rubio.

How would you know that? asked the analyst and his fingers
poked like a pitchfork into the desk.

His drugs were a problem, said Rubio, but I saw so many like
him.

There wasn't any reason for Destouches to die, said the man.
He never bothered to see what might have pleased him and instead
he hanged himself.

I agree, said Rubio, and he pulled his ashtray from under
Destouches's file.

I don't think you do agree, said the analyst. I am telling you
that this is an interesting case.

Rubio felt the word *interesting* repeat again. The word was an
industry in its own right, one of the classically useless words, one
of the great breeders of sloth.

He grew up in Germany and then moved here, said the analyst.
A little emotional neglect, a bright boy but lazy, ends up with
aspirations that are guaranteed to come to nothing. He thinks that
journalism is going to give him what he needs and even at the age
of 38 it's too late. He comes to see you and wonders what kind of
depression he's got because he thinks that it's to do with drug
withdrawal. He's really got a different depression however, he's
actually got the one that he started with and you send him to me, I
don't know why. I help him deal with his depression but by now
he can't be bothered facing it. It's like he's started too late, he's
handicapped and everyone else is far ahead. So the intelligent man
has one last experiment to try. Destouches's not frightened of that

and so he hangs himself. It shouldn't have come that far however.

Rubio listened numb. One critical view of a young man's life, the disquisitor at work, the chilly person of the analyst.

Do you know why he really killed himself? asked the analyst.

I didn't even know he had killed himself, said Rubio in answer.
He killed himself because he didn't believe that anybody cared for him, said the analyst.

He brought forth this light statement as a revelation, as the wooden conclusion of his diagnostic.

I expect that Destouches was even happy much of the time said the analyst, so this was a punishment for all the people that he felt weren't paying him enough attention. What I don't understand is why you've sent them to me?
I didn't, said Rubio. Your name is on that list. I give them the list and if they come to you then it's your bad luck.
The analyst leaned back, his head forever grey, and there was a smile, his first statement of willing. He took his glasses off and folded them, predictably slowly.

What I'm considering, Doctor, is an interesting phenomenon, he said. A significant number of your surgery are now dead.

Rubio unfolded his legs and blunted the cigarette in the ashtray.

I'd be quite happy to talk about it, he said, but I've other work to do.
There's no implication that you are bad at your job, said the analyst, I'm merely on the path of personal research.

Rubio looked into the pious care of the man's suit. He was like a lens for all the pity that crept through people's minds – the more they went to see him, the more unmeaning there walked abroad.

My question is this, said the analyst. Assuming that there is more unhappiness in our society than we know about, why are so many of them living around here?

Rubio stood up.

Not on my time, he said.

Rubio took the files from the desk and watched the analyst's pen roll off and land on the floor. The analyst lay back in the chair.

We'll speak again, he said. I think that in these cabinets lies an enormous bulk of material most of which has not been read let alone seriously studied. More to the point the six suicides that have passed through your surgery in the last year and a half have all been ill for a variety of reasons that we do not know, so we owe it to them. The collegial project of dealing with depression as hermetically sealed in the individual mind, is obviously not valid in Sarcelles. That interests me.

This is obscene, said Rubio. I suggest you score your name off my list, he said, and leave us all in peace.

Rubio pointed a finger at the window and the analyst raised his eye. He rose from the desk and offered Rubio a hand.

The cigarette burned near Rubio's finger, dying and withering. As the analyst stood up, Rubio forgot his words and slapped him in the face, allowing the cigarette to smash to pieces and fall in many hot timbers across his suit.

How exquisite the thrill of violence, thought Rubio.

Get out, he said and the man stepped quickly away from the desk and straightened his glasses.

The analyst spoke quietly. You'll have to live with this you know.

Leave it, said Rubio and he stared in disgusted delight at the uncertain elements of the analyst's face as his visitor pushed towards the door.

The door slammed and Rubio began to pick at the files that had been disturbed, the many sad and weary griefs of Sarcelles. He pushed them aside and examined his hand where he had struck the analyst.

The hysteria of the depression doctor, thought Rubio and from the window he watched the analyst walk the avenue towards the station, away from the possibility of several thousand case-notes, out of the inert city of Sarcelles and for the mild amity of Paris.

•

Paradise was white, while in its alleys, children picked through bottle and brick, where rubbish gathered in ponds of dust. Adults laboured home while gangs of children hustled them for small change or favours. The kids outside the Pizza Hut were near delirium, curious at the outcome of the war. Rubio pulled Daniel into the rattle of the street. He guided the kid away from the madness of Tahrir Square where the street children taunted the arriving police.

On a trestle table sat a line of typewriters, their carbons slender and grey. A ring of smokers examined the machines while on blankets were pressed shirts and carved stone cats' heads. A wall-eyed Egyptian guided Daniel and Rubio with a long arm towards these items, and Rubio pulled the kid away into a road of arched coverings. The kid faced into the sky which burned heroically hot and patient.

We can still get something to eat, said Rubio. We can get anything that you like. Daniel was unmoved.

I know a hotel, said Rubio. I stayed there before. We'll get a mosquito net and then we'll go to the hotel and see if we can get to France.

Dad kills mosquitoes with his newspaper, said Daniel.

The kid made a delicate motion to imitate his father, the mosquito cut short by a refined pat. Rubio copied the curt motion, and faked a smile.

Whack, he said.

The kid didn't look up and they kept on walking.

They walked past courts of dust, patios where the sun struck walls and doors. Word of life flowed from the crowd and occasionally they saw a narrow passage or arcade where men on mats bent before God in converse.

Are we going to France soon? asked the kid.

Rubio nodded.

Yes, but until then.

Rubio searched ahead with regardless eyes while Daniel held his hand.

I'm hungry, said Daniel, his tune repeated and familiar.

We'll sort everything out, said Rubio.

He led Daniel across a junction where a stampede of boys descended from an open gate, bold-eyed boys from the dark of an arcade, running through the traffic to the other side, street children, a numberless host, all across the light at one moment and in the retreat of an alley the next. Rubio worked his way through the cars until they arrived among the dingy atoms which marked a small public square. The main road trembled with vehicles and they crossed into an older part of the city, the walls were knuckles of stone and the nearest road unpaved.

Rubio bought more water from a street seller, he felt deaf as he looked into the copper drum the man had tied around his body. Light and sound knocked off the drum but Rubio's hearing was dying, the muscles were wasting away and all he could make out was that hum.

He seemed to be having an argument with the man about money. The man took what he wanted from Rubio's hand and Rubio listened to the clack of his voice, the crunch of his words. A spiral spring of water dropped from the seller's canister into a cup and Rubio looked into it. Rubio gave the cup to Daniel and lit a cigarette. He pointed to the nearest mosque and they began through the grid of stalls to where the markets gave way to a clearer plan of streets. The voices of the street sellers turned to hints and innuendoes and Rubio and the kid drew up in a small square where the kid folded his arms and sat on a stone, like a throne of spotless light.

Here, he said, this is it.

Rubio's breath grew short and he looked in ragged age upon Daniel. The boy looked like Mitard, his father, and the guilt rested on Rubio like an association of ancestors none of whom he knew. The kid scowled at Rubio for the last time and Rubio stood on the sad verge of saying something.

From across the road there was a cry and a slam, the noise of a coffin shut fast. There was a click in Rubio's head as he coolly took up the image of a café which was emptying of men.

People ran like shadows from the door of the café while its glass reflected the shrinking hours of the afternoon. The boy looked up in regret as if Rubio were the failed pupil and Daniel were the teacher, while another four men spilled out of the café warning people away. Lastly and in silence, another man ran towards them. He carried a wooden box of the driest flax, the rusty iron coins of his customers. The man with the cash box stumbled, tripped on his apron, and seeing Rubio he changed direction towards a nearby lane. At the café front, the tables were on their ends and an abandoned sheesha trailed smoke into the air. A man with the stick stopped in the street, about half way between Rubio and the café. What he said was not elaborate, but it had the sound of a threat, and Rubio put his arm around Daniel and drew away. The same man with the stick turned on his good leg and shouted. The others had long gone and Rubio's heart beat one plump ejection of blood in which it looked to him to die. The man struggled with his stick and hopped to one side to shout something down a lane. Rubio was going to tell Daniel that it was okay, he was even going to forget about the mosquito net and the hotel, he was going to say that it would be food and water, toys and chocolate, the aeroplane home – and he looked at the hard-bone face of the kid and wanted to embrace him.

His heart was keen. Everything was ready. He looked at the café. There was no reason to be there and he thought that he saw somebody still inside.

The man with the stick moved faster than the cloud of dust and brick and flew brusquely past and was presumably killed when he knocked into the wall behind. There had been no warning, the air had snapped like a switchblade. Rubio remembered thinking how lucky he had been not to have been hit by this body which tumbled past him. The man's words had vanished into the same ringing, the same white blindness that afflicted Rubio's ears with a roar and crash. The brick that followed had been different and Rubio had seen the opportunity to avoid it. There was a cauliflower of yellow dust and the earth shook in the cavity around him. The café windows shattered and in the same fuzz, they became a part of the ashes. The brick had been visible from that point onward as if it had cut its own window in the dust and marked its destination in this manner. As it shelled through the air, the brick became the sole object of Rubio's attention and although Rubio's hand had gone out to save Daniel by covering him, his mind was still locked in the impending duel with the brick.

Where was Daniel?

Rubio had his hand upon the boy's neck, although when the brick came to light through the glowing ball of dust he couldn't be sure of it.

When did the brick come to light?

At first a speck, but a discernible speck, and then after that, a shape on a trajectory. He kept his eyes on the brick and his hand on Daniel's neck. The brick loomed, there was no doubt that its edge was aimed directly for his head, as if a wire had been drawn in that acoustic cloud of masonry dust, through the ground-rocking force of the explosion. The crowd had vanished, all of the buildings, even the sun had been blocked by the phosphorous blast of sand. In the death between the beat of his heart, the brick had seen its opportunity and ensured its aim was true. Rubio now recalled the figure in the café, the cruciform man with the open book. He had waved as the first thick fudge of dust had shattered out the windows. Many thousand hammers descended at the same time and a wave of sound burned out. Somebody had planted an explosive or detonated themselves. The same hostility as elsewhere in the world, here with minor variants, there with the meat of hatred, almost a cultic observance in itself. A bomb in the South, Arabs shelled by their cocksure enemies, a small puff and a click of smoke into the hemisphere, the mangled consonants of holy books taken everywhere in vain. A bomb in the North, a cloth-headed Catholic with a yard of powder blows his neighbour's family into a lake of fire, beads of stone and glass falling like broken jewels. A bomb in the West, a small chord chimes, another trail of smoke, terror in the United States, a blip in the stock market, the bodies spittooned to the pavement. A bomb in the East, a trail of smoke, the sound of gunfire, the conveyor obliterated, those in the vicinity killed, maimed, traumatised, eight kilograms of TNT and five of nails, a twisted heap of metal and lasting despair. A suicide killer, a homicide bomber, the message in the mortar, our war against the people, the people bombing back. Explosives made in garages, pipe bombs, nail bombs and incendiary bombs, wiping the air of human life, every bomb launched at humanity by humanity, and always at the wrong target.

And please not me! thought Rubio. Bomb someone else. . . !

Bomb the politicians, not the doctors. Blast the politicians and the churches of religion, bomb the agents of grace and godliness and their polarised opinions. Blast the beards of the serial cursers and the hornets' nest of their parliament. Blast the scoffers and the freethinkers, the nonreligious and Pyrronhic, burn the Mullahs with the Church Triumphant, blast the Staunch. Bomb the dogmatists, the Venerable, the deanery, the canon and the Reconstructionist. Blast the Saints, the atheists and the reprobate, just don't hurt me with this arriving brick. Blast the blessed and the tinkling bells of Paris, blast those who crave a good fight, the baldric of their armed forces. Blast the Martyr Breed, blast anybody but the passers by. Blast the scum of the upper house, the justices and the jury boxes, the kadi and the bar, bomb sarcasm and excise the village virus of opinion from the planet. Blast the beardies and their small dogs, anyone who fails to make the peace by speaking up instead. Rubio could see it coming, the clear edge of a brick about to ruin his day, and with the brick came guilt. It was as if he had planted the bomb himself.

And stationed on the edge of the brick was a mosquito!

There wasn't a lot of time to speculate, but staring at the thrilled grin of the insect as it rushed at him on the end section of the brick, Rubio forgot to move aside.

Probably, he thought, the targets of this bomb were humans.

Rubio prepared for the brick but it was too late. It smacked him in the face, just as he and Daniel were showered with sand, rubble, sharp metal, powdered metal, and a shock wave that ran into them like a troop of horses. The brick knocked Rubio between the eyes and as his eyes dried, the street went black, nothingness. Rubio had been lanced by a chuck of stone, a pale spike of it in his face. The shock wave knocked him down and he felt the rest of the rubble falling on his body, burying him as he fell.

Above him, strangely, the remnants of his postcards, fluttering out of his pockets and into the fire, a haphazard collection of material.

that will   With respect   Rubio
or any   only say that
seen (!) – Rubio   sue.   I pression that is
slowing me down,

                              rious, as if a formerly unconsciou
end of the holid   affections of on
seen the sphinx or any

Colleagues! Why should   not our who
Muslims? The two objec   tions are as follows

Rubio   The words of Nap
        or me but comple

                        a strange cha   grin, a mil
        I cannot easily pu   's honour ha   d taken a sl
        Require, but I h   anable toi tr ack down th
                        in those in carcerated vo

Once more, in the teeth
                        of my tor

                        y pen to write you. It might be,
                        ild depressio

                        ut my fin   ger in th
                        rhaps by   the en

yram   ids, but ne   ither I
        gu ess h   ave they seen –   ubio
                                (!)

                the heat
                cannot eas
                        ho   lid   ay   that   will
                        hin   x   or   any

The explosion was like the lash of a heavy iron chain. The street was invisible where the bomb had been and Rubio fell on a broken table and waited in the chill while shapes unseen approached and sirens sounded.

The last of the silver glass fell and voices rose into the black mist which blocked everything.

So it's happening, thought Rubio, wouldn't you know – tossed panting into the rubble, on a whitening strand, under thunder, swept from the wreck of my holiday, which lies ransacked and strewn – because a bomb – pointless, because I have never so much as seen a terrorist or imagined they existed!
Let alone considered they might be out to get me!
Of all people. . .

I should be grateful, thought Rubio as the dust fell on the buildings and the cars, the people who ran in bulk towards the scene.

It may prove too much, thought Rubio,
but at least I am alive. . .
at the end of my resources. . .
in tears of envy for every other living person. . .
in six thousand square miles of featureless, friendless city, in the knowledge that I am alone by my own design.
The bomb will, I trust, at least prove that I am in good mental health, proof of my readiness to face the cruelties of my fate and. . .

The first policemen arrived with their guns waving and Rubio stretched for his cigarettes, glad that they were intact. The beauties poked their white tips into the dust and Rubio drew a loving finger along the line of their resting place. Medical and military activity began where the ruined gut of the building rose and Rubio noticed that even the mosquitoes had begun to prowl.

The first cigarette was lit and Rubio lay on his front and watched the rescue until he choked on a coil of dust.

By some hydraulic facial power, by an improbable muscular pulling in the cheeks, he smiled. The smile arched into Rubio's temples, as if needles in his cheek bones had risen to puncture his eardrums. The units of sound drilled onward, the piston power of the ringing increased and the smile dug into his skull as if that battalion of bone might be compacted into a grin forever. Daniel was gone, buried or fled. The cigarette was inscribed to the memory of the cross-bearing demon who had destroyed the café across the road, that and the forces that had saved Rubio's life. Somewhere in the city, the kid was running, crossing those dried-up streets in the Islamic area, the valleys and the teeming womb that made up the markets and the motorways. He had escaped to somewhere from the cold grasp of Doctor Rubio and his attempts to drag him back to France. He had vanished, exploded, run away, rejected the doctor's company.

The ringing in Rubio's ear precluded thought, each idea was interrupted as if a buzzer were pressed by somebody insisting on his attention. He hit the ground to dislodge the flies. There was a crack and a pain in his finger indicating that something had come undone.

It is as if, he thought, my medical knowledge has now been erased, meaning there shall have to be a full inquisition in the Star Chamber by the Health Minister. It means that I can retire at last and not have to prescribe and cure any more, thought Rubio.

Why have you been turning people off of newspapers? asked the Health Minister.

Rubio was tied to her operating table.

248

The bad news, he said, is that there's a new language in town, *odium mei*, the language of depression. It's taken over I'm afraid, and none of your doctors can deal with it.

We'll have your job for this, said the Health Minister and she slammed down a White Paper.

A policeman took Rubio by the arm and pulled him a few feet away, where he was set down. The air was still fragrant with dust and fire.

I can manage said Rubio, and he squinted back to the cigarette packet where it had landed on a broken rock.

A minute later, hobbling gamely away from the scene of the tragedy, Rubio turned the corner where a row of empty tables sat in the crevices of the walls, the buildings as dreary as his patients.

He walked, looking for a crowd. In the direction of Ramses the road was blocked with both people and traffic and the sun cooked him as it had done before the explosion. Up ahead was a great mosque, like an airport emptying of many hundreds of people, every figure moving in the model. He searched the crowd for Daniel while men bumped him on their way to pray. Faces watched as the river of road traffic ran beneath the smog ahead, the people changed form, rose in thousands and gathered under the awnings. Rubio had a body as strange as theirs, and he took care not to bump into anyone. Arches linked with arches and underneath these were ranks of children pestered by the police who were moving them with sticks. Rubio took a cigarette and headed round the square to where the children were.

Daniel! he called, and the image of the kid's face kneaded quickly into a knot.

The rough-hew of the towers dizzied Rubio until he turned a corner from the arches into another jumble of a road. He stuffed the nearest payphone with coins and dialled the number the French student had given him at the Nile Hilton, stabbing the numbers until he heard the boy's voice. The student was uncertain who it was and Rubio babbled that he'd lost the kid in an explosion. He picked at a thread on his torn shirt, and said *we've got to find the boy*. Rubio forgot his words while he listened to the young man's voice. He stared at the empty square of sky above the phone box, the sight restored something to him. What was distinct about the sky was that Rubio had never looked at it before, he had seen its colour but not its virtue, a curtain of blue that he'd always accepted he couldn't see through.

Get over here, said Rubio. I need your help, I want to ask your help.

With the phone call over Rubio squatted on the pavement to wait. Soon to get new cigarettes, he thought, working his foot into the dust. While nothing was happening, it was appropriate to smoke, to forget what was going on, to shrug off another human exchange. It was about all the proof Rubio had left that he had been at one time, a civilised man.

●

The great mosque rose through the prison-bars of the traffic and Rubio sat beneath its steps with a cigarette burning in his hand. Four hours after the explosion and the floral lures on the walls of the mosque hypnotised him with their geometry as worshippers appeared in their hundreds and proceeded towards the door. Traffic passed on wings of soot and Rubio's mind fell to his favourite game of calculating how long he had left in Egypt, based on the amount of money owned, a game that had as its centre value, the sum of three hundred dollars remaining from the purchase of his airline tickets. He palmed at the notes and muttered, doling them from one hand to the other, and the sun hurt his eyes when he looked up to check if anybody was watching.

Here was one hundred dollars, four days of peaceful accommodation by the Nile – postcards to the colleagues full of self-regard and squibs – a trip to the museum to see the lewd treasures of the ancient world – and here was two, a round trip out of Cairo including the base of the sphinx. He could write more postcards perhaps, offer a glimpse of something too intimate to maintain psychological equilibrium – describe in no more than twenty words how much you dislike the recipient and wish that they were not so stupid. Describe in ten words what a lovely time you are having on your holiday.

Three hundred dollars were counted, representing the last ports of call, wherever they may be, perhaps a night between Charles de Gaulle and Sarcelles, a day in Napoleonic Paris hunting down some Second Empire shop-fronts, fluted wooden pilasters and statues to the foreign dead.

Rubio folded the money and returned it to his pocket, taking measures to ensure it was secure. Men entered the mosque in their hundreds, pleased with the mercy of their god like slaves. Rubio stood up, never to see Egypt again, an agreement between himself and Cairo that in time he would have forgotten the city and that Daniel was lost within it. Which way to turn and what as a frame of reference? How much did Daniel matter while Rubio was continually undoing himself in order to protect him?

Above him Rubio detected an aeroplane, remote over the towers of the city. Beyond the slope of the dead land to the south of Cairo the jet shot dimly towards its conclusion. Paris didn't need Rubio back but the potency of these aeroplane engines would take him there nonetheless.

He climbed the steps of the mosque and turned to inspect the city street. He blinked and searched the crowd until he noticed the male model posing near a coffee house. The student wore the same black T-shirt and trainers like two fat loaves. Easily recognisable among the brightening millions of Cairo, he stood in the shade of a brick awning and smiled when he saw Rubio. Rubio trailed down the upper steps to meet the student with a cigarette leaning out from his mouth, the humming in his ear increased and he remembered there was no Daniel beside him and that he was alone again.

Thanks for coming said Rubio, ever the gentleman.

It's cool, said the student, tossing a chocolate wrapper on the ground.

The two men shook hands and Daniel the elder inspected Rubio's cut where the brick had sliced a sun-glazed thread through his hair. Once satisfied the student pointed towards an old shopping arcade, an alley with the same ironwork and dirty glass that Rubio recognised from home.

I reported Daniel missing at the Hilton, said the student and this is what they gave me. These are just from this week. I thought you'd like to come here because this is the kind of place that stray children get to.

Rubio glanced at the paper data, inky images of young faces that had been facsed too many times, Arabic curls and the children's names in English.

The list ran for several pages, there was a number to telephone and a block of information for each entry. Suddenly Rubio was glad that he was going home, that his judgements and opinions would at least survive the journey even if they had failed him in Egypt. All the children on the list were the best consolation for his failure – bar oblivion.

Rubio stopped at the corner where the arcade exited to a broken roadway which led to another courtyard.

Let me look at this, he said, and he reached for the cigarettes.

Daniel the Elder shrugged and said sure and began to operate his phone, full of self-consciousness.

Buerij may be in the company of his non-custodial mother. He has a mole on his lower back and walks with one foot turned inward. He may be wearing glasses and may go by the name of Michael.

Sameer has a scar on her inside left knee about two inches long.

Jamal's photo is shown age-progressed to 19 years. He and his 8-year-old brother were last seen playing in their neighbourhood. His brother was later found murdered and Jamal has not been seen or heard from since. He was last seen wearing white tennis shoes and a grey and red baseball jersey.

Mari had a stainless steel crown on one of her front teeth.

Aos 12 anos Jose Carlos saiu de casa para buscar emprego na cidade de Cairo e desde entao nunca mais se comunicou com a familia.

Sayid can be identified by a front tooth that has darkened to near black and a brown scar on the left side of his waist.

Tabgha has braces on her top and bottom teeth.

Harpeet was last seen in Tanta and is of Jordanian descent.

Asha went missing from the police post on Midan al-Widha. He was wearing a green sweatshirt, grey pants and had one tennis shoe. He also has a gap between his teeth.

Jamling was wearing a t-shirt with 4 Mutant Ninja Turtles on the front.

Berenia nao retornou da escola para casa. Sua mae acredita que a mesma fugiu, por nao aceitar limites impostos pela genitora.

Mahhamat as wearing glasses, has some computer skills and is very good at football and table tennis. Mahhamat disappeared after leaving a note to his mother and father apologising for not being able to live up to their expectations.

Risa has a chipped tooth on the left top of her mouth. . .

I have an idea, said Daniel the Elder as he gazed into the influence of his mobile phone. If the kid's still about, he said, we should ask some of the other kids if they've seen him.

A mild boom rocked the distance, the air maintained its poise as the pale texture of the broken arcade became clearer to Rubio

Give me one more try to find that kid, said the student.

The student's smile maintained, his teeth a row of shields. A further thunderclap over the city announced another aeroplane was leaving.

Let me come too, said Rubio, and they began to walk through the arcade.

Rubio's feet scratched the ground. He thought about going home and what he may say to his patients. Government inspectors growled at the door of the surgery in Sarcelles. Rubio's feet grated against the stones, in the arcades of Cairo. Have we no projects to realise, he wondered, that might give intelligibility to this brute existence? The airline tickets were squeezed in his trouser pocket, Daniel's would remain unused, meaning that the adventurer was returning with no comfort and no great alibi.

I have a good idea, said Daniel the Elder. I don't think you can find him now.

I don't think so either, said Rubio.

If you can't find him then don't look, said Daniel the elder. If you've got to take a child home to France then choose another one. That's the thing, otherwise you just go home alone.

In the centre of the arcade various passages broke into an avenue up which Rubio could see people, families perhaps, and Rubio thought he heard the shriek of children playing.

You go up there, said Daniel the elder, and you'll meet more children than you've ever seen. There are hundreds of them live in these arcades. I could find you a child and then you could go home like this.

Daniel the elder placed one foot on a yellow sack of corn, his smile was warm, two cigarettes appeared and he offered one to Rubio, Rubio took it and they began to smoke. After a moment, the student spoke again, his voice was music, he waved a finger up the arcade and said, go on. Rubio looked to the end of the passage where boxes and drums blocked the route, the drumbeat dominated his hearing and yet his head felt clear.

I'll wait here, said Daniel the elder.

An aeroplane passed overhead, the very sort of jet to take him to Sarcelles, where he would start consulting again.

It's our day's work, he thought, that keeps us from panic when confronted with our dereliction in the world and our sense of solitude and abandonment, of being launched from nothing into nothing. It is work that gives us the strength to see this unavoidability and to bear it.

Garges Sarcelles, the pealing, rumbling cars, the head-register of the television, the knock and rap of the civilised world, the moaning from the sewers that had chased him away in the first place. The aeroplane blasted off and Daniel the elder grinned like the fool he was.

And so fortified by work, thought Rubio, we can, when faced with the possibilities inherent in the nature of things in this absurd world of brute existence, take courage enough to chose the authentic – though rooted in the explicit sense of our situation and despise the automatic reflexes of those people around us with no conception of the fact that they are depressed . . .

I'll wait here, said Daniel the Elder, and Rubio stared, forgotten in the march of his thoughts.

In the first courtyard children approached, older boys and then the younger ones, naked from the waist down, some with fingers in their mouths, a filthy and scraped together collection of kids, now harassing Rubio in cracked voices. There were children all ariound, all speaking at the same time, one with an eye missing, the other side of his face jarred and torn. There were very few girls in the group, and one of them suddenly spat on a boy and ran off.

Hello, said Rubio and an angry cry went up. The children pushed into him, and he continued forward.

Hello everybody, he said.

Hands dragged Rubio by the pockets and he felt himself carried towards where he had come from. The ringing burst in his ear and he felt dizzy as if the crowd of chest high infants had taken control. Daniel was there somewhere, maybe dead, maybe living it up. Rubio could make out nothing the children shouted, the pushing had became a game, an attempt to topple him. He could still make out the younger kids, the sicker ones, crouching under their plastic awnings, under the fallen stones, undetermined eyes, thin and sharp faces. Tinny voices spoke but the ringing in his ears had increased to such a state that very little else made sense.

Rubio thought of Burneto and Burneto laughed. The sound ran through Rubio's centre. Burneto's laugh was a snorting laugh, not unlike Virginie's laugh, and behind it was the laughter of a soul which had eluded pain, the soul that had flirted with him for years until his mother died.

Some people never have children said Burneto, they remain quite happy you know.

It was supposed to be advice, thought Rubio, but the fact is that creeping into middle age without children is as good as dying aged forty. The dread widens to encompass all possibilities and cannot any longer be localised into anything in this world, he thought, and one is left contemplating the capital possibility of death.

Burneto laughed at the café where he was telling everybody

about the curiosity of Rubio and every man listened carefully, every oaf in question rooted in their longevity by the fact of their children somewhere nearby.

I don't know where Rubio's gone, said Burneto, but I understand he's taken early retirement. I saw him when his mother died and that was that. He was supposed to be going to Egypt for a holiday was he not?

We must continue to take care of ourselves said Rubio, and recognise that everything is contingent, devalued, and above all remain on the alert for the authentic.

Burneto played with his napkin and drank his coffee, perfected motions in the repertory. The colleagues were interested, they suspected that Rubio's mother dying may have played an important part in his sudden decision to run away to Egypt and they pressed Burneto for information, and with an unprofessional sincerity he continued.

When his mother died, said Burneto, he applied himself to her affairs in the same way that he applied himself to everything else. He emptied her house as if he were redecorating, he couldn't even permit himself an emotion. He collected what he needed from his mother's house and disposed of the rest. He threw out the photographs without so much as a look. He said to me one time that he couldn't understand why people kept photographs, such great albums of them. So he sold his mother's house and that was his mother buried without a blink of the eye.

I wasn't unhappy, Rubio interrupted. Do you think I'm some kind of monster that could feel nothing in the presence of my mother's body? It's beneath contempt.

Certainly, said Burneto, the reaction to her death was muted. After all, when his mother died, Rubi then phoned his wife to ask if she wanted to come back. That was despite her being engaged to another man.

The colleagues listened carefully while Rubio cursed them. He cursed their lack of empathy and their desire to take refuge from the human plight in the bovine warmth and comfort of the approved mode of existence – the family.

I made a commitment to my wife, said Rubio. It may have been foolish but I believed it. You make me out to be a monster, but look at yourselves. Look at your ship of fools. I'm sticking on the dry ground of existentialism.

He worked hard at his practice in Sarcelles, said Burneto, and he went to the café now and then but he hated those ritual gatherings. He never liked any of us, we were a sign of failure. He only saw us to remind himself that he was in fact, alone. He never went to the cinema, because people enjoyed the cinema, he felt that cinema was for children, just like music was for children.

Performance of music *is* for children, said Rubio, but Burneto rubbed his brow and shook his head.

He thought that everyone was a child except himself, stated Burneto, and the colleagues, flumped in their café chairs, yawned and smiled.

How many times, Rubio asked, have we witnessed in social situations, a person paralysed by self doubt pick up an instrument, a violin say, or sidle up to a friendly piano and impose their childish fluency on the adult grouping in an attempt to engender that warm bath of applause and sympathy that they remembered from childhood? Is this not why most concert performers are invariably inarticulate fools, less at home among adults than say, your average accountant?

The arguments were always well-rehearsed, said Burneto, but ridiculous. It was amazing that his wife stayed with him for so long. I mean everyone has the right to a normal life, don't they?

The colleagues at the café agreed with this. They sat in the unpretentious strategy of care, waiting to see what Burneto would tell them about the departure of this man who hated them.

So here he was, said Burneto, a man asleep. How many of these are there walking Paris at any given time? Walking the banlieue in his case. He hated his patients because they were immature as well. He told me that he wanted his wife to come back but he hated her too. The moral rectitude appealed to him, his commitment to her.

What happened? someone asked and Burneto slid back in his chair.

He went to the airport and flew to Egypt, said Burneto, off on the trail of his true love, Napoleon. He closed the practice, kept the nurse on paid, and vanished to Egypt!

Rubio picked himself from the ground and found a coin in his pocket. Daniel the Elder's arm picked him up and he felt the man's youthful thinness, and suddenly asked him for a pen. Rubio turned to where the children had retreated and held a coin before the sunny face of the nearest innocent.

If you take me to the post office, said Rubio, I'll give you a dollar.

The boy sat down to wait while Rubio looked at the face of the Sphinx on his postcard. Natural erosion and destruction at the hand of man had altered the Sphinx's form, originally drawn with wings, the body of a lion and an ox with the face of man. On the card only the face of a man and body of a lion were apparent. The Sphinx faced the rising sun and was carved out of a single piece of stone weighing hundreds of tons. It was about as long as a city block and was about seventy feet in height, an androgynous being showing that all partake of the positive and negative powers of the gods.

Is there not a time for everything? thought Rubio, pleased with his feelings of dislike for the waiting child. Can I not take heart that so far I have not allowed myself to be subsumed by or delivered into the great alibi, the ubiquitous dictatorship of everyday human affairs, of family life? Have I not done well to get so far without fathering any child? he thought, and he pictured the colleagues tip back their heads and return to the colours of their newspapers.

Is there not a time for everything? he thought, picturing the colleagues' respectable company, anonymous prisoners to established usage, judgements or opinions.

Rubio tore through young Daniel's airline ticket and dropped the shreds at his feet, a relief.

Is there not a time for everything, he thought, now that I have avoided the magnetism of human herd-safety and at the risk of continual crisis in my personal life, have refused to take refuse in the warmth and comfort that those colleagues so prize?

Rubio reached for the postcard and traced out Burneto's address for the last time. While Daniel the elder made small talk with the street orphan in Arabic, Rubio wrote a holiday postcard to his oldest friend.

Dear Burneto, I'm in Egypt and thinking of your greatest asset, your childish simplicity. I admit to a little devilish advocacy and pot-stirring in writing to you to break contact for ever, but it is plain to me that you have always been an idiot, and more than that, in the wrong. What's left for you now is your child's childhood and yes, the rest of your own.

Yrs with no regret, Rubio

•

In order to eradicate the sound of opinion from his ears, Rubio's analysis began by enlarging the field of human intercourse to include the totality of information about all facets of the social, spiritual and material lives of the Parisian group. As for opinion, he no longer sought it at the level of ethics or in the motive forces of the people that he fled from. Rubio understood it as a method of controlling the specific absence of religion. He simply suggested therefore that one arrived at one's opinion by means of chance, and therefore that all opinion was an accident of circumstance.

Just across the canal from the gardens was one of the finest buildings in Paris, the Hôpital St-Louis, and over its steep pitched roofs was the St Odile Church, the skyscraper of the Somme, battered by the wind, the high point of the Levallois district. Voices carried over the rooftops from Clichy, St Justin, St Benedict and Rubio stared meanly at the sun's white glue and lifted his hand over his face. He blanked out Paris by looking directly into the light where there was no threat of becoming lost.

Behind the architectural cacophony of Paris was a canal and then a 600 million dollar motorway with a new housing development that melted in a half-hearted eminence of stone blocks into the northern section of Sarcelles, reinforced by walkways that accelerated towards the vanishing point and were gone.

On Saturday, Virginie called to say that she was pregnant again, her voice as upright as a sunbeam, spoiling the melancholy that Rubio had painstakingly gathered to himself that weekend. She hadn't phoned him during the first pregnancy but now it was different. She wanted to meet him while the husband was away in Germany, lobbying vigorously for his job at one of his many overseas conferences.

It was settled that Rubio would meet Virginie in a restaurant in Paris, so Rubio travelled to the city on the shelved seat of an old train, imagining that he might even enjoy himself. The restaurant stood in a quiet arcade backed up in a frock of litter, and behind the lettered glass was a hall of diners, light-hearted and slim, lit in pearls of candlelight. He entered and approached Virginie while two waiters prepared his place.

There you are, she said, the sickly milk of motherhood already present in her voice. I'm glad you found the place.

Rubio sipped a glass of wine and listened to Virginie's news. Together, as if in their own wedded love, they accepted a raclette dish and Rubio joked about the small pensioner who played the violin, calling him a racket like a car braking.

Who are these people? whispered Rubio. Who the hell comes here?

You're here, she said, and like the words of a fatal song Rubio reflected on the trap that he had entered.

Everyone merited some spit or other and Rubio picked them off. They were such easy targets, vegetarian couples, thin on water and carrots, wholesome parents and absorbed young lovers, the more he drank the more he offered a thread of insults under his breath. Virginie found it as amusing as she had done when they were twenty-four. She was light-headed with cigarette smoke and enlivened by Rubio's tight descent into acrimony. Ultimately only the waiters remained to insult.

Do waiters dream of coming to places like this? asked Rubio.

Virginie watched the waiter. The man's attention was superb.

They probably do, she said. He seems to like the people here, he doesn't seem nearly as persecuted as you.

I know for a fact, said Rubio, that if a waiter sat down in such a place it would cause his immediate demise. There are things about being a servant that have been forgotten entirely. It should be a matter of pride to be a servant. It would be typical of these people for example to exploit the idea of service. They drain people like that waiter and throw them away. The waiter could never enjoy coming here.

How do you know that? asked Virginie.

She watched the waiter who bestowed himself well on everybody within his charge.

I know it, said Rubio, because it's practical to serve

I don't understand, said Virginie.

Look at him, said Rubio. A man who I'm sure shares with me the most acute sensitivity to a fellow being's mental comfort, meaning that for each of us here supposedly enjoying ourselves, he has a plan and an intention.

Is that psychological? asked Virginie, and she spilled a drop of wine or her shirt and swore.

No, said Rubio, it's just a point.

What is the point? she asked, and she dabbed on her shirt without looking for an answer.

The game was over, Virginie had drunk more wine than her reeling brain could compete with and the novelty of Rubio was wearing out. He took her coat and she rolled her arms into it. They fought about who was going to pay until Rubio filled the waiter's hands with notes and pushed him out of Virginie's reach.

Save your money for the baby, said Rubio, but Virginie stood strong-shouldered, with her eyes darkened by cigarette smoke.

I don't need the money, she said.

They walked beneath the gargoyled eaves of Paris until Rubio remembered she was pregnant again. The thought solemnised the scene and he led her to where she could find a taxi. Again she tried to get Rubio to take some money.

Here, she said, but he waved his hands politely.

Something for you to spend, she said, but Rubio folded his arms.

Let us live in the present, he said. Have we not sufficient in the immediate world to keep us preoccupied, concerned? Is there not a time for everything?

What are you talking about? said Virginie, and she stepped away from the taxi against which Rubio had boxed her in.

The sky spawned a black spot that remained steady and then spilled into Rubio's vision. A buzzing bloated his ear and he could think of nothing. Virginie was there, they were just out of the restaurant and it had been an awful meal.

Super, she said. It was super to see you too.

The sky was darkest at the edge where it met the rooftops of the private apartments, Rubio stared at the bruised remains of the clouds above Paris and thought of Virginie's child and from a strange eminence he'd not felt before, he imagined that it was his own. A feeble note broke free from his mouth and he asked her to keep in touch. The scene passed into Rubio's heart and Virginie stood on the brink of the curb, near him like an old companion.

You'll have to tell me about Egypt, she said. You never told me what you did there.

You didn't ask, said Rubio, and his glance at her lips revealed to him that he had been expected to tell nonetheless.

Don't worry about it, she said. I'll give you a call when the baby's born if you want to come and see it – and she gave him one of those kisses on the cheek that he hated.

You do that, said Rubio and he waited on the bank, slender and grey, unhappy until the yellow taxi drove away to the secret place on the Seine where Virginie made her home.

OBESA CANTAVIT

Other titles
from Thirsty Books

also by PETER BURNETT. . .
The Machine Doctor
1 902831 33 0 288pp pbk £9.99

". . . an exhilarating and anarchic comedy" **Scotland on Sunday**

". . . an ambitious, multi-voiced satire" **The Journal**

Whit Lassyz Ur Inty
ALISON FLETT
1 902831 72 1 80pp pbk £6.99

Volcano Dancing
OWEN O'NEILL
1 902831 67 5 64pp pbk £6.99

The Republic of Ted
EDDIE GIBBONS
1 902831 65 9 64pp pbk £6.99

Available in bookshops or direct from Argyll Publishing,
Glendaruel, Argyll PA22 3AE Scotland
For credit card and other enquiries
tel 01369 820229   info@argyllpublishing.co.uk
or visit our website
www.argyllpublishing.com